"Is any danger involved in the use of the talisman?" the Lady Ais asked.

"That is hard to say," replied the mage thoughtfully. "The talisman is a fragment of dense obsidian, a form of volcanic glass like blackest crystal. Therein the wise Zoromé long ago imprisoned a goblin."

"Does the thing have a name?"

He shook his head. "Such creatures have no names. To reply to your first question, there is not the slightest danger that the goblin can escape its glassy prison, for Zoromé sealed the creature and bound it with seven-and-seventy potent and powerful spells. But, like the earth itself from which they were formed, goblins are dull and obdurate, and this particular member of its race furiously resents its imprisonment and its impotence to gain its freedom. When you command the goblin to perform whatever act you desire of it, you must choose your words with care and phrase your orders beyond equivocation. They are by their nature malicious and tricksome, so be warned and wary . . ."

Magic In Ithkar

Edited By
André Norton
And
Robert Adams

A TOM DOHERTY ASSOCIATES BOOK

MAGIC IN ITHKAR

Copyright © 1985 by Robert Adams and André Norton

First printing: May 1985

A TOR Book

Published by Tom Doherty Associates
8-10 West 36 Street
New York, N.Y. 10018

Cover art by Walter Velez

ISBN: 0-812-54740-3
CAN. ED.: 0-812-54741-1

Printed in the United States of America

ACKNOWLEDGMENTS

CONTENTS

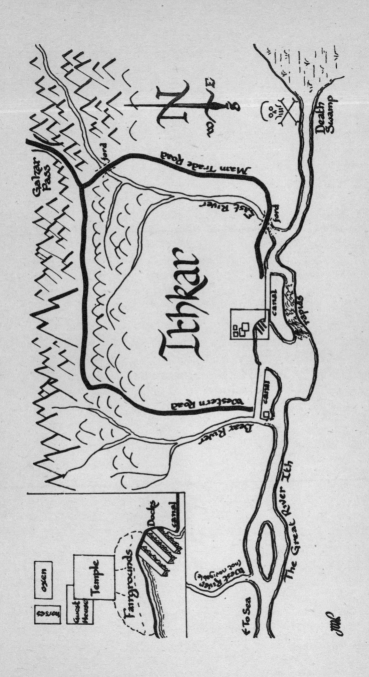

PROLOGUE

Robert Adams

The Three Lordly Ones are said to have descended in their sun-bright Egg and come to rest on a spot near to the bank of the river Ith. The priests of their temple reckon this event to have occurred four hundred, two score, and eight years ago (and who should better know?). Though the Three never made any claim to godhead, they now are adored as such, and for at least four centuries, many pilgrims have come on the anniversary of the day of their coming to render their worship and to importune the Three to return.

The Three are said to have remained on the spot of their descent for almost a generation—twenty-one years and seven months—though they journeyed often in smaller Eggs that, it is told, could move far faster than even a shooting star and so bore them in only a bare day across snowy and impassable mountains, across stormy and monster-infested seas, to lands that most folk know only in fable.

Since not even the learned priests can fine down the exact date of their coming closer than a ten-day, pilgrims came and still come all during this period, and centuries ago, the Ithkar Temple and its denizens lived out the rest of each year on the donations of the pilgrims, the produce of the temple's ploughlands, orchards, and herds, plus whatever edible fish they could catch in the Ith.

But wheresoever numbers of folk do gather for almost any purpose, other folk will come to sell them necessaries and luxuries. Pilgrimage Ten-day at Ithkar Temple was no different. Each year succeeding, more and more peddlers and hawkers gathered around the temple, the more astute arriving before the start of Holy Ten-day, so as to be well set up for business upon the influx of even the first day pilgrims. Of course, other sellers, noting that these merchants always appropriated the best locations, began to plan their arrivals even earlier to claim these spots for their own. Within a few more years, the most of the merchants were in place a full ten-day before the beginning of Holy Ten-day and many of the pilgrims then began to come earlier, in search of the bargains and rare merchandise often to be found at Ithkar Fair, as it was coming to be called far and wide.

Now, in modern times, the Fair at Ithkar has lengthened to three full ten-days in duration and still is extending in time even as it increases in size.

Nearly seventeen score years ago, the then high priest of Ithkar Temple, one Yuub, realized that the priests and priestesses of the shrine were mostly missing out on a marvelous source of easy, laborless income. He it was who first sacrificed the nearer gardens—betwixt the temple enclave and the river-lake—and made of them three (later, four) campgrounds for the merchants and tradesmen, so that they no longer surround the temple on all sides as in the past. He it was, also, who first hired on temporary fair-wards—local bullies and old soldiers—to maintain order with their bronze-shod staves, enforce the will of the priests, and collect the monies due for the marked-off shop-spaces during the fair.

As the Temple at Ithkar waxed richer, successors to old Yuub continued to improve the temple and its environs. A guest house was built onto the northwestern corner of the temple's main building in order to house the wealthier and nobler pilgrims in a greater degree of comfort (for which, of course, they were charged a more substantial figure than those who bode in tents, pavilions, or wagons, or who simply rolled in a blanket on a bit of ground under the stars). A guest stable followed shortly, then a partially roofed pen for draft oxen. The next project was a canal to bypass the terrible rapids that lay between the East River's confluence with the river Ith and the Harbor of Ithkar.

Two centuries ago, a high priest arranged to have huge logs of a very hard, dense, long-lasting wood rafted down from the northern mountains, then paid the hire of workmen to sink them as footings for the three long docks below the lower fair precincts, these to replace the old floating-docks which had for long received water-borne pilgrims, fairgoers, traders, merchants, and the like. Now these docking facilities are utilized year-round by users of the main trade road that winds from the steppes up the northern slopes of the mountains, through demon-haunted Galzar Pass, then down the south slopes and the foothills and the plain to the Valley of the Ith.

Southbound users of the main trade road had, before the building of the docks and the digging of the canal, been obliged to either ford the East River well to the northeast, prior to its being joined by tributaries and thus widened, then to follow a road that led down to a ford not far above the Ith, or to raft down the East River, then portage around the rapids and falls.

With the great success of the temple or eastern canal there clear for all to see, the great noble whose lands lay just to the west of the lands of the temple in the Ith Valley had dug a longer, somewhat wider canal connecting Bear River to the harbor and its fine docks, charging fees for the use of his canal and, through arrangement, sharing in the commerce-taxes that the temple derived from year-round use of its docks by the transmontane traders, hunters, trappers, and steppe nomads who tended to use the Bear River route rather than the main trade road.

Before Bear River was rendered navigable by an earth-quake that eliminated the worst of its rapids, the folk who used it had come down into Ith Valley via the longer, harder, western road, rather than the eastern through well-founded fear of wide-ranging denizens of the Death Swamp.

Many long centuries before the blessed arrival of the Three, it is related, a huge and prosperous city lay on the banks of the Ith somewhere within what now is deadly swamp but then were pleasant, fertile lands and pastures, vineyards, and orchards. But the people of this city were not content with the richness of the life they enjoyed, so they and other cities made war upon another coalition of lands and cities, using not only swords and spears and iron maces and bows, but terrible weapons that bore death from afar—death not only

14

for warriors, but for entire cities and lands and all of their people and beasts. It was one such weapon as these that destroyed the city, rendered all living things within it dead in one terrible day and night, left all of the wrecked homes and empty buildings not destroyed outright clustered about a new lake created by the weapon, a long and wide and shallow lake with a bottom composed of green glass.

In those long-ago days, it was, that lands surrounding the destroyed and lifeless city earned the name of Death Swamp, for many of the most fertile of the former city's lands had lain well below the usual level of the river Ith and had been protected from riverine encroachments by miles of earthern levees, but with no care or maintenance of those levees, spring floods first weakened them, then breached them and inundated field and farm, pasture and vineyard and orchard. Within a very short time, reeds waved high over expanses that once had produced grain-crops, while monstrous, sinuous shapes wriggled through the muck that had so lately been verdant pasturelands filled with sleek kine.

Monstrous beasts, kin of the mountain dragons, dwelt in many swamplands and in as many near swamp wastes—this was a fact known to all—but the denizens of Death Swamp were not as these more normal beasts, it was said, being deformed in sundry ways, larger, ofttimes, and more deadly. It also was said that the Death Swamp monsters were of preternatural sentience.

Descriptions of the Death Swamp monsters were almost all ancient ones, for precious few ever deliberately penetrated the dim, overgrown, terrible place that even the Three had warned should be avoided, adding that there were other places akin to it in lurking deadliness hither and yon in the

15

world, sites rendered by the forgotten weapons of that long-ago war inimical to all forms of natural life.

Of the few who do brave the Death Swamp, fewer still come out at all, and many of those are mad or have changed drastically in manners of thinking, acting, and speech, and seldom for the better. The sole reason that any still venture within the lands and waters surrounding that blasted city is the extraordinarily high prices that wizards will pay for artifacts of that ancient place, many of which have proven to be of great and abiding power. And magic is as much a part of this world as the air and the water, the fire and the very earth itself.

The fair precincts are surrounded by palings of peeled logs sunk into the earth some foot or so apart, and those entering the gates must surrender all weapons other than eating-knives. Be they merchants or traders, they and the wares they would purvey must undergo questioning, weighing, and scrutiny by the fair-wards and the wizard-of-the-gate, lest spells be used to enhance the appearance of shoddy goods. Some magic is allowed, but it must be clearly advertised as such in advance and it must be magic of only the right-hand path.

Those apprehended within fair or temple precincts practicing unauthorized magic, harmful magic, or black magic can be haled before the fair-court. The high priest, or those from the temple he appoints, then hears the case and decides punishment, which punishment can range from a mere fine or warning up to and including being stripped of all possessions, declared outlaw (and thus fair game for any cheated customer or other enemy) and whipped from out the precincts, naked and unarmed.

The Ithkar Fair is divided into three main sections, each of which is laid out around a nucleus of permanent shops and booths; however, the vast majority of stalls are erected afresh each year, then demolished after the fair. Most distant from the temple precincts lies the section wherein operate dealers in live animals and in animal products—horses and other beasts of burden, hounds and coursing-cats, hawks, cormorants and other trained or trainable birds, domestic beasts, and wild rarities, many of these last captured afar and brought for sale to the wealthier for their private menageries.

In this fourth section, too, are sold such mundane things as bales of wool, hides, rich furs, supplies for the hunter and the trapper. Here, also, are places wherein performing animals can be shown and put through their paces, offered for sale or for hire to entertain private gatherings and parties of the well born or the well to do. Of recent years, quite a number of all-human performing acts have taken to auditioning here for prospective patrons.

The westernmost section of the main three houses craftsmen and dealers in base metals—armor, tools, and smaller hardware of all sorts and descriptions. Once the folk dealing in the sundries of wizardry were to be found here as well, but no more. Farrier/horseleeches are here, as are wheelwrights, saddlers, yoke-makers, and the like.

The middle section of the main three holds dealers in foods, clothing, and footwear. Here are weavers, tailors, embroiderers, bottiers, felters, spinners of thread, dealers in needles and pins, booths that sell feathers and plumes, metalcasters' booths with brooches, torques and arm- or finger- or ear-rings of red copper or bronze or brass or iron. Cookshops abound here, some of them with tasting-booths from which tidbits can be bought, some of them offering cooks and

17

servers for hire to cater private parties or feasts. Also to be found here are the dealers in beers, ales, wines, meads, and certain more potent decoctions, with the result that there are almost always more fair-wards—proud in their tooled-leathern buffcoats and etched, crested brazen helmets, all bearing their lead-filled, bronze-shod quarterstaves—in evidence about the middlemost section.

The easternmost of the three main sections houses the workers in wood and stone—cabinetmakers, woodcarvers, master carpenters, statuette-carvers to master masons. Dealers in glassware are here to be found, candlemakers, purveyors of medicinal herbs, decoctions, scented oils, incense, and perfumeries, potters of every description and class, and lampmakers as well.

In this section one may purchase an alabaster chess set and, a little distance farther along, an inlaid table to accommodate it. Here to be seen and examined are miniature models of the works of the master masons and carpenters, with whom contracts for future work may be arranged; likewise, custom furniture may be ordered from the cabinetmakers.

Within the outskirts of the temple complex itself is a newer, much smaller subsection, centered around the temple's main gate. Here, where the ever-greedy priests' agents can keep close watch on them and on their customers, are the money-changers, dealers in letters of credit, public scribes, artisans in fine metals and jewelry, image-makers, a few who deal in old manuscripts, pictures, small art treasures, and oddities found or dug out of strange ruins or distant places. Here, also, are those who deal in items enhanced by magic.

There are a few scattered priests, priestesses, mendicants, and cultists from oversea or far distant lands who worship

18

other gods and are allowed to beg in the streets of the fair. They are, however, strictly forbidden to proselytize and are kept always under strictest surveillance by the men and women of the temple. One such alien god is called Thotharn, and about him and his rites of worship some rather odd and sinister stories have been bruited over the years; a committee of the priests of the Three is conducting secret studies of this god and his servants, while considering banning them from the fair.

Since all who legally enter the fair or the temple must surrender their weapons at the gates and swear themselves and their servants or employees to be bound by fair-law and fair-court for the duration of their stay, the well-trained, disciplined, and often quick-tempered fair-wards, armed with their weighted staves, seldom experience trouble in maintaining order.

The bulk of their work takes them to the middle section, with its array of pot-shops, or to the outer fringes of the enclave, where gather the inevitable collection of rogues, sturdy beggars, bravos, petty wizards, potion-makers and witches, would-be entertainers, snake-charmers, whores, and, it is rumored, more than a few assassins-for-hire.

And now, to all who have paid their gate-offering, welcome to the Fair at Ithkar.

THE GOBLINRY OF AIS

Lin Carter

The Lady Ais arrived with her entourage at the site of the great fair three full days before it would officially open. The reason for her early arrival was that she wished to reserve for her pavilion the very choicest and most advantageous position in that area where merchants, ship captains, and private citizens were accustomed to pitch their tents.

This was, in itself, more than a trifle unusual, since a temple building was set aside for the wealthy and for members of the nobility, and the Lady Ais was a member of both classes. Her motive for choosing the freeground over the more comfortable temple building was, however, easily explained: the desire for privacy.

Many of the earlycomers and fair workmen stared curiously as her gauze-veiled palanquin was borne by upon brawny shoulders. There was no question as to what notable reclined within, for her colors—pink, lime green, and silver—fluttered in bunched ribbons from each of the four posts of the palanquin. Many eyes stared, striving to catch a glimpse of the notorious lady through the veilings, which stirred a little before the breezes of late summer. They saw the silhouette of a slim, proud, full-breasted woman of regal, if languid, poise, the glitter of gems, or perhaps the profile of a luminous face, but nothing more.

In her youth, the Lady Ais had been a famous dancer, a celebrated beauty, the mistress of lords and princes. But that was long ago; as her youth and loveliness faded into legend, she had taken a husband, the aged but immensely wealthy Baron Inkus, whose fragile health had not by long survived their nuptials. It was believed by many, even by most, that it had been a subtle poison and not the inexorable accumulation of his years to which the infatuated and enfeebled Inkus had succumbed. A poison, some whispered, administered by the lady herself.

No one knew for certain. Save, perchance, for the Lady Ais, who inherited the whole of her husband's great fortune.

As her servants erected upon a hilly height her exquisite pavilion of floating and lucent silk, the lady conferred with her fair-agent, Borkis.

"You are entirely certain that the Mage Ioster has reserved tent-space at the fair?" she purred in silken tones that had, ere this, entranced earls and marquises.

"Entirely certain, Great Lady," he replied. "The space he has reserved is thus-and-such," he added, indicating a position in that area of the grounds traditionally set aside for those who dealt in sorcerous amulets, charms, and periapts.

"Very good. As soon as my pavilion is ready, I will retire

with my serving-woman. I wish not to be disturbed. However, inform me when the Mage Ioster has reached the fairground, and make ready to escort me to his tent."

It was not until the morning of the first day of the Fair at Ithkar that the Mage Ioster finally arrived, and the lateness of his coming hence was doubtless to be ascribed to the considerable distance that he must travel from his residence in the fastnesses of the remotest south. Nevertheless, the Lady Ais had endured without any noteworthy patience the interval between her arrival and his own. At her age, the relatively primitive accommodations of her pavilion were to be endured, not enjoyed. Moreover, a woman of her wealth and position likes very little to be kept waiting by anyone.

One of her palanquin-bearers she had soundly whipped for a fancied impertinence, and she had scratched with cruelly sharp nails the soft breasts of her serving-woman for being a few minutes late with her bathwater.

As might be imagined, Borkis was greatly relieved when the mage finally made his appearance on the scene. His employer was an imperious woman with a vindictive nature and a vicious temper, and he had not the slightest wish to incur her ire.

So, when at length her agent informed her that Ioster had erected his tent, the lady wasted little time in securing a private interview. She was, in point of fact, his first customer at the fair.

A lean man in narrow robes of black and purple, with thoughtful, hooded eyes, he greeted her at the door of his tent and assisted her from her palanquin. No less curious to observe her legendary beauty than had been the workmen, he found her veiled in silks so skillfully arranged as to conceal every inch of her form.

Ushering her into his tent, he begged her to be seated and asked in what way he might serve her wishes.

"It has come to my knowledge that you possess the Black Talisman of Zoromé," she stated. Curious as to how the Lady Ais had procured this information, which was not common knowledge, yet not daring to ask, the mage gravely indicated that this was true.

"In his epoch, Zoromé was a most distinguished practitioner of the sorcerous arts, in particular of goblinry. The talisman to which you refer entered my collection but recently, by a private transaction."

"Explain, if you will, the nature of goblinry, and the precise powers of the Black Talisman," she ordered. "My agents have told me much concerning both subjects, but I wish to hear of these matters from your own lips."

"Zoromé was a famous master of elemental spirits," said Ioster. "Goblins are earth-elementals and within the sphere of their powers fall such matters as the curing of impotence, the quickening of a barren womb, the restoration of health, the renewal of youth, physical beauty, the fertility of farm and field and orchard, the discovery of mineral treasures, and—"

She silenced him with a lifted hand.

"Enough! I have heard all that I need. I wish to purchase the talisman and full information as to its use."

"Alas, Great Lady, it pains me to inform you that by the nature of the transaction by which I acquired the Black Talisman, I am not permitted to sell it—"

The Lady Ais interrupted by naming a price so unheard-of

that it made Ioster blink. When he still politely, regretfully declined to let her purchase the talisman, she doubled the amount of her first offer.

"Great Lady, it is not a problem of price but of the arrangements under which I came into the possession of the talisman. But there is no need for you to buy the talisman, for I will rent it to you for a night. Whatever the use to which you desire to put the talisman, the rites of goblinry are exceedingly simple and the operation will require no more than an hour, at most."

"I see," said the lady in measured tones. "Is any danger involved in the use of the talisman?"

"That is hard to say," replied the mage thoughtfully. "The talisman is a fragment of dense obsidian, a form of volcanic glass like blackest crystal. Therein the wise Zoromé long ago imprisoned a goblin."

"Does the thing have a name?"

He shook his head. "Such creatures have no names. To reply to your first question, there is not the slightest danger that the goblin can escape its glassy prison, for Zoromé sealed the creature and bound it with seven-and-seventy potent and powerful spells. But, like the earth itself from which they were formed, goblins are dull and obdurate, and this particular member of its race furiously resents its imprisonment and its impotence to gain its freedom. When you command the goblin to perform whatever act you desire of it, you must choose your words with care and phrase your orders beyond equivocation. They are by their nature malicious and tricksome, so be warned and wary."

The mage opened a small chest and withdrew several objects. These were a sheet of fresh parchment, an inkhorn and a new-cut quill, and one thing more. It was the last object that caught and held the fascinated gaze of the Lady Ais. For this was an irregular chunk of black glass wherein could be but dimly glimpsed a squat and grotesque minuscule form.

"I will set down the instructions and the ritual itself, Great Lady, and rehearse you in them to make certain that you perform the rite without error," he said.

Returning at once to her pavilion, the Lady Ais commanded her serving-woman to leave and ordered that she was not to be disturbed for any cause and that two armed bearers were to stand guard over the entrance.

Then she placed the piece of black glass on a low tabouret and fondled its slick, cold surface with greedy but hesitant fingers. The chill of the crystal gnawed at her bones, and within, the stooped, shadowy figure stirred a little as if sensing her nearness.

She then lit three black candles and burned some pungent herbs in a small brass chafing-dish, stripping entirely naked. In her state of nudity it could easily have been seen, were any other present, that few remnants of her famous beauty remained. She was thin to the point of gauntness and her breasts, once released from the undergarment that lifted and supported them, dangled flat and wrinkled.

Only in its classic bone structure and her enormous amethyst eyes did the face of Ais retain aught of its legended loveliness. Where it was not thickly painted with cosmetics, her skin could be seen as sallow and dry, and the ugly brown spots of age stained her bony, shriveled hands.

Performing the ritual with care, she addressed the talisman.

"Can you hear me?"

A voice dull, harsh, and grating replied in slow and sluggish words.

"I, can, hear, you."

"Can you see me?"

"I, can, see. What, do, you, want, of, me."

"When I was young I was very beautiful, very graceful, very much admired and desired by men. So supple was I in the dance, possessing a fluid and boneless grace, that princes were entranced. So white was my skin that lords and barons swore the petals of white roses seemed sallow next to my flesh. At thirteen I became the mistress of a great baron. In the springtide of my youthfulness I was deemed the most desirable woman in the realm."

"Tell, me, what, you, want, of, me," said the dull, deep voice.

"I wish to be in the springtide of youth, my white body fairer than before, the supple grace of my movements even more graceful than they were when I was young."

"It, is, done," said the goblin.

A milky radiance filled the dark glass, and swirled from it to envelop the naked old woman. It tingled with a delicious warmth as it seeped into her flesh. She felt a momentary thrill as it sank into her very bones, and then . . .

She uttered an involuntary cry, between a gasp and a moan as her body reshaped itself uncannily. And then she gave voice to a shrill shriek of pure panic, which the guards at the door could not help but hear. They looked at one another apprehensively.

They had been commanded not to disturb their mistress on any account. But thieves and assassins were not unknown,

27

even at the great fair. So the younger of the two men raised his voice.

"My lady? Do you require assistance?"

There came no reply from within. Summoning up his courage, the guard parted the flap of the tent and peered within. He saw the usual appointments, but no intruder. The silken raiment his mistress had worn was draped across the back of a carven chair. But the Lady Ais herself did not seem to be in sight. There was nothing else strange to be seen but a dully glistening chunk of black crystal upon a tabouret.

The burning candles and the parchment and the smoking herbs in the brass dish he did not even notice. For his gaze was fixed almost instantly upon the carpeted floor of the pavilion.

There a slim white figure writhed with supple and boneless grace. It was small and slim, and whiter than fresh cream or even the petals of the white rose, and its eyes were amethystine. It was very beautiful.

With a cry of revulsion and alarm, the young guard sprang into the tent and crushed the narrow, wedge-shaped skull of the young white serpent under his heel.

In the gloom of its dark prison, the goblin smiled a slow, slow smile.

TO TAKE A THIEF

C. J. Cherryh

Sphix meant a small sly animal; a thief and nuisance in fowlyards and brooderies. And Sphix meant Sphix himself, who was lean and long-eyed as his namesake, as hungry and as full of hubris when hunger drove him.

But not straight to the target. To go any straight line, his master Khussan had taught him, was predictable; and to be predictable was to be dead (no matter that Khussan was lately dead himself, swinging from the gibbet far down on dockside, far from nobles' tents and merrymakers and the festive business of the commons).

Thus for mistakes. And ambitions.

Sphix moved the way Khussan had taught him, all ease and smiles—handsomer than Khussan, coming up on manhood but not yet arrived. He had the long eyes of the east; the dark curling hair of the west; the swarthy complexion of the north—in fact, Sphix imagined all sorts of lineage for himself. His mother had no memory, she said, where *she* had come from, only of wandering the aisles of tables amid the color and the noise 'til old Melly took her in and taught her serving; and she had a thousand lovers (some lords) of every land in all the world.

Mostly he remembered drunken louts and his mother dying the hard way, of one of Melly's cures; but those were the bad days—his father was a lord: his mother told him so. Her last lover was Khussan, who beat her when he was drunk and made her laugh when he was not.

But his true father *was* a lord: his true father was all of Ithkar Fair. Like the fair he was seasonal—starving most of the year and living in gray misery; going sleek and fine and gay-coated at fairtime—

Wear good clothes, Khussan insisted. When a thing's snatched, they look for poverty.

And smile at the ladies (Khussan would) and look thoughtful at the tables (Khussan would ponder a thing oh so carefully, and something would fall off a table right into his pocket when he moved).

Bones, by now, he was.

Never go direct to the target. Move not arrowlike, but like the evolutions of the snake.

Even if one's belly ached with hunger.

The temple hove up ahead, above the gay-striped canopies of the aisles. Here and there were real buildings. Here the crowds were lords and ladies, Ithkar folk in stiff, brocaded robes; foreigners in silk; veiled folk and the gossamer-dressed Khoi. There was a gradation of wealth within the aisles. It began with trinkets and gold-washed brass, proceeded to semiprecious stones, and worked its way to the rarest and most fabulous of goldsmithing and gem-carving, in shops that had all their displays safe inside, bars upon the windows and guards with quick eyes and no sense of humor at all. Such shops catered to the gentry. The sale of even one such fabled gem was a days-negotiated event, as much for the prestige of the purchaser as for the profit of the treasure merchant; and the object might be worn in the glittering society of the pavilions, the rites of temple, to the awe even of lords.

Sphix knew these things. He was no beggar to keep his eyes on the mud; no common cutpurse to think only of the movements of his prey, and snatch and grab and swill down the meager take in some ale tent down by dockside, penniless by sunrise. Sphix was a *thief,* which, Khussan would say, was part magician, part entertainer, part lord.

He did not, for instance, look about with nervousness. His moves were all-gracious, his stopping at a counter got a merchant's hopeful glance, and gave him time to cast that backward look only another thief might know for the backtrail-watching it was.

His clothes were not stolen; they were bought. And they were fine enough to walk the aisles in and smile at the ladies and gentlemen in. He knew to a nicety how far up those aisles they would take him. He kept a few small pebbles in his purse to make a convincing weight—nice, bright ones to be sure. (Why, sir, he would say were he ever apprehended and his purse turned out—mere luck-pieces! I tossed my last in a harper's cap, I do forget where—should a man walk the fair with gold in his purse? There might be pickpockets and cutpurses, so I've heard. . . .)

31

He weighed a bracelet, smiled at the old merchant, and put it back. He felt a jostle from the crowd and turned in indignation—no, not deft enough a move: he could not palm the brooch. He caught himself on the counter and gave it up: no second try at the same booth. The merchant had not followed the crowd motion, only him. The man was too alert. He smiled, chaffered a bit with the old man, got his face to relax—"My mother had such a brooch, all set in rubies it was, with the blessed Evin's face—"

"Garnets," the old man said, running a gnarled finger around the rim. "Fine garnets. Mark the setting, set firm, here, rub it across your sleeve—see, not a snag. That's my craftsmanship. Hold it to the light."

"Oh, it's very fine. Very fine. I like this." He felt dizzy, the brooch held thus against the sun, the light shining in his eyes with the white, white brilliancy of late summer. He felt his knees go weak, the penalties of hunger. He blinked, lowered his arm, handed the brooch back.

"Young gentleman?"

"I haven't the funds just now—truly—" He looked left and right, scanning the crowd while his knees wobbled and his stomach felt as empty as his purse. He did not clutch the counter. "I'll remember this booth; I'll be back for it—could you save it for me?"

"No, no, young gentleman, first come, it's bought; a man has to— Are you well, lad?"

"The sun—I think I've forgotten to eat."

He wandered off, steadier now. Hunger did that, came and went, along with the wobbles. But he knew a panic gnawing as famine.

Khussan hanged. He had crept up later to the gibbet; and the sight haunted him, the twisted shape against the sun.

His nerve was gone. Four days he had not scored, not the least trinket. He had felt the unsteadiness in his moves, known his every flaw. A dead man had taught him. The best that he knew was hanging in the sun, food for birds. Khussan had failed—all his laughter, all his studied good humor, all the skills and tricks had not saved him. Something he had done was wrong and Sphix did not know what it was.

He did not know. And day by day, as the thought had been growing in him from the day Khussan died, he grew hungrier, and more driven, and (Khussan's precepts advised him) more a danger to himself.

Don't steal hungry, Khussan would say.

Don't work sick; or mad; or cocky, either.

It's an *art*, lad.

But those thoughts were dead. The birds were picking them from Khussan's brain, through empty eyeholes.

And day by day the hand that had faltered from fear grew unsteadier still with hunger.

Fool, Sphix told himself with Khussan's inner voice. *Fool*—walking up the aisle, remembering he should not be hurrying. (Where was he hurrying? to what? from what? He did not know.) Ahead were the too good shops, the too fine lords; the priests in black and glittering brocade, where even merchants wore robes fine enough for the jewels that they sold. His clothes were not good enough for this. He turned aside, bumped a shopper, and stammered a plea for pardon, walking on. The man likely checked his purse after. Suspicion. All it took was a finger pointed, a cry raised, and they would take him like Khussan—

Voices buzzed in his ears. The sun beat down on his head, making a red blaze behind his lids when he blinked. Sell his fine clothes, that he could do—there were the secondhand booths where he had gotten them; but such things always bought dear and sold at a pittance: the dealers knew the desperation of those who traded for their rags. A meal or two if he dealt sharp, a solitary meal; and after that, going in some worse garments, confined to a territory where thieves were more common and more guarded against, and the eyes of the merchants sharp indeed. Oh, Lords, he already had the wobbles, had already backed off from one gullible old man—

No. No. No.

Think calm, lad, Khussan would say.

Go at it calm. Laugh. Laugh gentle. Feel it. Be it. A true thief's an actor, juggler, artist. A true thief has pity, has a heart: steal what's little missed, steal from them as little miss it, steal from them as deserve to have it lost. Then the laughter comes, then you can laugh from the eye outward, and love them you steal from. That's the way.

He smiled. He dallied with a new counter, ignoring the gold-washed glitter, a professional eye going past all of that to the opals, the cameos in onyx, the ring—tourmaline; the jade, milk and green; the precious tiny coral that was worth everything on the table—never steal that. *That* would be missed. He smiled at the merchant and blessed the arrival of a clutch of teenaged girls, which diverted attention one precious instant—

Not long enough. The easy move with the fine opal headed for his sleeve—the worst of all moments. The merchant's head turned, his nerve broke: he hurried the move, the unforgivable sudden, suspicion-drawing inconsistency; and knew it. He melted backward in the crowd, knowing every move the merchant made without seeing it, the quick dart of the eye over his well-known counter, the opal— Oh, Lords, he was a fool, it was mnemonic, a set of three he had broken—

"Stop that boy, someone stop that boy!"

He kept melting away (don't run, don't run, the crowd would not know what boy the merchant meant). There was a general stirring as the crowd examined itself for fault, and he was mostly through it, easing away.

"*That one!* Stop him!"

He broke and ran as he had run when he was fruit-nipping in the autumn-market, when his legs were short and the tavern-keepers who kept the few permanent inns had not tried hard to catch him—no finesse in those days, none now, but a heart-thumping race, jostling fairgoers, oh, Lords, himself well dressed and moving wrong, drawing every eye, the fine clothes that had protected him now become the thief-catching mark, individual, describable—

His head swam. Startled ladies dodged him, he them, a knot of priests called out at him—he dived aside, through a curtained tangle of guy-ropes and pegs, and, weaving through the maze behind the tents, hid himself, hugged himself, faint and tucked up as he had hidden beneath the tavern stairs—

"Sphix," his mother would call. "Oh, Sphix, come out of there, I know where you be, imp—"

He bowed his head and squeezed tears from his eyes; looked up in a flood of sun against the flap. Shadows came and went like the puppet-plays, all strange with dazzle. He thought that he would faint, but fainting was not so easily achieved. Panic passed. No one came. Just the shadows. The hue and cry died down. He was trapped there, in a young gentleman's clothes, in a place no sensible young gentleman would get himself, in a place no thief ought to, and himself gut-aching with hunger and exhaustion, while the shadows dimmed and the day waned, and the ground beneath him went cold.

The voices grew fewer: there were the shouts of merchants to apprentices, closing down.

(Oh, Lords, don't let them move the flap aside.)

The voices grew louder, though fewer: the walled shops shut their iron gates and barred their shutters for the night; the lords and ladies of the pavilions sought entertainments among their own rank; the merchants of the tents rolled up their displays and betook them to safekeepings the temple provided (for a fee), to roister or commiserate the night away down among the taverns. Ithkar Fair changed its dress and became carnival, ceased glitter and became torchlit gaud. The gimcrack dealers ruled the night; the sellers of gold-washed trinkets, of glass gems and tinsel crowns, of luck-pieces and charms of spectacular bad taste.

But some jewelers merely changed displays, or put apprentices on duty, or rented for the night.

Into such a transformation Sphix crept, from beneath the overlap of two canvas displays; and if he staggered, it was not unlike the young bravos (some of them nobility pretending otherwise) and ruffians (some pretending nobility they had not) who careened through the aisles in this quarter beneath the temple's very walls, their wits and their manners left in the ale tents. They shouted and laughed, jostling him this way and that.

He walked—he knew only direction now. He lost whole

tracts of the course, passing through the aisles, knocking into drunken celebrants; and thinking, thinking how quickest to turn the stone to some few coins, to fill his stomach; roust old Tomek out and trade these clothes before the dawn—

The tents and booths began to be those of clothiers, like the gimcrack arts of near-the-walls, the cheaper goods left on display, the gaudy, the tawdry, the well used. He looked about him, dazed, trying to know where he might be. A set of carousers bore down on him.

One caught his arm, swung him with them—he tried to fling out again, feigning merriment. The arc swept on, imperiled tent-pegs and ropes, bore him stumbling beyond the torches of the aisle.

Then he struck and darted to escape in panic; but one seized him by the sleeve—it tore. He ran, stumbled on a guy-rope, and sprawled among the stakes.

They hauled him up again. "It's Khussan's lad," one said. He knew that voice without the torchlight that filtered through the tents and showed the black-bearded man, the broken nose, the gapped teeth. "Eh, pretty boy? What's it have? What's it take today? It gives it to us, eh?"

He said nothing. They found the stone; he knew they would. He knew they would hit him then, Coss and his little band. Not while Khussan was alive; but the master thief was dead, and the carrion birds moved in. He shut his eyes, squinted one open again.

"Coss, I got to have a copper—you want me thieve for you, I'm hungry, Coss. Lords, I got to get something—"

Gone the lordlings lisp; it was dockside cant, Coss's own. He had strength in him maybe to cock his leg and shove it where it would do Coss least good; but the other two had his arms and Coss would get up again. There was no choice left, no choice in all the world. Coss patted him on the cheek, ever so gently. "Let 'im go, lads, let 'im go—an' no, lad, ain't no copper. T'morrow there be a copper. Maybe a twain, if you brings us the likes again. Khussan got hisself hung: we got a guard or two looks the other way. We got this. We names ourself a thief and turns you in; or you thieves for us. It's us or it's Luttan; you works the fair, you pays your cut to someone, lad; Khussan you ain't, is you, now?"

"No," he said. And: "Coss, I got to have that copper."

They hit him then and kicked him when he fell among the tent-pegs, several times.

Then one took his hand and put a coin in it. "So's you knows where it comes from," Coss said.

There was that noise which in the night, in the lowest haunts of the fair, always attended private troubles: the laughter, dead a moment, picked up; the prudent went away quickly and by now were gone.

Sphix moved and closed his fingers on the coin in panic, for there was someone there with him, in the light that slipped through the tents, on the great flats of tent-sides and panels. He knew that he would be robbed again, perhaps of clothes this time; certainly of his coin; foreseeably of his life. But for that life, he could not stir his limbs beyond a feeble twitch, a halfway successful lurch onto his side to protect his vitals from a kick. He was cold, oh, Lords, cold and sick and to lose the copper was only a slower death—

"Son." No one had ever called him that. He risked an eye out of the protective squinch. Perhaps in the great justice of the Three Lordly Ones his father had arrived, the great miracle of his life, or he was quite crazed. This man that knelt down by him sounded old. Dim light shone silver off his hair and the brown shoulders of a homely robe. *This* was not the father he had dreamed of. He drew his hand to his waist, palming the coin to a slit in the belt, all the while the old man laid hands on him and felt his limbs and, Lords, gathered him up, cheek to a rough-spun robe, and held him like a child.

He had no strength to waste. He rested, figuring to hit when he had to. Be smart, Khussan would say; fight smart; meaning not at all when you can run. "How are the ribs?" the old man asked. "They break any?"

(Lords, what's he want?)

"Can you get up?"

He tried; the old man helped. It was—Lords, he saw the light glancing off the rough-spun brown—a friar; one of the wandering priests. He was safe, then. His knees nearly left him on the spot; but the old man's arm was there.

"Where can I take you?"

"Nowhere. Nowhere." Then a thought came muddling through: He thinks I'm quality. Hopes for some lot of alms. "They took all I had. My father—I ran away to the fair— they took all I had."

"Brother," the old man said. "I'm not a priest. Just a lay brother. Come on."

"Where?"

"Out of this place, before something worse happens."

"I'm hungry—"

"Hungry, after that?"

"I've *been* hungry, Father." The hope got tears from him—no need to act.

"We'll get you fed, then."

It was rescue: he limped along among the guys and tent-pegs, leaned on the old man, believing in miracles, that a thief could find an old man so crazy. "Bless you," he kept muttering, "bless you, Father—"

"Lords bless you, too, boy; mind your feet."

It was a flaky pastry, a cup of milk—*Ale will put you on your nose in it, son. Take the milk.* Sphix had wobbled up to the noisy little zone of benches and tables with the friar's arm firmly locked about his own: the friar had set him on a bench at the other end from doting parents placating a squalling youngster. Sphix blinked and winced at the screams, but he was too unsavory—they moved and took the howling brat. He shut his eyes, opened them again with a jerk as the bench rocked and the friar was back with food.

He ate, picking at the crust and letting his stomach know something was on the way: no rushing. There was meat and gravy inside. He still had his copper. The clothes—there was another benefit to fine clothes: witnesses saw the color, not the man. Tomek would trade off, if he could get to Tomek's booth. The outfit, split up, would never be recognized.

Coss—Coss was another problem. A permanent one. He could go to Luttan and his lot; but Luttan was worse. Nothing like Khussan.

Tears ran down his face while he numbly chewed away and drank the warm milk.

"Where are you staying, boy?"

He blinked; he shrugged then, because he felt the tears cold on his face and had no wish to look that way. "Dunno," around a mouthful.

"A weaver lets a corner to me, after hours. A place to sleep."

He blinked again. It was a dream of his, to prowl the tents after hours and not be caught; but he was not that skilled, to bypass the night-warding charms of the rich places: that took a minor magician, a special kind of thief. "Sure," he said. (But a weaver's shop—nothing to pocket there. He could see himself with some great bolt of cloth, staggering away.) "Sure. Thanks." He sipped at the milk.

The bruises hurt. His ribs and gut ached. He would be slow for days. And Coss—Lords, Coss expected profits.

He forced the last of the pie down and swallowed the last of the milk. He looked at the friar, who finished his and got up.

"Come along," the friar said.

He got up. His legs felt battered. He was sore everywhere. But he walked on his own, with the old man at his side through the crowds, the laughter of the young, the pranks.

A boy jerked the friar's sleeve. "Cut it!" Sphix yelled and aimed a kick, proprietary.

"No need for that," the friar reproved him.

"Brat'll have your purse," Sphix muttered. It was one of Oin's lot, no proper thief. Beggar. But opportunist.

Another ran up to stop the friar, a fat woman from a booth who pressed something in his hand. He touched her cheek, blessinglike. "Here's a coin," the friar said, opening his palm when they walked on. "They come to me. What if one were taken?" There was another beggar, another, and another. To an old woman the friar gave the coin.

Rage swelled up in Sphix, longing for that coin. "Lors-

41

sakes," he cried. "Father, that woman's no more blind than you."

"I don't need it," the friar said. "I've eaten. I have a place to sleep. She has to have something to give her guild . . . doesn't she?"

Sphix opened his mouth. Shut it. A tiny alarm rang deep within his heart. But the friar took his arm. "This way."

It was a wagon-tent, one of the down-Ith kind that pulled into the grounds at the start of fairtime, turned its draft animals to the livery, and settled deep into the appropriate rows. It extended awnings and all the appurtenances and produced a marvelous lot from its insides, which in this case was not alone a great lot of canvas, but skein upon skein of wools, carding-combs, folding chairs, peg-tables, vats, hanging-frames. It smelled of wools and warmth, of cookery and charcoal; it was a maze inside of hanging fabrics, blankets, like laundry of a hundred lamplit hues: stripes and plaids, checks and embroideries.

The merchandise flapped as they came in and gave up an old, old woman as gaudy as her trade, striped skirts, ripple-weave shawl, grizzled braids done up in yarn. "Who's this?" she said.

"I don't know," the friar said. "Son, you have a name?"

"Sphix." The blankets hanging leftward moved; a dark, frowning boy stood there; another move: on the right a man, huge and black-haired, with bare arms the largest he had seen on any man. Oh, Lords, the place was aswarm. No knowing what ambushes. "Sphix, ma'am." His eyes went back to the grandam in the braids, his smile immediate, winning, and tragic. "The good father said—"

42

"Of your charity," the friar said. "The lad was beaten. Robbed. I fed him." The friar was dragging him through the maze, the grandam left behind; there was a corner of the tent, a pallet. "Mind your manners. You're in Grandma Nosca's tent. Wipe your feet; don't tread the blankets."

They were pursued. The boy came bringing blankets, fine, new blankets. The friar handed them Sphix's way and Sphix clutched them, gazed perplexedly at the religious, remembering the fat woman and the coin. So now there were blankets.

"You a magician of some kind?" Sphix asked, half-afraid to hear the answer. "*Everything* come when you want it?"

"When I need it. Mostly." The friar sat down, kicked off his leather-and-wooden shoes, revealing gray woolen socks. He lay down and flipped the blankets over his rough habit. "To sleep, lad, sleep, that's what we're here for."

Sphix made his bed—never such a bed in all his life, not with first-time blankets. He worked his boots off (no socks), prudently tucked them under the blanket edge, and lay down with a great sigh.

Coss tried to haunt the edges of his sleep; there was always, last before sleep, Khussan's eyeless face. But he was too tired—too helpless, he told himself.

Then even fear for his life was too little a fear. His stomach hurt, but it was that good kind of hurt rich food gave it. He tucked up and shut his eyes—

—opened them again with the before-light bustle of activity. His boots were still there and likewise the coin in its place in his belt, which he had not even loosened.

He rubbed his eyes. The friar stirred and sat up.

He smelled coals.

"Breakfast," the friar said.

Sphix began to sit up. The beating hurt enough to bring tears to his eyes; but it was of no consequence. He smelled fresh bread and imagined wondrous things, like jam and butter, tasting them in his memory of special days, the tavern table and old Melly's preserves.

Oh, Lords, to be a priest, he thought; and eat jam and butter.

When the friar got up and made up his pallet, he took his cue, smiled his winningest smile, folding up his blankets. "Breakfast, Father?"

The old man did not smile, not all the way. Sphix knew such smiles, was a connoisseur of expressions; and that look frightened him, that wistful, I-know-you-lie look.

"Tea," the old man said, "and bread and butter. That suit you?"

Oh, mightily it suited.

"Yes, Father." He levered himself to his feet, staggered this way and that, and made the tent shake, wobbling into it. He kept the idiot cheerfulness on his face because the friar had an impatient look; he played the fool, because a fool could make laughter, turn questions, lie a bit.

And get out after breakfast.

"Who beat you?"

"Father—" Instant, owlish sobriety. "I've no desire to know."

There was Nosca, eldest; her son, Olf (Blackbeard), western and broad-faced; and Olf's wife, Tiggynu, eastern and flat-nosed, with small dark eyes and dusky skin and red enamel on her canines when she grinned. The imp was Stynnit, half-and-half, father's nose and mother's eyes and no one's freckles but his own. Sphix scowled at the brat and the brat grinned, having everything all his life and eating bread each morning.

Of a sudden, between the cakes and the second cup of tea, his aching ribs caught up to him, and it was hard to get up again.

But all good fortune ended.

There was the door. He thought of palming *something,* like a fat skein of wool, worth a penny. But he had no quickness left. He would botch it all. Besides, they knew his face.

"Good luck," the friar said when they both stood outside, the sun coming up pink and golden, the tents spreading themselves like newborn moths. Cattle lowed. A bird laughed. Fair folk began their own rushing about after supplies and water and taking slops out to the wagon.

Into this bustle the friar set out. Sphix caught a breath, danced on one foot, committed himself, plunged after. "Father, where are you going?"

"Oh, about. Up and down. Wherever." The friar never turned his head. Sphix faltered, fell behind. Hurried a second time.

"Mind if I join you?" Coins came this man's way. And blankets and breakfasts. And he hurt, Lords, he hurt; it hurt to run, hurt to walk, to breathe. He could not face a day of stealing. "I *know* the fair."

"So do I."

He dropped back, defeated.

The friar stopped, turned. "Well?"

Sphix caught him up, breathing like a winded horse and holding his side. But there would be supper. Maybe a place to sleep again. He swung along beside the friar, matching

45

strides and remembering—oh, sweet Evin, the *clothes*. The clothes he wore. He was hunted, up near the wall.

And suddenly—suddenly he spied one of Coss's folk, just sitting, the other side of the slops-wagon.

Three-Fingered Tok they called him. Small and lean, like the vermin that haunted grain bins.

Tok winked.

He kept walking, limped his way up even with the father and stayed there.

There were fair-wards, brass-hats, with their staves; they wished the friar good morning.

There were priests: they did not.

"What do you do?" Sphix asked, meaning what the friar did in his walking about.

"I'm doing it."

"Is this *it*? Walking around, picking up coppers, handing them to fake blind beggars?"

The friar turned on him a look very like Khussan's, all quizzical, as if he had said something very peculiar indeed.

And he walked, that was all, walked until Sphix was limping; until they were very near the walls and Sphix limped more and more.

"I hurt," Sphix said. He should not go closer. But to let the friar go his way and lose supper and a bed—to face Coss without a coin . . . "Father, I'm sick."

"Are you?" The voice was only concerned.

"I think—think I'd like to find shade and sit."

They sat. They sat and sipped fine ale at a booth, for a coin the friar had.

All the day was like that.

And in evening, when Sphix was limping in dead earnest: "Father—wait—"

"Coming?" the friar asked.

Sphix looked. A brass-hat was looking his way, just standing there leaning on his staff and looking at him in the twilight. A chill went up his back.

He came, in all haste, limping all the way.

"Is it Nosca's?"

"You want a place to sleep?"

He stopped dead; not for nothing he read human faces, knew humor at his expense. Begging, the old man wanted. He would have said no.

But there was Tok to think of. He had only a copper coin. He had clothes that marked him thief for any witness. And Coss—Coss had that opal, enough to get him hanged.

"I guess," he said, victim of his pride, "I guess I can find one."

"Boy."

He looked back, mouth open. Saw a sorrowful smile.

"Want supper?" the friar asked.

They shopped among the counters. They sat in evening in the benches of the pastry booth; ate pies; drank ale.

"This being a priest," Sphix said in deep contentment, "pays—"

It was Tok. Coss. Standing beyond the rail.

The friar turned his head, or started to.

"Hey." Sphix put his foot up onto the bench opposite. Sweat broke out on his bruised sides. "Father. . . ."

"You worried about something, son?"

Sphix took a sip, studied the ale in the mug. His heart beat triple time. He looked up again. "Maybe." (Lords, the old man was a fool. Never saw. Helpless. Frail as aged bone.) "Maybe we ought to stay here a while. Walk real careful. There's something over there I don't like the look of."

"Someone that you know?"

"*Don't look*, for lorssakes. You stupid?"

"No," the friar said. "Never was."

Sphix stopped in midsip. Just froze, alarms banging away in his heart and gut. Resumed the sip. "That so, Father? You know them?"

"Man named Coss. Who doesn't?"

"You do know the fair."

"Ought to. I work it, too."

"You really a priest?"

"In the sense you mean. Yes."

He did not look at Coss. They were waiting for their payment. Waiting for what he would have stolen in the day. But hassling Coss: that was asking for a knife. Weapons never passed the gates. They were made secretly. Inside.

"Got an idea?" the friar asked.

He looked at the old man. Sweated. "You got money, Father? How much?"

"A few coins—" The friar reached for his purse.

"Lorssakes, don't *hand* it me. Not in front of them. I'll get it." He took his feet from the bench, set the ale mug aside, drew the friar to his feet, and palmed his own small razor. "You want to take those mugs back, get our coin, huh?"

"Son—"

"I'll be here." He brushed close, severed the thong in the same motion. "Go on." He walked on to the rail and laid the hand with the purse in it on the post. Tok came up.

He lifted his hand. Tok's maimed hand replaced it, and the purse was gone. "Light," Tok said critically. "Ye c'n do better, chick."

"I'll do better."

"Old man got money; priests allus got money. Ye gots yeself a religious, eh? Ye don't goes an' drinks it all, eh, chick?"

"Get!" Sphix hissed.

"Wants a *big* purse t'morrow, we does. Eh, chick?"

Sphix pushed off from the rail and walked back into the crowd, caught up the friar.

"My purse is gone," the friar said plaintively. He had a coin between his fingers, what he had gotten for returning the mugs to the counter. He seemed not to know what to do with it. "Here." He handed Sphix the coin. "You manage it."

"Father—" He was disgusted. Harried and terrified. "Let's go." He caught the friar's arm and dragged him on through the crowd, past laughing folk, past an escaped pet, a shrieking child.

Tok and Coss were gone.

There was time left at Nosca's tent; the nighttime with the carousers and the nonsense, the counters drawn in and the flaps thrown down (for Nosca sold no cheap thing): the fair went by outside; and there was tea, and talk, and the blankets removed from Nosca's great loom, which she worked and thumped away at; while Tiggynu and Olf spun yarn and young Stynnit carded the loose wool.

So did the friar work at carding. And handed a carding-comb to Sphix.

Sphix worked at it with a vengeance, listened to the merry

talk: Tiggynu laughed and flashed her enameled teeth, supervised Stynnit a bit in spinning. "This lad might learn," she said of Sphix. "He has good fingers."

Sphix forgot his ready grin. Remembered it too late and felt not at all like laughing, for he had looked over everything in the shop, measuring with an eye to value; and truth—there were valuables all about. But none for his kind of talent.

"Here," said Tiggynu. "I'll show you."

It did have its tricks, this spinning, sending the yarn out just so. "He has an eye," Tiggynu said—for artist that Sphix was, he rejected his own mistakes, worked and worked 'til he had done one perfect string. "Well," Tiggynu said. "Well." It was the first thing ever he had made, that he could remember, that little red yarn. He felt a small glow of pride for it and so wadded it up with the rest of his mistakes. "Not enough of it, is there?"

The loom stopped thumping. Nosca left her bench, clapped her hands. The outside had grown quiet, or quieter. "Bed, bed, bed," she ordered.

So they went there.

"It's not fair," said Stynnit. "He got it first time."

"His hands are older," Nosca said.

"Not as old as yours," said Stynnit, cozener, being shoved off to bed in the maze of hanging blankets. His voice diminished. The light persisted, reflected along the tent-top.

The friar reached their corner and started making his bed.

So did Sphix, with complete attention, back turned. He sat down, pulled off his boots with a vengeance, determined to be beneath blankets, cover his head up, try to forget Coss, and avoid the friar's questions.

"Son," the friar said, behind him.

50

He said nothing, but loosened his belt, half turned to seize a blanket corner and arrange it.

"Son."

"You're not my father."

"You ran away from him."

"I did."

"Coss, I mean."

He was surprised into looking. Met the old man's eyes, as sad as before, as crazy soft. He flung himself around in the friar's direction, knees up, arms clutching the blanket to his chin. "Look, old man." He kept his voice down, mindful of Nosca's folk. "They think you got money. That Coss is *crazy*. They see you get money, they see you pass it out, they think you've got *plenty*."

"I—"

"Do. Sure. *Lorssakes*, Father. They'll cut your throat for a copper. They think you're rich."

"I—"

"Am. Lords! You're a lunatic!"

The old man grinned, a boy's grin, all laughter.

"It's not funny. That Coss *isn't funny*, Father. They know you've got money."

"Do you want to know?"

"Have you?"

"Better." The friar reached within his collar and drew a cord over his head, which held a small pierced stone veined with blue.

"That? That's a river-rock!"

"It's a wish-stone. A holier man than I am blessed it. It's good luck."

"I'm no fool, Father. It's still a river-rock."

The slyest smile touched the old man's eyes. He took Sphix's hand and closed the fingers on it. "Coss won't be interested in it. But I want you to have it. Who knows? Maybe you'll walk down the street and things will come to you."

"*That*'s not why; it's that by-the-Lords priest's habit. And Coss—"

"Wear it."

He put it on, defeated. Thrust it inside his shirt.

"See," the friar said, "already someone's given you something."

"Father. *Listen* to me. I got to get money—"

"How do you do that?"

He had his mouth open. He shut it, quick, before something got out.

"Where will you find it?"

"Hey. I thought it was supposed to come to me, huh? Look, Father—you hang around that Olf tomorrow. You don't leave this tent. Let Coss forget you."

"Where will you find it?"

He sat very still, trapped in the old man's sight. "I'm a thief. You've known it from the start."

"I was there in the aisle. I saw it. I couldn't stop it. Where are you going to get the money?"

"That's my business."

"Where do you work?"

"You one, too? You conning me, Father?"

"No. I'm not a thief."

"Brass-hat?" His muscles clenched up, aching around the ribs. "You after thieves?"

"No."

52

"*You're not my friend, hear me?* You go being my friend, old man, Coss'll cut your throat for sure. I'm getting out of here." He rolled over, snatched his boots, and flung the blankets off.

"You don't have to worry over me."

"Sure, sure." He pulled the right boot on, shoved down on the heel, and struggled with the left. "You stay by Olf, old man. Coss figures I talked, figures you can finger him to the brass, you're dead. *Dead,* old man." He jammed the right heel home and got to his knees.

"You're not like Coss. Why work for him?"

"I got no choice, I got no choice, that's all." His ribs hurt, his bruises hurt. He mourned lost meals, lost bed, lost comforts. Anger made a lump in his throat, and memories welled up, Khussan's face. "They hung my master. I'm *good,* Father. I'm a *good thief,* an' they're not."

"What's a good thief?"

"Lissen—" He hunkered there, held up the hand Tiggynu called agile, worked the fingers. "You ever feel that purse go? No. That's just a thing I can do. I'm not even good at that. Not like the other things. I can lift things no one sees, things drop into my sleeve, you'd never see them go—"

"Never hurt anyone."

"I never hurt anyone." He dropped harder on his haunches, planted himself, arms between his knees, furious at this pursuit. "Father, I'm a *thief;* Coss is dirt, real dirt. Come on, you believed that gentleman I played."

"It's a good speech you can do."

"I got the manner, got the moves. Old man, I know stones good as the jewelers do."

"You must."

53

"I can—" He remembered the family, caught his breath. Lords, the lights were not blown out, and it was quiet elsewhere. Listening, they were. Huddled terrified. Or Olf . . . But the friar's eyes were dark, absorbing wells. "I can tell a fake, tell the best, Father." He lowered his voice: he wanted, Lords, wanted Khussan back. "And I never take the best; likeliest that's got a spell on't. I never break a set; these merchants, they got their ways to remember, patterns, how they set the stones out—" The eyes drank on, dark and wide. All his wounds ached. "I tell you something else, Father; it's a game. They know there's thieves; I know they know; I never, *never*—took nothing they'd grieve for. I could take something big. Really big. Take one of them lord-jewels, I could; but that'd bring down the brass on all of us thieves, stir up the law, get me hunted— Smart, Father. That's the difference between me and Coss. I never hurt no one I take from."

"But that's the thing, son. You do *take*."

He blinked, drew in his breath. It hit him in the gut, that the old friar wanted a sermon after all. "Huh," he said. He was not even angry, only hurt. He reached out and patted the old man's arm. "You tried, priest. You're quick. I give you that." He put on the gentleman again, stood up, faked a grin. " 'Night, Father. Mind what I said. And you bring the brass on me *I'll* cut your throat. Huh?"

With that, out of the corner, through the blanket maze, out the tent-flap.

He looked sharp, then—a quick dart of the eye to the shadow, still slightly nightblind from the faint light inside. He stood still in that condition, missing the watchers outside and wishing they were in sight.

But he imagined the stir behind him, too. Lords, the eavesdropping family would be at the priest in short order, angry and apt to bring down the watch. *How could you bring him here?*

So maybe the friar would lose a bed for it. He, Sphix, he lost a whole part of the fair he would never dare walk: the weavers knew his face.

Should have taken the blanket. Fool.

He had lost his edge. The priest had dulled him, that was what.

He started walking, no slink, but the walk of anyone going through the aisles; time enough to run if they raised the hue and cry and the brass-hats got into it. He was good at crowd mingling, if the tents turned out.

A shadow flowed into his path, in the dim glow of inward-lit tents, the torchlight persisting from down the way. It waited for him. He spun half-about and cast a look behind.

More shadows. Bad news. A dive off this strip into any between-tents space would find others: Coss was stupid, but no fool.

He walked on. More shadows flowed outward to join the one. Lords, Lords. He hurt already. Another beating he could not take; it was time for glibness.

He held his hands outward, approaching Coss, for Coss it was, centralmost of the thugs. Grinned charmingly. "Dear master."

"Master, be I? Where's the money?"

Rough hands searched him, bypassed the stone, got the coin; pulled him aside to shadows to do the job more thoroughly—he hoped only that. He let them. There was nowhere to hide, not in all the fair, if Coss was after him, and he had no connections.

The search got rougher. They jerked off his boots and turned them out; held him by both arms.

"Come on, Coss, my feet are cold."

It got him a belly-blow. His breath whistled out. He doubled as best he could with his arms locked on either side and came up with Coss's fingers in his hair.

"You got real cozy with them folk, eh? *You talks to that religious, does you?*" (A knee to the groin. A jerk upward on his hair.) "Admits you's a thief?"

Oh, Lords, they'd been up against the tent wall—

"You's a fool, boy." (To the gut this time.) His knees went. He sagged, beyond controlling his legs to fight; Coss jerked his head up again. Dinner tried to come up. "A by-the-Lords real fool. Now we gots two ways to shut them folks up. One's killing you. But boy, you's trained real good, real nice, nice face, nice manners . . . killing you's a waste. We just solves your problem for you, ain't that nice? Then you knows who your friends is."

Another blow, to the gut again. The wind went out of him, the light next, and he came back with his face against the dirt, such a numbness all over that foretold pain when it stopped.

Fool, Khussan said.

And it was the friar's face. Tiggynu's enameled grin. His knees were moving, driving him up on his hands. The earth met his face; he pushed up again and vision came back in a muddle of dark and light.

Lords, no time to be sick. He numbed himself and held his gut and ran a few off-course steps, fell, and heaved up, one spasm after the other—got to his feet again and drove his legs to movement.

"Murder!" he yelled down the aisle of tents. *"Wake up! Murder in weavers' row!"*

He kept going, barefoot. Panic rose in the tents, no word that he could hear. It was a fool would come out to mix in trouble: it was for the watch he cried.

Fire blossomed orange in the dark ahead, Lords, *fire* in the tents, a spark at first. "Fire! Fire! Fire!" voices yelled ahead; shrill and deeper screams.

"Father!" he yelled. The light blurred on dark figures. He sucked wind, drove pain away, and ran.

Folk came pouring out of the tents. "Fire, fire, fire!" the shout went out across the fair. Shadows struggled in the light, one tall man laying about him with a stick at a ring of three that darted at him. Tongues of fire went up the tent-side. "Buckets! Water!" the cry went up. "Wet down the tents!"

"Olf!" Sphix cried. It was the tall weaver so beset: Tiggynu, too—she laid about her with a pole, braids flying, shrieked something foreign and defended Olf's back, but not her own. *"Tok!"* Sphix screamed, and hit the knifeman full on. They both went into the dirt, Tok squirming beneath him. He found the knifehand, pinned it with both hands, used knee and elbow at groin and throat 'til Tok stopped struggling. There was a great hiss: another: "More buckets!" the cry went up.

He staggered for his feet. "Here's one!" someone yelled, and he was grabbed on either side. A brass-hat moved in, gathered Tok up.

He blinked, saw one fire dying, another waving—torches

of the Watch, the gleam of light on brass helmets, brass-bound staves. He twisted his neck: two such had his arms and dragged him over to stand with Tok and Coss and One-Eared Fix.

He kicked, never mind his ribs. He wanted free, not to hang. Pain exploded across his ear. He went half to his knees. "Hang on to that one," someone said; and Coss broke away, went pelting through the night. Sphix lurched up, tried to run, but they had him fast. Faces showed in torchlight, figures in the swirling smoke—Olf and young Stynnit reunited; Tiggynu unharmed—

"Father," he cried. The fair-ward pulled at him to take him away. *"Father—"* For he saw the friar nowhere, and he twisted in the brass-hat's grip, trying to look behind him, in the crowd that rallied there. *"Father!"*

The crowd came between. They hastened him through the gathering mob that shouted for rope and hangings.

"Wait," a great voice cried. "Wait!" A huge arm snatched him and crushed him in a grip like iron. "That's my son you've got."

Sphix gaped up at him, at great black-bearded Olf. "That's the weaver," someone told the brass. And Sphix hung there in Olf's embrace. His knees went.

Lords, his *father*? But his father was a lord. To such inanities his mind went. Then, Sphix-like, they went to practicalities. The weaver lied—for some crazed reason the weaver lied, but the neighbor-merchants would raise an outcry.

"That's Sphix," they would say, "Sphix the thief."

But no one did.

"We've been looking," the brass-hat said, "for a boy of his description—"

"Couldn't be my son," Olf the weaver said.

"Shame," someone aged cried, "shame, they burn our tent, the watch takes up our son—"

The crowd muttered.

"You swear to him," said the fair-ward; and hands that still held his collar let go. "Mind, if he's in trouble again—"

"Come on, lad," Olf said.

Sphix tried. His legs went; and Olf simply dragged him by a hand within his belt through all the commotion. There was light; there was the stench of burned wool; truth, there was nothing savory in himself, with moisture bubbling from his nose and running in his eyes, his knees failing at every other step.

Then they braced up, for there was the friar sitting on the ground in front of the tent with a cloth pressed to his brow.

"Con artist," Sphix said when Olf had dragged him up to the friar and dropped him there. "*Fake*. You're not dead—"

He fell on his face and wept.

They patched the tent up—Lords, Olf even found his boots. The water-carts made the rounds off hours, replenishing water-jugs, enabling a little scrubbing-up; but Grandma Nosca's remedy was wine and herbs, both on the cuts and in upset stomachs. "I can't," Sphix protested on the third round, getting up. "I've got to go—" There was precious little dark left for one with so far to walk.

"Go where, pray?"

"Oh, down the road." He kept his voice light. He ached, not alone in his bones, but in his heart. It seemed unfair, in one night to find he loved an old man and lose him and the fair forever. "They'll be hunting for me, every thief in Ithkar; Lords, I know their faces, don't I?"

"Would they come here?" Olf asked.

"No, not likely. That Coss, he's crazy. But he'll be out that gate and down the road. Folk'll love that one like the plague, the brass knowing his face now like they do. No. Thieves is thieves. Takes care of our own. And I'm for the road myself."

"I think he should fix the tent," Tiggynu said.

"He'd have to learn weaving," said Olf, "to do that."

He stared at them.

"Is he staying?" asked Stynnit.

He sat down again, wincing with bruised ribs.

"I guess he is," said Nosca, and puffed at her pipe. "Mind," she said, motioning with it, "you keep a sharp eye out to the merchandise. No one ought to light-finger us. We got our own thief. Afraid of work, boy?" She tapped the ash out. "To bed. We'll sell double tomorrow. Crowds'll come to see our burned spot, won't they?"

He blinked, because it was true, and the old woman no fool at all. Like Khussan, she was.

And in the morning, in the grayest early dawn, full of fresh bread and salted butter:

"*Lorssakes*, Father—" Sphix caught the old man up halfway down the aisle, limping nigh as bad as he was. "Where you going?"

"Oh, a little turn about the rows. Not far today."

"I'll walk with you."

"Haven't you got a tent to patch?"

"Haven't you forgot something?" He fished in his collar for the stone. "How would things come to you, else?" He hung it about the friar's neck. "So's the pennies come, old man."

"It's just a river-roçk."

"Old fake."

The friar grinned, a boy's grin. "Worked this time, though."

He walked off. Sphix stared after him, then walked back up the row with a swagger in his limp.

He was scared, that was what. He had never left Ithkar Fair, bright disappearing summer and gray, drab winter, when the fairgrounds shrank to a huddled village of permanent buildings beneath the walls.

He had never been beyond sight of the temple, the taverns, the docks.

Nosca talked of downriver; of dealing clear to the sea in winter.

Son, she'd called him, too, this morning, giving him an extra bit of bread and naming his duties.

He was caught, fairly snared and tangled.

And he found a tune of Khussan's and whistled it up the street.

JEZERI AND HER BEAST GO TO THE FAIR AND FIND MORE EXCITEMENT THAN THEY WANT

Jo Clayton

"Ow!"

Her mother ignored Jezeri's squirming and used the end tooth of the ivory comb to tease loose a stubborn tangle in the mop of hair that sun and wind had dried to the color and consistency of straw. "If you did this yourself a bit more . . ." she said.

"Oh, Mama."

"Oh, yes." She stepped back and stood tapping the comb against her smooth brown cheek. "I suppose you'll be safe enough on your own."

Jezeri wiped her nose on her forearm, scuffed her boots across the brittle dirt, quivering with anxiety lest her mother change her mind about letting her go.

"Ah, well, soon enough you'll be going into skirts. Let me see your hands."

63

"Oh, Mama."

"Hands."

Jezeri rubbed her palms down the sides of her sleeveless undershirt, held out her hands.

Her mother turned them over, inspected the backs and fingernails, reversed them, and sniffed at the palms. "I thought so. Reeking of horse. Wash. Now."

"They aren't dirty."

"Soap and water. Now. I'll have your tunic ready when you finish."

Jezeri slouched around to the back of the wagon where the tailgate was lowered to make a washstand. She dipped lukewarm water into a basin, added a dollop of soft soap, sniffed at the soap clinging to her fingers. Scented with oil of coolblue, it reminded her of her mother, of the garden at home with its herb beds and disciplined riot of flowers, of crisp cool sheets on a summer evening. She didn't really mind washing, what she minded was the waste of time, her time, the first night of her first fair.

Interfering relatives (more often than not Uncle Herveh; he went through life looking for things to complain about) came and chided Miles Kunisca for letting his daughter run wild.

Her father said: What's the harm? Let her be.

He said: Jezi is a better hunter and horse-trainer than her brothers. I'd be a fool to change her. And she's a good girl.

He said: My mother was just such a flyabout. Tell me to my face she turned out bad, hunh! Time enough for harness when Jezi's under Moon's Rule.

Her mother snapped the tunic through the air, then tugged it over Jezeri's head, stood back as Jezeri wriggled her arms into the sleeves with an explosion of elbows and some hard breathing. She settled the tunic on her daughter's shoulders with a few brushing pats, smoothed the hood into a neat fold. "Your brothers." There was amused exasperation in her voice. "They took care to go off before I could tell them to look after you." She shook her head, the braided coils over her ears shimmering like gold shields, brushed a few wisps of hair out of Jezeri's eyes. "Don't talk to anyone but the venders in the stalls and that only if you're buying something, you hear? This isn't the Vale and these aren't homefolk who've known you all your life. Any trouble—any, mind you—you yell loud for a fair-ward. Bronze-shod staves and brass helmets, remember?"

"Aieea bless, Mama, all I'm going to do is look around."

"Hah. I know you, little-fall-in-the-mud-when-it-hasn't-rained-for-a-triple-moon." She ran her thumb across the band of embroidery that outlined the tunic's unfastened neck opening. "That beast of yours, he's been chewing on this." She looked around. "Where is he? Don't tell me you're going without him."

" 'Course not, Mama. Old 'Un's watching him for me."

"So . . . you be careful, hear?"

Jezeri sighed, smoothed her hands down her front. "I hear."

Her mother laughed, a soft rippling sound. "Oh, I know, Jezi. Right now it's all pains and fuss and no pleasure being a woman. Just you wait, though."

Dark amber eyes smiled into dark amber, mother's eyes and daughter's eyes creased into laugh slits, crescent-shaped under thick blond brows. Then her mother turned away. The moon was low in the east, swimming in the violet afterglow of sunset. She pointed. "You've got till the moon's in the

65

paws of the Pard, then I want you back here. Not a minute
more, you hear?''

"Oh, Mama.''

"Oh, get along with you.''

With a chuckle and a shapeless wave of her hand, Jezeri
sauntered away from the wagon, coating her bubbling excitement with transparent nonchalance.

Under the thatched roof of the open-sided horse shed a
dark figure sat cross-legged by a fire of dried dung, bent over
a chunk of wood, working at it with a small knife whose
blade was little longer than his palm. As Jezeri came up, he
gathered a handful of shavings and tossed them into the fire,
sat watching the dance of blue and green among the red
flames. His scarred hands were turned to ancient roots by the
play of firelight and shadow, his face to a gargoyle's mask.
He looked up as she ducked under the edge of the thatching,
his mouth twisting into the lopsided smile he saved for her.
"Your mum finally let you loose?''

"Uh-huh.'' She squatted across the fire from him, watched
him ease a long curl from the wood. "Where's Tanu?''

"Picking fleas off Jet's back.'' He turned the chunk over
and began working on the other side. "Last time I looked.''

"Ah.'' She rubbed at her nose. "Wagon-draw's tomorrow
midday.''

"Ah,'' he said.

"Been looking 'round?''

"Some.'' He detached a long curl from the chunk, played
with it a moment, tossed it into the fire, where it gave a sharp
resiny smell to the acrid bite of the burning manure. "Pair of
bays three barns down. That way.'' A nod of his head.
"Only ones that look like giving your father a hard time.''

"No pair's as good as Jet and Nightlord."

"Mmm," he said. "The draw's the decider."

"Mmm." She sniffed at the smoke blowing past her face. "That's a good smell; what's that wood?"

"Got it off a sailor down to the wharves. Load of aromatics in." His mouth twisted into a bitter downturn, his eyes half-shut, he tapped the wood on his palm. "From the forests of Estarin-Over-the-Water." With a quick flick of his hand, he tossed the wood to her. "Highland cedar."

She stroked the smoothed places, sniffed at it, tossed it back. "Mama's linen chest. You going fairing?"

"No." He sat staring down at the wood he was turning over and over in his hands. "You taking Tanu?"

" 'Course. Why?"

He set the wood aside, clasped his hands over his knee. "Folk here from all over. Some might know what he is. Get nervous." He hesitated, stared over her head at nothing or at memories that brought him no pleasure. "There are those, Little 'Un, who'd pay ten times Tanu's weight in gold. Hassle you. Try to take him away from you. Temple priests apt to know. You keep away from them. Why not just leave him here?"

She scowled. "Someone would pay, you said. Who? Why?"

He stroked a knobby thumb along his jawline. "You don't want to know that, Little 'Un."

"I wouldn't ask, didn't I want to know."

He shrugged but said nothing.

She itched to push him for answers but he was her dearest friend and she had to respect his silences. Besides, being born and bred of practical Vale stock, she wouldn't waste her breath putting questions she knew she'd get no answers to.

Even for her, Old 'Un wouldn't talk about anything before he came to Vale.

Disgusting old Uncle Herveh started picking at Old 'Un, complaining that no one knew what or who he was, complaining that he never answered questions, hinting that the stranger would murder and rape them all given half an opening.

Her father said: He don't want to talk, that's his business. He does his work and keeps himself to himself, which is more than I can say about some folks here.

He smiled his lopsided smile and she felt better. "Look, Little 'Un," he said. "If you won't leave him with me, then you keep your eyes wide and watch your back."

"You and Mama, hunh!"

His low rumbling chuckle was just louder than the hissing of the fire. He tested the knife on his thumbnail, slipped it into the flexible sheath he'd made for it, reached across the fire. "Stick this in your boot."

"But that's forbidden. Papa said—"

"Not big enough to matter, this knife. Besides, what the priests don't know won't hurt you." He dropped his hands on his knees. "So get you off. Enjoy your fairing."

"If you say so." She slid the knife into her boot, jumped to her feet. Whistling breathily, hands clasped behind her, she sauntered past black geldings snuffling at oats and straw in the manger, jerking their heads up as a stallion some distance away bugled a challenge or a dog howled at the moon, nudging each other for comfort of kind.

The five-year-old stallion Jet was the fourth one in. She rubbed his nose. "Bays, hunh. They're never as good as you. You show 'em tomorrow, hey? You and Nightlord." She scratched his face between his wide-set eyes, smoothed the shaggy lock of mane falling forward between his ears. "Tomorrow Mama and me, we'll polish your hooves until they shine and braid red ribbons in your mane and in your tail and you'll be the most beautiful horse at the fair." She gave him a last pat, stepped back, and called, "Tanu. Tanu."

With a warbling squeal a small brindle beast came lying from somewhere near the roof, landing with a solid thud in Jezeri's arms, golden eyes opening and shutting slowly, flower-petal ears twitching, blunt black nose twitching, long sinuous tail swaying back and forth, horizontal stripes of umber and amber down to a hairless black tip that was a finger as dexterous as those on his hands. Jezeri tickled his stomach, laughed at his song of welcome, then settled him into the roomy pocket her mother had sewn inside her tunic. Tanu scratched about until he was comfortable, popped his head through the tunic's neck opening, closed his hands on its sides, slid his long tail about her neck. He sang his contentment to Jezeri, then settled into a vibrating expectant silence as she began threading through the stock sheds, the wagonloads of cages filled with birds of all sizes, coursing-cats, hounds, and more exotic beasts, creatures she'd never seen before—though none remotely like her Tanu.

The fledgling night was filled with sound. Voices—talking, laughing, shouting, singing. Snatches of melody from a guitar at one shed, a flute at another playing another tune, a mouth harp buzzing away at a third. Dog barks and ox bellows. Horses snorting, neighing. The mewling of assorted cats. The shriek of a night bird soaring high above the river lake. Jezeri laughed with the joy in being alive and young and about to explore the greatest fair of all and Tanu echoed and reinforced her laughter.

At the edge of the stock section she stopped and frowned into the night. On her left were the sounds, the bits and pieces of bright color, the dancing shadows and glimpses of marvels from the fringes of the other three precincts of the fair; these beckoned to her, but ahead of her something else caught her interest more strongly. The docks and ships from lots of places, some from Estarin, maybe a chance, just maybe, to discover clues to the Old 'Un's past. Tanu began singing to her in his cheerful imitation of her speech patterns. She scratched behind his ear. "I know. Plenty of time for both. The ships first, yes—though there's probably nothing there, you know. Old 'Un's luck. Still, we go hopefully." She giggled as Tanu's tail-finger tickled her cheek. "Stop that, you. This is serious investigation."

The wharves were sunk in the shadow of a huge crumbling warehouse, a roofless relic damaged in a quake and long abandoned for the tighter and more suitable sheds built closer in to the waterside. Scattered lanterns hanging from masts cast scattered pools of light that made the darkness all the blacker in the open sheds and the barred sheds fronting the docks. Jezeri strolled along the walkway, her boot heels thudding dully on the warped, worn planks.

The ships at the first dock were dark and deserted, but at the second, a man and his sons were unloading wheels of salt like full moons from a riverboat like a crescent moon with its high peaks fore and aft. A lantern swung swaying from the single mast, the shadows it cast dancing to the beat of music wafting from the other sectors of the fair, the jars of the competing tunes and instruments mended by distance. The salt wheels rose in squat towers on the dock beside bales of seaweed, the salt smell cool and fugitive, the seaweed tangy

70

and medicinal. Jezeri knew what the dark leathery leaves were, though she'd never seen the sea. Traders brought rolls of them now and then to the Vale and her Aunt Jesset, who was heal-woman at Aieea's shrine, used them in her medicines.

Jezeri prowled on, weaving between piles of wood, some of it turned into rough-cut planks, the rest left in trunks with the bark still on, though the small limbs had been trimmed away. She smoothed her fingers over the cut ends, reveling in the mélange of smells, letting Tanu sniff the wood, wondering if the more exotic woods might wake memories in him, though he was such a tiny thing when he crawled out of Old 'Un's shirt.

The neighbors came to call: Where did he come from? Who is he? What is his rearing? Is he dangerous?

Her father said to some: Out of nowhere.

He said to others: Jezi found him.

Aunt Jesset came to tend him. She said: What's your name, friend?

He smiled at her. He said: Pick a name.

Her father said: What can we call you, friend?

The stranger said: What you will.

The neighbors said: What's his name?

Her father said: We call him Old 'Un. Fits well enough, he looks older'n the oilberry tree Grandma planted by the string door.

He came out of the dawn. Jezeri (three years of willful mischief) came on him when she was poking about the milkers' corral, getting underfoot and into a lot of things she had no business bothering with. She was startled but unafraid and curious. He was torn and burned and battered, starved,

71

parched, a miserable tatter of a man with an odd remnant of grace. He used the corral gate to pull himself erect, bowed to her with an elegance that delighted her, and collapsed at her feet.

Tanu crawled from his shirt and tottered to Jezeri, a pathetic bit of bone and fluff. He huddled against her bare foot, clasped her littlest toe with a small black hand, and won her heart forever.

As she lingered with the woods, she searched the silent ships that had brought them for a sign of anyone she could talk to, but their lanterns were unlit, the crews most likely tasting the delights of the fair. Tanu groused with her, then reached up and patted her chin, making her laugh, sang his own laughter in response. "Like I was afraid of," she said. "Nothing. Oh, well." She strolled on, leaving the unhelpful wood behind, peering into the barred cells at the treasures sequestered there.

Bales of fine woolens, silk, linens, their glory gleaming through rips in the more plebeian outer wraps. Piles of artifacts from the ancient places. Boxes of porcelains and stoneware. Rolls of tapestry. Scrolls housed in fine vases. Glimmering mirrors and other glassware. A thousand wonders from a thousand places whose names she didn't know; she didn't know much of anything outside the Vale. It seemed to her these things exhaled a fragrance that brought all the world crowding into her body when she breathed it in, that once she'd breathed it in she'd never be small enough to fit back into the Vale—then her Vale-bred practicality reasserted itself and she laughed at her fancies.

A cluster of men knelt on a blanket near the end of the line of sheds, stacks of coin in front of them, tossing the bones in a desultory game where skill vied with luck and neither mattered much and the piles of coin were exchanged with good-natured cursing and friendly threats.

Jezeri stopped to watch. She'd played that game with her brothers and the hired hands—till they chased her off because she won all the time. The bones seemed to whisper to her fingers when she threw them. She followed them as they skittered across the blanket and knew how they would land, clapped her hands when the man who threw them raked in the stake.

He looked around, grinned. "Eh, boy, sit in. Just a friendly game."

Tanu voiced his disapproval in loud and emphatic song. Sometimes he was worse than Mama the way he tried to protect her. She stroked him under his chin to shut him up, wanting to accept the invitation, knowing she could win, but wary of traps. She took a good long look at the men on the blanket.

All but one wore short, striped trousers that ended raggedly at midcalf, sleeveless canvas shirts laced up to the throat. Some braided their long hair, others pulled it tightly back and tied it at the nape of the neck with gray fraying cords. All but one had knotty bare feet, arms ropy with muscle, looked as tough and about as trustworthy as the crippled direwolf that cornered her a few years back. A friendly game all right, she thought. Long as I lose.

All of them sailors off the ships. All but one.

He was staring at Tanu, pale eyes flat and unrevealing as carved eyes in a carved face, fine soft black hair fluttering a little in the breeze that followed the river. He was smaller than the sailors, with a slim body that somehow made her think of supple, slinky things like ferrets or weasels, with a narrow gaunt face that reminded her of someone—she didn't know who until one side of his mouth curled into a mirthless half smile. Startled, she sucked in a breath and held it. Old 'Un, she thought. Not like he is now, but before. Bloodkin? She let the breath trickle out. No. His kind, but not his kin. She narrowed her eyes, searching for a way to ask questions that wouldn't betray him, but a chill around her stomach warned her off that track.

The sailor rattled the bones in his massive fist. "Not cut loose from your ma yet, boy?" he taunted her. "Eh, be a man."

She broke her gaze from the interesting enigma of the odd man, grinned at the hopeful gambler, delighted to be taken for a boy. "Find another flat," she said. She walked off, had a thought, called back an old Vale proverb, laughter bubbling in her deliberately roughened voice. "Do a friend, that's a shame; do a stranger, that's fair game."

She rounded the last shed and slouched along beside the ruined warehouse, scratching behind Tanu's ears, staring up at the massive stone walls that seemed as ancient as the earth under her feet, man-made cliffs with much the same enduring feel as the stone bones of her home mountains. Tanu chittered suddenly, came out of the tunic pouch, and climbed on her shoulder to ride there, peering into the darkness behind them. Jezeri chewed her lip, the darkness frightening now in a way she didn't quite understand; she walked faster, then broke into a nervous lope as she rounded the warehouse and moved into the temple garden between the Pilgrim Way and the palings that fenced in the merchant precincts. The peeled logs were a foot or so apart and she could have wriggled between them, but there was a gate close by and she could see the brass helmets of the fair-wards. She trotted to the gate, grinned at the aspirant collecting gate-offerings, flipped him a copper, and sauntered into the noise and excitement beyond.

Acrobats, their faces white ovals, glitter paint about their eyes, red mouths like bloody gashes. Three high, hands touching hands, two towers circled with stately grace in a vertical dance. Man on man, the girls on the topmost shoulders waving silversilk to catch the light, round and round the towers went. A rattle of a drum, a flirt from a tin horn, and the towers crumpled, the girls whirling over and over, caught by their partners, whirled over a last time, landing feather light, arms outstretched, red mouths smiling. A clatter from the drum, a blare from the horn, and all six flew about in twisting leaps and tumbles, crossing and recrossing the small open space, wild as wind-tossed tumbleweeds. Then the girls took collecting bowls and walked through the crowd, moving with an oddly touching awkwardness as if uncomfortable when tied so close to the earth.

Jezeri dropped a copper in the bowl as one of them moved past, thinking the pleasure they'd given her well worth one of her scant hoard of coins.

She drifted on, past dancing dogs and fortune-telling finches, past fire-eaters and freaks—and stopped to stare as she caught the glitter of silver swords. She pressed her leg against the side of her boot, suddenly all too aware of the hidden and forbidden knife. She edged closer, elbowing her way through the gathering crowd. When she'd pushed and wriggled to the edge of the low stage, she saw with disappointment and disapproval that the silver was only paint on wood. She

75

watched the fighters posture, attack, retreat, joined the applause of the crowd at the end of a spectacular exchange, rubbed at her neck, swung around to see who was watching her, saw nothing, and decided she was imagining it. After a time she grew bored and pushed out of the crowd.

A dancer. So nearly naked under crimson gauze that Jezeri blushed as crimson as the gauze. A bored man sat at the back of the low stage, tapping a steady rhythm on a small double drum he held between his thighs. Another sat beside him, drawing a humming tune from a fat single-stringed fiddle. Jezeri stared at them, wide-eyed. They were blue. All over. A deep rich blue like the dye her mother pressed from ridda leaves. Where the skin was tight over bone, the blue lightened to a gleaming sapphire. Their eyes were blue. Even their teeth were blue. Their heads were shaved, their bare torsos decorated with white lines that set off the hard, ridged muscles. The music they made was strange, but the woman danced powerfully to it, entranced by it.

Jezeri felt hot and uncomfortable watching her, but she couldn't help sneaking quick, embarrassed peeks at her. The dancer was a sleek, powerful creature, a rich dark gold with gold-streaked umber hair, a coarse mane as wild as Nightlord's tail after a run through thorny brush. Fidgeting from foot to foot, always on the point of leaving, Jezeri stayed until the music stopped and an arrogant young apprentice dancer walked out among the watchers, shaking her tambourine under their noses, demanding rather than requesting payment for their entertainment—and getting it, heaps and handfuls of coin.

Jezeri grinned and drifted on.

Snake dancers. Tanu hissed his disgust, so Jezeri hastened

past these, eyes widening at women shaved bald and tattooed all over.

Mouse races—little gray runners scurrying through mazes.

A sly little man with three shells and a pea and a following of adolescent boys, her brothers among them. Jezeri watched a moment, feeling comfortably superior. She had, after all, overcome just such a temptation. She sniffed with disgust as her brother Calley lost a copper bit.

Jugglers.

Puppeteers. She stopped to watch one play but got tired of being elbowed or squeezed near flat. Anyway, what she managed to see embarrassed her more than the dancer had and got worse as the bellows of appreciation from the crowd got louder, men and women alike urging the puppets on. She stared at hot red faces and decided this was some kind of grown-up thing she might appreciate when she was older.

A minstrel strolled by. She sensed his interest, though he said nothing as he walked beside her a moment. He stared at Tanu, but that didn't bother her after the first prick of fear, since she could feel his puzzlement. Then he quirked a brow at her, bowed quickly, gracefully, and passed on, the only one of them all to see she was a girl in spite of her trousers. His curiosity quickly faded as he moved away, plucking idle chords from his guitar, subvocalizing words as he sought the songs to match the mood of the crowd.

The sense of him trickled off as she left the fringes for the area of stalls and booths where cookshops and sweet vendors turned the air as thick as stew with what they sold, where other vendors sold wine in throwaway clay cups and beer cooled by ice magicked down from the mountains. Jezeri and Tanu drifted along in an ecstasy of sniffing and staring, entranced by the glimmer of mirrors, the shimmering colors of the silks spread out on counters with folk haggling over them, the spices in pots and crocks that perfumed the air every time a customer lifted a lid to test the taste and aroma of what he or she was buying.

A woman with a round sweaty face, her hair tied up in a linen coif, was stirring a glutinous mass in an iron pot, muscles like melons in her heavy arms. She pulled the ladle loose, eyed the brown threads dripping from it. Clucking her tongue with satisfaction, she emptied a cup of white powder into the pot, stirred a moment longer, then stepped back and watched the candy foam up until it filled the inside. She swung the pot off the fire, tilted it over a stone slab, and let the seething mass spread out into a brown puddle. There was another stone slab on the far side of the pot where an earlier batch was already cold. She took a mallet and broke this into pieces.

Jezeri bought a copper's worth of candy shards, coaxed Tanu from the pocket and set him on her shoulder, gave him a piece of the candy. They both crunched noisily and contentedly on their shards as Jezeri strolled on, immersed in the life around her, ignoring that little itch at the back of her neck.

People stood in clots, talking, arguing, buying, selling, all sorts of dress, all shades of skin—from a translucent white rivaling the moon's pallor, through shades of gold and brown, to a soft black darker than night.

Their helmets ruddy in torch and lantern light, fair-wards strutted arrogantly through the crowd, forcing others to step aside for them.

Priests were all over the place, like vermin infesting a granary, no two of them alike, from the one who wore an elaborate robe of black velvet thickly embroidered with gold and crimson thread to a dust-and-ash-plastered ascetic whose single garment had less cloth than a lady's kerchief. They chanted, whirled in off dances, jingled begging bowls, or stood about looking wise if they could, settling for mystery if wisdom seemed unlikely.

The itch got worse.

Jezeri licked her fingers and rubbed them dry on her trousers, spat on Tanu's hands, and used the hem of her tunic to wipe them clean. "No sticky fingers in my hair," she told him, smiled as he sang his protest. She eased him back into the pocket, rubbed irritably at her neck, calling herself many names, the kindest of which was fool. Despite Old 'Un's warning she'd let herself be so caught up in the pleasures assaulting her senses that she'd been slow to take serious notice of the itch. She couldn't ignore it any longer. Someone was watching her. Worse. Someone was following her, had been following her for a long time. She began walking slowly on, letting the noise and excitement flow unnoticed around her.

What to do? She wished her father was here, or her mother. They always had answers, even if you didn't like them. Hunt up a fair-ward? Bronze helmets enough about, mostly around the drinkshops.

Mama said first hint of trouble, yell, she thought, but . . . well, yell what? I'm being followed? And the ward asks who by. And I say I don't know, it's just I've got this feeling in the back of my neck. And he says get out of here, kid, I got no time for foolishness or he takes me by the ear and trots me back to camp. No! Artna rot him, I won't let him chase me

79

off. Besides, what can he do to me with all these people about? Hunh!

She moved her shoulders impatiently. Tanu tickled her jaw with his tail-finger. She grinned and pulled it away from her face and let him curl the finger about her thumb. In a funny way her follower gave a touch of spice to her enjoyment of her first fairing night. "He wants to play games," she told Tanu. "We'll play, too."

She began walking slowly, steadily, halted without warning before a stall, darted around it into another line of shops, tried to catch a glimpse of who was following her, but saw nothing. "He's done this before," she told Tanu. She strolled casually along, then suddenly squeezed through first one group of chaffering adults, then another; they smiled after her, granting her the first night indulgence her follower certainly wouldn't receive from them. She felt frustration billowing from him, a frustration reflected in Tanu's growing uneasiness. He didn't like this game. He was treading nervously at the bottom of the pocket, the hairs on his tail erected, rubbing stiffly against her neck.

She twisted and turned through the rest of the merchants' sector, riding a high of excitement and mischief until Tanu's distress began to rub off on her. The game was going on too long; the man's persistence began to disturb her. "Enough," she whispered to Tanu and nodded as he sing-muttered his agreement. She tried to break away from the man, but he was always there behind her. Nothing she did shook him off. She started looking about for a fair-ward and knew a spurt of panic when she saw how quickly the crowd was thinning. There were no wards about, not here. He's been herding me, she thought. Fool, fool, fool. Breathing hard, she scrambled to a stop as the palings loomed before her. She looked both ways along them, then wriggled through the space between two of the peeled poles and raced through the trees to the Pilgrim Way, which led to the great gate of the temple.

Late as it was, the Way was still crowded. That comforted her and also surprised her. Because she was not a pilgrim, because the folk of Vale were what they were, she had forgotten that the fair was the high point of the pilgrim year. Folk came overland and by sea to pay tribute to the Three Lordly Ones, to atone for sins real or imagined, to beg favor from the gods. To Jezeri all this seemed as much nonsense as the patter of the man with the shells and the peas. Jezeri's Vale folk paid respect to Aieea the Nurturer and Artna the Hunter; their rites were splendid excuses for feasts and games and general revelry after the hard work of harvest and the gray dullness of winter. There were no priests in the Vale. The folk there—sturdy independent farm folk and stock raisers—thought themselves quite able to manage their relationship with their gods and saw no point in feeding extra mouths. Aunt Jesset would snort with scorn if anyone called her a priestess. She had no authority over the lives of Vale folk and wanted none; all she asked was to tend Aieea's shrine, grow her herbs, use her healing gifts when needed, and to be left alone to live her life the way she wanted.

Jezeri plunged into the throng, wove through pilgrims until she thought she'd lost herself; the itch had died away almost completely. She slipped into an opening behind a clot of pilgrims from overseas and began gazing about with curiosity and a regrettable smugness.

She saw a few high ladies with long silk dresses trimmed with fur, jeweled headdresses, and gauzy veils that obscured very little of what they covered. But most pilgrims wore coarse somber robes with only a worn bit of rope as a girdle. Many of them had an exhausted, emaciated look, as if they'd walked barefoot across half the world to get here. Some were simply slogging forward, saving the dregs of their energy to get them to their goal; others had a glowing exaltation and were chanting, the various chants so mixed Jezeri couldn't make out the words. She rubbed absently at the back of her neck, stiffened as she realized what she was doing.

Her shadow was back. Calm now. Unhurried. Sure of her. She could feel him so strongly it was like a club whammed against her head. Mama, oh, Mama, why didn't I do what you told me? She shook herself calmer and and began to wriggle between clumps of pilgrims, trying to put more space between her and her shadow, looking anxiously about for a fair-ward. All back haunting the drinkshops, she thought bitterly. Tanu had gone silent, scrunched low in the pocket, his small black hands gripping the cloth of her tunic so tightly she could feel the ache in her own hands. She pushed harder against the bodies blocking her way, ignoring muttered irritation and scolds, brushing off hands that caught at her. If she could get to the temple, if she could just get there . . . He wouldn't dare try anything under the eyes of the priests. . . . Old 'Un warned her against going near them, but he hadn't known—

A thread of music, soft, tiny, like the singing of the wind. It began weaving in and out of the scattered chanting. A nothing. A bit of wind. But her feet stopped moving. A woman behind her bumped into her, hissed disapproval at her, and waddled around her. She struggled. Her legs were frozen. The music built a wall between her and the priests ahead.

She broke a foot free. She couldn't go forward, but she could edge herself sideways. She began stumbling across the lines of pilgrims, relieved that she could move. That relief went quickly as she realized she was being herded. Again herded. She opened her mouth to scream, to bring the fair-wards or the priests to her if she couldn't go to them.

The music added a harsh trill and her throat closed up.

As she knocked into people, flailed her arms, tried to close numb hands on robes, arms, whatever she touched slipping away from her, she saw people drawing away from her, faces shocked, disapproving, dismayed, fearful. They thought she was a twitcher throwing a fit. She understood that after a while, tried to plead for help with her eyes, her groping hands, but they all were deaf to these.

She staggered sideways until she was off the Pilgrim Way and back under the trees of the temple gardens, tearing through bushes, stumbling through wind-whipped shadow.

When the music began forcing her toward the water, her surge of panic wore off and she felt Tanu's fearful grip on her tunic loosen. The piper was somewhere behind her, but he was as silent as one of those shadows. Though she could hear the squeak of the grass under her boot soles, the creak and rasp of the dirt, she couldn't hear him at all. He's a hunter, yes, he has to be, she thought. She won a step closer to the palings, grinned fiercely into the darkness, and began pushing against the lock the music had on her body, working her way closer and closer to the pales. The fair sounds and the flicker of its lights teased at her. She tried a sudden jerk for freedom, but he reeled her back. A darkness ahead. The

old warehouse. She tried to ease her head around so she
could see him, but her neck muscles were as stiff as frozen
ropes. She set herself to wait while she slogged along as
slowly as she could. She was no tame prey like some of her
female cousins, helpless and scary and as easy to do down as
a woolie's calf. As she touched the wall of the warehouse
and moved along it, she blessed Old 'Un for giving her the
knife; still, she had to have a plan or the piper would take it
away from her and use it on her. She had no illusions about
opposing her strength to his. A knife. A plan. And Tanu.

*Her mother said: She takes that beast to bed with her, she
even talks to it. What is it, Miles? Is it dangerous?*

*Her father said: Looks like a cross between a coon and a
cat. Dangerous? Even-tempered little beast. Don't bite even
when she pulls its tail. Besides, you'd have trouble getting
him away from her, and what's the need? Let them be. He's
teaching her what responsibility means, teaching her to finish
what she starts.*

Jezeri said: What is Tanu? Old 'Un said nothing.

*The crippled direwolf they were tracking from its latest kill
cornered Jezeri between a cliff with an unstable slant of scree
at its base and a river plunging through rock-filled rapids.
Tanu wriggled away from her, ran up the scree, and launched
himself at the wolf, his overlarge hind legs sending him
arcing over the intervening distance onto the back of the
beast. He drove heelspurs Jezeri didn't know he had into the
wolf's sides, leaped away. The direwolf fell dead. And Tanu
came singing contentedly to her, the poison spurs retracted
into their sheaths, his soft, small hands patting her to comfort her.*

They buried the direwolf and tacitly agreed not to tell her parents how it died.

Jezeri said: What is Tanu? You've got to tell me now.

Old 'Un said: Better you don't know. Safer. He'll never hurt you, that's all you need to know.

Tanu was stiff and angry; caught by the music, he couldn't move or make a sound, but rage was pulsing through him. He understood as well as she that they were under attack. Jezeri could hear in her head, though not in her ears, the hissing whistle he'd made when he'd struck at the direwolf.

The music changed. It built a box about her that shifted her around and pushed against the stone. She stood with her back tight to the wall and saw for the first time the face of the shadow.

The odd man on the wharf. Old 'Un's kind, she thought, and was surprised to find herself so unsurprised.

He lowered the flute.

She thrust her hand inside her tunic to quiet Tanu. "What do you want?" she said, remembering almost too late to speak gruffly, like the boy she was pretending to be.

He ran his thumb along the flute. It was bone white in the dusty shadow. Someone's legbone, she thought. Gahh, how sickening. "Kneel, boy," he said. His voice was so soft she had to strain to hear him. Boy, she thought. Good. That means he's not as smart as he thinks he is.

She knelt, her mind going very calm, very clear; she knew exactly what she was going to do. On her knees, trying to look passive and frightened, she waited for him to make his next move, baiting her trap inside his, stalking her stalker. Artna guide me, she thought, make my throw straight.

The odd man reached inside his tunic and drew forth a

85

black bag of some heavy material that hung in stiff folds
when he held it out. "Put the beast in this," he said, and
threw it at her. And turned too quickly away, twisting his
head to look over his shoulder at the dark bulk of the temple
rising above the trees.

She fixed her eyes on the bag, struggled to suppress a grin
when it fell short.

The odd man swung his head back around, started cursing.
"Pick it up, fool," he snarled at her, his voice held to a
whisper in spite of his anger. "Get a move on. Why does it
have to be the village idiot!" Once again he looked over his
shoulder. Jezeri began to worry a little herself. Stories she'd
heard said that the priests of the temple could see anything,
anywhere, any time they wanted. Aieea send they're much
too busy with the pilgrims, she thought. Now that it was a
fight between her and the piper, she wanted no priests snoop-
ing into her business, especially if they'd take Tanu from her
like the Old 'Un said.

Shifting clumsily on her knees, she moved forward,
hesitated, disciplined a rush of excitement when he said
nothing; pushing her luck as hard as she could, she lurched
closer to him. Sweat popped out on her forehead, began to
drip in her eyes. She wiped it away with her sleeve, chanced
a quick look at him, saw she'd reduced the distance between
them by nearly a third. It was enough. Maybe.

"Mind-lost idiot." His whisper was harsh with urgency
and menace. He brought the pipe to his lips, played a few
notes that froze her and sent pain coursing through her.
"Faster, or you'll get more of that."

She picked up the bag, more shaken than she cared to
admit. The material was heavy, slick, like oiled silk but

much thicker; she played with it a few moments to flex her fingers and calm her tightening nerves, then began to uncurl Tanu's tail from about her neck. "Be ready," she whispered to him as she eased him from the pocket and set him on the ground beside her knee. The piper stared at him, breath hissing between his lips, his eyes wet with greed and fear.

Fumbling at the bag to cover her movements, she slid the knife from her boot, slipped off the sheath, held the knife with the blade pressed back against her arm as she worked the mouth of the bag open. The piper shifted impatiently, looked away, back along the wall.

Jezeri scooped up Tanu and flung him at the piper, felt the powerful thrust of his hind legs as he kicked against her hand, then launched herself in a low dive at the piper's legs, knife flipping over to slash at his hamstrings.

Warned by weasel-instinct, he sprang aside—but not quickly enough or far enough; she missed the hamstring but scored him deeply on the calf as she brushed by him.

She landed heavily, awkwardly, all her weight coming down hard on her shoulder, her head slamming against the earth, the knife knocked out of her hand, the wind knocked out of her body. Behind her she heard a scrabbling on the ground, a bubbling scream that broke off suddenly, then nothing.

For what seemed an eternity she couldn't move, could only lay gasping, but finally she rolled over and came up onto her feet, looked around for the piper.

He lay in a contorted heap, as dead as that long-ago direwolf.

Crooning his bliss, Tanu perched on the dead man's hip,

preening the fur on his hind legs, obviously very pleased with himself.

Rubbing at her shoulder, Jezeri stood gazing down at the odd man. I never got a chance to ask you where you came from, she thought. I don't even know your name. Artna rot you, you cheated me. You're dead. You made me kill you, and there's no asking you anything anymore. She shuddered, swallowed several times as sour fluid flooded her mouth. "What do I do now? Aieea help me." Sick and more than a little afraid, she glanced fearfully at the temple, wondering how much longer she had before everything fell on her, shivered as she remembered how the piper kept doing that. She wanted her mother, her father, Old 'Un, even her idiot brothers, Aunt Jesset, her father's sister—and even awful Uncle Herveh, who'd somehow managed to marry her mother's sister. She wanted to feel safe and ordinary again, wanted someone, anyone, to take this burden off her shoulders.

But there was no one. Only Tanu and the wind and the trees. And the dead man, who still threatened her even though he was so very dead. "I killed him," she said aloud, and was startled to hear herself say the words so calmly. She tried over in her mouth one of the spitting curses the piper had flung at her and felt an intense satisfaction at the sound of it, though she had no idea what it meant. "Probably something obscene," she told Tanu. "Haschundapri!" she repeated, liking the way it let her explode out her woes. She said it a third time as she looked around for somewhere to put the odd man's body. If the priests found it . . . she didn't know what they'd do to her, but it'd sure mess up her family. She ran along the wall, turned the corner, and headed toward the canal, keeping the wharf sheds between her and the docks, stopped on the bank of the canal, looked both ways along it. Most of the pilgrims were up closer to the temple and the sheds blocked the view of anyone on the docks. The water slid past, dark and secret, moonlight scrolling silver lines on the shifting black surface, the muted whisper of the water lost to the wind that teased at her hair. "Mama says all the time pick up after yourself, Jezeri, don't leave your stuff lying around." She giggled, bit her lip, dragged her sleeve across her face. After a last glance along the canal, she raced back down the weed-choked alley, rounded the corner of the warehouse, and stopped beside the piper's body.

"Pick up, pick up," she breathed, began giggling again in tiny gasping bursts as she bent and grabbed hold of the man's collar, hoping he'd been practical enough to buy good strong cloth. Her stomach lurched, but she got command of herself and started dragging the body toward the canal.

Like Jet and Nightlord hauling an extra-heavy load in the wagon-draw, she dug in her heels and heaved the awkward weight along, inch by inch at first, then faster as she built up momentum. Fighting waves of dizziness and the pain in her shoulders, sweat on her forehead again, trickling into her eyes again, she pulled the body over the crackling weeds, the dry withered grass, the sounds thundering in her ears with the groaning of her breath. With a last explosion of effort, she got him lodged at the top of the bank. She straightened, stood rubbing at her back, her arms and legs as limp as old leather rope.

A rustling in the grass behind her. She swung around, frightened, but it was only Tanu bringing her the knife and sheath. She sheathed the knife and stuffed it back in her boot. "Thanks, little friend. Just a bit more and we head for camp.'' Tanu sang of pleasure and patience and went trotting off again. Jezeri pushed the damp hair off her face and nudged the piper's body with her toe. Its eyes were half-open, the whites glistening in the moonlight like wet mother-of-pearl. At first she didn't think she could touch it again. She closed her hands tightly, so tightly her fingernails bit crescents into her palms. What I have to do, I can do, she told herself and fought to make herself believe it. Trying not to think about what she was doing, she wound her fingers in the fine black hair and heaved.

For an instant the dead man resisted her, then, with a sickening sucking sound, he came loose and rolled over into the water, pulling with him a rattle of loose gravel and clods of dirt. The current teased at him, dragged him away from the side, drew him downstream, his body gathering speed as it sank below the surface. The last she saw of him was a flapping white hand.

Gulping, gasping, she collapsed on hands and knees and spewed out everything in her stomach. When the spasms were finished, she crawled away from the edge, tore up handfuls of dry grass, and scrubbed at her face, wiped her hands hard across the clumps of grass. Wearily she got to her feet, drew her sleeve one more time across her face, feeling empty but somehow cleaner, as if the canal had taken him and hidden him but cleaned his traces off her. ''Tanu?''

He came lolloping from the alley, sat on his haunches, and held up to her the odd man's bone flute. She took it from him and thought of tossing it into the water to follow its master, then she changed her mind and stuffed it into her money pocket, pulling her tunic over the part that stuck out.

She looked for the moon. ''Haschundapri!'' she breathed.

It hardly seemed to have moved since the last time she'd looked, sometime around the middle of the chase. She thrust her hand up—yes, more than a handspan gap between the moon's front edge and the first stars of the Pard's paws. "What do you know!" she said, wonder in her voice. A shred of cloud blew across the moon. She dropped her hand and watched it and others like it scud along. The wind was getting stronger, with a damp bite to it that hinted of rain before morning. A good thing that would be, she thought, frowning at the drag furrows the body had dug in the dirt and weeds. She kicked at the ground, sending a spray of soil into one furrow, shook her head. Enough is enough. "Let's get out of here." She clucked to Tanu, grunted as he leaped into her arms, settled him in the pocket. "Old 'Un's got some explaining to do," she said. Tanu didn't bother answering; he was curled up, more than half-asleep. She ran nervous fingers through her tangled hair, smiled ruefully as she thought of the scolding Mama was going to give her for making such a mess out of herself. With Tanu murmuring sleepily against her chest, she edged around the end of the shed and started back along the wharves toward the livestock sheds and the place where her family was camped.

FLETCHER FOUND

Morgan Llywelyn

Born a fletcher, I. Born light-boned and long-muscled into a tribe of knotty, barrel-chested smiths and squat, sinewy miners, I had no choice but to learn the less strenuous art of fitting feather to shaft in order to support myself.

My people lived in the cold and arid mountains far above the Galzar Pass, wresting a precarious living from holes they gouged into the earth and raw materials they shaped into the weapons men always seem to require. Ours was a homeland of blowing granular ice and icy granular wind, and my people had long been numbed into bitter subsistence and nothing more.

But they were not really my people. Even as a small child I suspected it. My place was not among head-bowed, back-bent folk who groveled in front of traders and snarled at one another over a few coins.

Does every child think he has been raised by the wrong parents, shipwrecked among strangers? Or perhaps not born at all, for the old women told no tales of my mother's labor and never spoke of Weenarin as having been a red and mewling infant. So . . . into this place by another route I had come. But from where? And how could I find my way back?

Then one season, just as my first beard started to itch, a trader told me the city people's legend of the Three Lordly Ones who had descended to earth in a silver dwelling from the stars and been hailed as gods. Good and kindly gods, incredibly clever and capable of stunning feats of magic.

Light-boned and long-muscled, that was how the trader described the Three Lordly Ones. And when his words touched my ears I knew at last who I was. Whose foundling.

The Three had landed at Ithkar and subsequently vanished from there, leaving a riot of legends behind to be celebrated each year at the great fair which had sprung up around the earth scorched by their appearance. And in my heart I knew they had left one of their own behind them, a descendant born but for some reason unclaimed—stolen, perhaps. Lost in some tragic way before they returned to their starhome. Yet surely the Three knew of that child's existence and were watching for him with the infinite wisdom of gods.

Must get to the place where they had last been. Must find a way to signal to them, to summon them back for me!

Kept this knowledge to myself, I did, because the others would tease me cruelly if I whispered a word of it. But from that day I planned to go to Ithkar, and when my chance came I took it gladly.

The year had been harder than usual, and traders scarce. There began to be talk of sending some of our wares to the great fair, for we had need of many things. Stout leather for boots and potions for sickness—and even I needed a replacement for the piece of glass I screwed in my eye to allow me to study the exact angle and set of feathers as I affixed them to the arrow shaft, for the one I had inherited from my predecessor was cracked. It is no easy thing to be a good fletcher and give an arrow wings.

Begged to be allowed to go to Ithkar, I did. No one else volunteered. No one else was anxious to be scorned and spat upon as mountain folk were in the lowlands. He who called himself my father scowled at me from under the thorny overhang of his eyebrows. "For what purpose you, Weenarin? Ithkar is far away and the journey is dangerous. Smarter men shrink from it, stronger men than you."

Still I persisted, and at last they gave me an ass with a pack of tools and weapons strapped upon her back, bows and my arrows to sell, daggers, links of chain, hammers. And I faced into a howling wind and headed down from the mountains.

No one came out to bid me good-bye. That was their way; I understood.

The journey was even harder than I had imagined. The ass was stubborn and smart and made me many times angry, but I kept going. Below the Galzar Pass we came upon a metaled road with signposts I could not read. Miners and smiths are not allowed bookteachers; city folk do not want them to be wise. But stopped other travelers along the road, I—merchants and pilgrims to the shrine at Ithkar. And asked directions, and was told.

Told which fork of the road to take, where to pay tax or toll for crossing some border no one could see, what magics were prohibited at the fair. All of this was on the signposts, but someone had to tell me.

"Do no magic, I," I protested. "My tribe would not live at the farthest reaches of misery if they could do magic."

Was not even sure what magic was, but knew I had never done it. Had no intention of doing it at the fair.

Before I had half completed my journey a band of nomads set upon me and cuffed me about, laughing, until they tired of the game and took the best contents from my pack and most of my food. Good daggers they took, and axe heads, too. They left me with nothing I could sell but a pouch of small arrowheads fit only for bird shooting, and no payment but the memory of their hard fists and kicking feet. "Troll from the mountains," they called me, not knowing who I really was.

Could have gone back to the mountain people and told of the robbery, they would not have been surprised. But then I would never had gotten close to the Three Lordly Ones. So slogged on and on, dragging my beast with her depleted pack, searching for something to eat and something I could sell to earn admittance to the fair.

We eventually came to a marshland of still water and waving grasses, and there I let the ass graze while I daubed mud on my wounds. Hungry I was, and growing desperate, when a flock of birds flew in over the marsh. Great gray creatures with long necks and voices of haunting sweetness. In the mountains, a fletcher takes his feathers from hawks. Never had I seen birds such as these, with such plumage. It seemed to me that killing one would be a monstrous thing, though mountain folk would not have thought so. Kill or be killed was their simple law. But I saw beauty in these strange gray birds and mourned in my heart, even as I tore one from the air with a stone in an improvised sling.

The bird lay at my feet, stunned and dying. It stretched out its long neck and rolled one glazing eye upward, looking for its killer. My heart leaped with pity. Dropped to my knees in the mud, then, and tried to find its wound, tried to undo what I had done. But the bird was already departing on another journey and I could not hold it back. My tears fell upon it as my hands explored it with more gentleness than I had known I possessed, but it uttered one soft cry and went limp. In dying, it had extended its wings to their utmost, so I could see the fine quills, the gloss and perfection of each feather. And I swear the bird was still watching me when the light went out of its eyes.

That night, beside my campfire, I skinned the bird and cooked its flesh, though I had little appetite for it. But I carefully cleaned the feathers and set them aside, and the next morning found me hard at work, making arrows from the wood of the young trees that grew at the fringe of the marsh. Fletching the arrows with the feathers of the great gray bird. Sniffling a little, like a weakling, because so much beauty was dead.

The mountain tribe would have scorned me, had they seen.

When I had a sizable bundle of arrows I looked at them with pride. No shafts had ever been so true; no feathers had ever been set more evenly. Took the only bow my assailants had left me, a poor thing with little power to it, and tried one of the arrows. It went straight for a target so distant I could hardly see it, and I found it dead center there, though everyone knows Weenarin is an indifferent archer.

But the astounding thing was the flight of that arrow. It

97

sang all the way, a melody of great beauty such as the birds had sung in their flight.

When at last we entered the region of the fair my ass became nervous, which was a new thing for her. She stamped her feet and rolled her eyes, and when a gilded wagon with curtained sides passed us enswirled in dust my beast bolted, dragging me a goodly way.

Someone laughed behind the wagon's curtain. Laughed at me, not knowing who I was. Rippling, mocking merriment, unmistakably feminine—and though I had never heard such a sound in the arid mountains, I recognized the voice of wealth and privilege.

At the gateway I was halted by a condescending guard who eyed my person with contempt. "You're a fletcher, an arrowsmith?" he asked coldly. "Did no one tell you weapons are outlawed at the fair?"

"Brought only arrows for hunting birds," I answered truthfully, momentarily forgetting the bow out of sight at the bottom of my pack. "The arrowheads are too light to penetrate anything much bigger."

He picked one up and turned it over in his hands. Too late I remembered the bow. Meager thing that it was, would he still call it a weapon? Would he search my pack? But just then he began humming a pretty tune, deep in his throat. Took a step backward, I, thinking he might be going mad. We saw much madness in the cold mountains. He looked and met my eyes.

"What, you still here? Why haven't you taken your place?" He caught me by the shoulder and held me like a child while he pinned a badge on me, then directed me to a distant clutter

of merchants' stalls on the borderline between the area reserved for food and clothing and that of the metal-workers.

A shabby fletcher could not hope for a stall of his own, but
I was allowed to tuck my things into one corner of a painted
canvas lean-to shared by a mercer and a pair of identical
twins, two wizened crones who sold salt in leather bags.
Tall, bony women who said I might tether my ass behind the
tent.

The mercer was a spindle-shanked, potbellied man with a
wall eye, but there was no meanness in his voice. "This is a
good location," he assured me, "though our pavilion isn't as
fancy as some. But you should do well here. What's your
name, lad?"

No stranger had ever asked for it before. Mountain folk do
not speak of themselves, nor hand out their names like gifts.

Then I remembered: the laws of the mountain tribe need
not apply to me.

"Weenarin," I told the tent-holders in a bold voice, not
bowing my head.

"What kind of name is that?" asked the mercer, mopping
his domed forehead with a square of fine fabric.

One of the old women pressed forward. She had wispy
gray hair and more gaps in her mouth than teeth; her eyes
were as bright as a ferret's. "A mountain name," she told
him. "This fellow is dressed like the trolls from the mining
district; a strange people, surly and—"

"They're not my . . ." I began, but then I swallowed my
words and my secret. The old crone seized my words like a
terrier seizing a rat. "What's that?" she said. "You're not
from the mines?"

Lowered my eyes then, as I had been taught all my life,

though pretending inferiority burned me like fire. "From the northern mountains, I come," I muttered.

The mercer shrugged. "That's an end to it, then."

"No, wait," said the second crone. "There is something about this fellow. I cannot imagine him standing over a forge, or wielding a pickaxe."

"Fletching is my trade," I said, willing to give them that much. "My stock is bird arrows for dove or pheasant." And was glad my assortment of real weaponry had been stolen, for with it I would never have gained entry to this place.

"Can you demonstrate your arrows for me?" asked the mercer. "If I like your wares, I might buy some myself; we do a bit of birding where I come from."

Reluctantly took out my bow, glancing over my shoulder all the time for the authorities. The two old women hung up a salt sack in the weedy lot behind the tent to serve as a target, and by the time I set arrow to bowstring a small crowd had gathered. People at a fair will crowd up for anything.

Felt the weight of judgment in their eyes. They saw how slender my arm was, how small the bow. But when I held the arrow and saw the gray feathers sleeking back from the shaft, I deliberately moved back from the target so many paces that someone snickered. "That lad has delusions of grandeur. He'll take no pheasant on the wind, he'd be lucky to shoot a hen on the ground at his feet."

Spread my legs and braced my body; drew my elbow straight back in line with my ear. And arrow left bow with an exultant hum that became winged song as it flew.

The onlookers gasped. Shaded my eyes against the sun and tried to see the target, but too many people were crowding around it. As I trotted up they were saying, "Dead center!" "An incredible shot for such a bow and a arrow!"

"Incredible indeed," said a different voice belonging to a hulking, flat-faced man wearing the uniform of a fair-ward. He carried a weighted quarterstaff and his eyes were constantly shifting, alert for trouble. He jerked the arrow from the salt sack and handed it back to me. "You broke our law by bringing that bow in here," he said angrily. "And there are only three explanations for the shot you just made—accident, skill, or magic. From the looks of you I doubt that it's skill. And I discount accident. That leaves only the possibility that you are using magic to enhance your wares, which is an even graver offense than carrying weapons. Since you broke one law you may well have broken another and we'd best know it now, so shoot again, boy! Just as you did before. And if your archery is a magician's trick, it will cost you your goods and you will be declared outlaw, driven from the gate, and thrown to the mercy of the people."

Driven from the gate. Denied access to the Shrine of the Three Lordly Ones before I even had a chance to see it. That was a far worse threat to me than mere outlawry, for mountain folk were treated little better than outlaws anyway and were used to it.

"His arrow sings a strange song in flight," someone in the crowd murmured. "I heard it, and I say it must have been magic."

"Shoot!" roared the fair-ward, doubling his fist at me.

"Do no magic, I!" I protested. But how could I keep the arrow from singing or flying true an impossible distance? The magic was in it and not myself, though by now I was certain of its existence. Certain of it and doomed by it.

101

They made me stand where I had stood before, too far away for any normal shot to succeed. My heart hammered at the base of my throat as I notched arrow to string. Could have pulled the shot, of course, and let it fall short, for my skill was enough for that at least. But when I held the gray-feathered arrow a sort of integrity moved from it into my hand, and I fired the best I could.

The arrow arced up, up into the air, climbing as if it spurned the earth forever. Then suddenly it bent in its flight and coursed off to one side, toward the gathered crowd. In helpless horror I watched as it sank straight into the shoulder of the fair-ward, in the joint his breastplate did not cover.

He yelled and clutched at the shaft. "Now you've done it," the mercer said to me in a low voice. "I thought your arrow sang too strong to be meant for sparrow hunting. It's capable of piercing a man; you will be sorely punished for this. If you run quick, though, you might make the river before they seize you. . . . I know of caves where you could hide. . . ."

Running I was, but not to the river. Running toward the crowd and the fair-ward, as if my feet had a will of their own. For beyond that shouting throng of people was the shrine, and if I was to be exiled or killed, I would at least see it first, somehow.

But when I drew near the fair-ward I found an astonishing thing. He had pulled the arrow from his shoulder, and in spite of the good bronze head I had affixed to it my weapon had made hardly any wound. A little blood oozed, then stopped as if the skin closed up. And the man was smiling!

Stopped still and gaped at him, I.

"That was a clumsy shot, young man," the fair-ward said,

handing me back my arrow. The head was still warm where it had been heated in his flesh. For some reason I thrust it through my belt instead of putting it back in my quiver. "You're too thin to be a bowman," the man went on. "You need fattening up if you're going to be able to demonstrate your wares impressively. Here . . ." He dug into a pocket and took out a fistful of coins, which he pressed into my astonished hand. "Go to the food stalls and buy yourself a decent meal, will you? And then get some clothes that look like something; we can't have beggars in rags at the fair, it isn't good for business."

He grinned at me as if I were his dearest friend, then turned his back on me and began breaking up the crowd, calling names, punching noses, threatening to break heads if they did not move along. A fair-ward, surly and short-tempered. My arrows could be used as weapons against men and he had felt the proof of it, yet seemed to have forgiven and forgotten at once, almost as soon as the shaft had entered him.

What to do? Took the money and ran, as fast as my legs could carry me. When I had gone far enough to be out of his sight I opened my fist and found more coins than I had ever seen at one time before.

It appeared I could do some sort of magic—or magic could do me, since I had no control over it. That was yet another proof of kinship with the Three Lordly Ones, was it not? And now I was very near the place where they had entered this world. Soon I could be standing just where they had stood. . . . Stuffing the coins into the little leather purse that had hung from my belt like an empty bladder until now, I headed toward the sacred precincts.

Felt the hackles rise on the back of my neck. No one needed to tell me where the sky-descended dwelling had rested; even without the fenced-off enclosure and the reek of incense and the muttering of priests I would have known the place. Needed no stone cenotaph to guide me. Would have found it by the lines of force surging up from the ground, catching my feet and drawing me forward.

Surely this was the heart of the universe, the place of perfect centeredness. As I drew close to it I felt myself on the verge of a breakthrough into unimaginable abundance. At this point, the Three Lordly Ones had achieved immortality by becoming gods to us. And wherever they had gone, in their infinite and godlike wisdom they must be aware of me. Would surely reach out and gather me in, now that I was here. Would lift me up—

"Stop that, you beggar, what are you doing here?!" Harsh hands grabbed me, pinioning my arms behind my back. Angry faces surrounded me. Eyes were flashing, mouths were stretched wide with yelling, but I hardly heard. Kept concentrating on the Three, calling desperately to them to come back to me, feeling almost confident, almost safe, for the first time in my life. Had got so far against such odds, I.

Then someone hit me a mighty blow on the side of the head and I tumbled off the world.

When I woke up, I was lying in a stone cell bedded with filthy straw and slimy refuse. No head ever hurt worse than mine. The room was dark and stinking, worse than any mountain hut. Shut my eyes tight and willed myself to be somewhere in the silvery vault of the sky with my true people. When I opened my eyes again, however, I saw only

104

a scruffy rodent no more than a handspan from my face, watching me with dispassionate assessment.

Sat up abruptly and the creature scurried back, but not very far. A quick inventory of myself showed they had taken my purse, my bow, and my quiver—but somehow overlooked that last arrow, the one I had thrust through my belt. My ragged tunic must have concealed it.

If I possessed magic, this was the time to prove it—and legally, too, for was this not self-protection? Flung my arrow straight at the rat, like a killing-dart. Saw it hit the mangy hide and bounce off harmlessly, falling into the straw.

Where was the magic?

On hands and knees I crept forward and reclaimed my only weapon, while the animal watched me. In dark corners, his littermates chittered and rustled the straw.

Footsteps on stone in the corridor, and the heavy door grated open. Someone thrust a lamp into my cell and an old woman hurried forward to bend over me. The door was shut behind. Even in the dim light I recognized her as one of the twins, the salt peddlers from the fair.

"You're accused of invading the shrine, Weenarin," she said in her cracked voice. "It's a serious charge, the priests want you executed. Is there anyone you can send for who will pay for your freedom?"

Pay for my freedom. The mountain folk? No, I had no resources with fat bribes in their pockets. I had nothing at all. It seemed even the Three Lordly Ones were not interested in me. That had been a childish fantasy, I saw now; this prison cell and the hungry rats were the reality.

She saw my shoulders slump. "I thought not, lad. You must do for yourself, as we all do. You are alone among strangers.'' An odd look flitted among the wrinkles of her folded face, and she dropped her voice to a whisper. ''Alone as the Three Lordly Ones were when they arrived here, no doubt, and had to depend upon their wits and skills to survive.''

My face must have mirrored surprise, for she cackled a laugh. ''Did you think they just sank to earth and were immediately hailed as gods? How little you know of life, Weenarin! Don't you suppose it more likely they met a hostile reception at first? Judge by your own experiences. They were strangers and very different from the natives; they were probably attacked and captured, imprisoned maybe, and had to disguise themselves very cleverly in order to escape. And then the authorities, to cover their embarrassment at being outwitted, may have surrounded the advent of the Three with all sorts of supernatural tales, which became myth and miracle in time. . . .'' She clamped her jaws on her words like a trap snapping shut. Instinctively, I understood the danger there must be in telling tales so at variance with the dogma of the priesthood.

The old crone leaned closer to me, thrusting her face into mine until I shrank back, which made her laugh again. ''You think I am ugly, Weenarin? This wrinkled old visage displeases you?''

Kindness curved my tongue. ''Your face is the map of your years,'' I told her. ''The landscape of a life is an honor to its wearer.''

She straightened up. ''Come,'' she said briskly. ''It is time to leave this place.''

''But how? I am imprisoned for a crime—will they just let me walk out of here?''

"Of course not, no one ever *lets* anyone do anything. Just bring that arrow and follow me."

Set in the door of my cell was a narrow window, high up, just large enough for the face of a guard to peer through. The old salt peddler went to this door and knocked, and when the guard looked in she told him, "I'm through now, let me out."

"Is this a relative of yours after all?" the guard asked. "Will you pay for his release?"

She snorted. "Of course not, he's a mere nobody from the mountains. I was mistaken."

The bolt was drawn and the door swung open just enough to let an old woman walk out; a tall, gaunt woman wrapped in a voluminous cloak. She did not wait for me or offer any suggestions.

A slender fellow, crouched down, could almost hide himself in her shadow. Made my decision and scurried after her, squeezing through the doorway with her body between me and the guard, shielding me. The corridor was almost as dark as the cell had been, and we had left the lamp behind on the straw. The guard did not realize what had happened until we were several paces beyond him. But then he let out a yell that would bring skeletons out of their graves.

The old crone darted forward, carrying me in her wake like a whirlwind. There were men rushing after us, but she dodged this way and that, down twisting passages and through narrow openings that I never noticed but that the old woman found unerringly. Like rats in their warrens, she seemed perfectly familiar with the dank stone fortress where I had been imprisoned. She knew it better than any of our pursuers, in fact, for when we at last emerged from some abandoned storeroom into a courtyard overgrown with brambles, there was no one behind us. Far off, I could hear the ringing of alarm bells, but we were free.

Wanted to express my gratitude to the old woman, but she shrugged it off. "The oppressed learn many skills," she said. "And sometimes we are able to use those skills to help a fellow creature. It is nothing, only common decency."

Common decency. Never before had I heard that phrase, and it pierced me like an arrow.

In the clear light of day I could see that she was very pale and her breathing was labored, and I felt guilty for having put an old body to such strain. But she refused to rest. She set off in a westerly direction without looking back, and I trotted like a dog at her heels because I had nowhere else to go.

"How will you care for yourself now?" she asked after a while. "Your goods were confiscated."

"In my bedroll—which was poor and shabby and not worth taking, I hope—I still have a supply of the gray feathers I used to fletch arrows," I told her. "If I can get them, surely I can find wood for shafts. My bronze arrowheads are gone, but there is flint in the hills and I know how to chip it into arrowheads if necessary."

She turned and looked at me, and her eyes twinkled in their network of wrinkles. "You have a fallback position, I see. I like that, it speaks well for your thought processes. There is a deserted farmstead not too far from here where you may hide, if you like, while I return to the fair. Salt must be sold, business must be done—you understand. My sister and I can send you a little food later, and we will get the mercer to see if he can find your bedroll and feathers. If you are fortunate, no one has bothered with them."

"Never been fortunate, I," was my reply. A miner's son, no sky-born princeling . . . but then I thought of the gray feathers and the singing arrows and bit my lip. Thought of the old woman and her brave kindness and regretted my words.

That night I lay shivering in a half-collapsed cow byre, hidden from the nearest road by a stand of woods but close enough that I could hear the clatter of hooves and the frightening sounds of what might have been a search party looking for an escaped prisoner. Sometime before dawn I finally fell into a troubled sleep, and when I awoke the wall-eyed mercer was standing over me, with my bedroll tucked under one arm and a pail of broth in his hand.

He watched in amusement as I gulped down the soup. "I've forgotten what an appetite a growing lad has," he remarked. "It's been so long. . . ."

When my belly was tight and round as his, I put down the empty pail and wiped my mouth on my sleeve. He had squares of fine linen for mouth-wiping, but he did not offer me one. "Now that you're fed and have your belongings, such as they are, I must leave you," he told me. "I must be getting back to the fair."

Back to the fair. Rested now, and a little less afraid, I, too, yearned to go back to the fair! To stand for just one moment more at the sacred shrine and feel the sweet glory roiling through me; to believe myself to be part of something splendid instead of a mere troll from the mountains, outlawed now and futureless as well. But I said nothing of this. Pride was strong in me and would not ask for pity.

Perhaps that is why he hesitated before leaving me there. If

I had asked for help, would he have abandoned me? Will never know, but sometimes I wonder.

"Weenarin," he said at the entrance to the byre, with one foot already out into the sunshine, "I've been thinking. You have a skill, and—perhaps—some small gift for magic, though I confess I do not know exactly what sort of magic it is or how it should be used. I cannot take you back to the fair with me, for you would be arrested on sight and I as well, for harboring you. But in less than a ten-day the salt peddlers and I will be returning to our own valley, many days distant from here.

"We are not much bothered there by the authorities, the sheriffs and tax assessors and their ilk. It is a pleasant place, but those of us who live there have to work hard to maintain ourselves. You know how to work hard, though, don't you?"

Nodded. Could not trust myself to speak.

"Very well, then. If you can continue to hide yourself successfully until it is time for us to pack up and leave, you can come with us if you like. We can use a good fletcher. We don't offer you more than you're willing to get for yourself, you understand. But the only other option you have is to try to get back to the mountains, and that would be a hard journey for a lad alone, impoverished, and with a price on his head."

This was not the choice of my dreams, the radiant beings in their silvery palace, holding out a hand to their true son and asking forgiveness for having left him behind. Offering luxury, offering godhood. No. Nothing I had come to the fair expecting had happened as I'd imagined it would. Instead I had been robbed, imprisoned, and brushed with an odd touch of magic over which I had no control, and now I was offered a life of continuing labor among strangers in a strange place.

No sky-born lordling, I—and I sneered at myself for ever thinking otherwise. The mountains that had made my tribe hard and bitter had failed in their duty to toughen me; had left me with a burden of compassion for injured birds and old women. So probably I should not try to return there; was not fit to live among stronger folk.

That is how Weenarin came to be in this caravan heading west, muffled to the eyes in a salt peddler's cloak, carrying a heavy load of fabric bolts belonging to a potbellied mercer. In my bedroll lie the gray feathers, sleek and shining, and when we reach the distant valley I will make arrows and put them into the service of these people who have befriended me.

Do not know what I can do for them; do not know if the very arrows I make may not someday turn against me, for they have a strange power beyond my understanding. But at least I will be with three friends who are not bitter by nature, though they are as ugly as I am, a scrawny mountain troll. And mayhap I will grow to be content in their company. Though not happy; I do not expect to be happy, since I am not who I dreamed of being.

Born a fletcher, I.

WELL MET IN ITHKAR

Patricia Mathews

The noise and bustle of Ithkar Fair went unnoticed at the rickety stand where Corielle the jeweler was finishing a bracelet of bronze. She sensed several people approaching, and an acrid, unfamiliar reek met her nose. In the next stall, Daramil the baker muttered, "So the priests of Thotharn have added alchemy to their other wickedness?"

The voices of the priests of Thotharn came closer; one, hard and jovial, nagging at the edge of familiarity. The priests appeared only as a blur to Corielle, who was nearly blind, but she listened as she checked the bracelet over with practiced fingers. Feeling a slight roughness, she picked up an abrading tool and began to work. The priest of Thotharn spoke, sourly.

"That is what I mean, brothers. The places that could be given to master craftsmen are now cluttered up with the likes of this bedraggled wench, who has somehow managed to lay her hands on some craftsman's tools—the fair-wards must be as blind as she is to let her get away with it!—and sits aping the motions she must have once seen her master make, in hopes the ignorant will mistake her trash for honest trinkets. Were it our fair"—the voices trailed off as they moved on—"we'd deal with her as with a common beggar. . . ."

She heard another voice, soft, answer but could not distinguish the words. If only I had my sight again, she thought uselessly, and touched minds with the scarlet bird on her shoulder. "Go look, Pawky. Bad smell, angry voice. Go see." The bird flew off, squawking. Then she indulged the luxury of anger.

She had once been a slave. Only now, two years later, could she call it "the fortunes of war." Her poverty was evident and, in any great marketplace, despised. But her work was good, and slowly the discerning would come to see it, for she had been bred to the trade and knew her worth.

Pawky flew past the priests, and one tried to swat him out of the sky. "That trinket wench's pet," the hard voice said impatiently. Through Pawky's mind Corielle could see an image of herself and her bird, a sorry contrast to a soft, silken lady in a soft, silken room, with a tiny golden bird in a tiny golden cage, cagebirds both. Pawky flew past the man's face, and then Corielle was sure who he was.

"Lamok," she whispered, packing all her work into a heavy, battered wooden box and locking it. She whistled for Pawky to return, asked the baker to watch the box for her, and set off across the fairgrounds as proudly as if she were still a master jeweler in a great house.

She found Niall the fair-ward by a wineseller's tent that

catered to out-of-work warriors, subduing one of that disorderly lot with his quarterstaff. When he was finished, he said cheerfully, "And how can I serve ye, Mistress Cori?"

"There is a proscribed wizard on the fairground among the priests of Thotharn," she answered. "I knew him once as Lamok, and heard him pronounced banished two years ago, after the wars. He was often a guest at the house where I was enslaved in those years."

Niall lightly touched the inflamed scar that slashed through her left eye, destroying it and thereby sorely weakening the right. People did not think of her as disfigured; they wondered what had happened to her. "The house where you got that?" he guessed. "At his hands?"

"At the hands of his bullies. It was not me he sought to punish, but I was in his way." Time had muted Corielle's anger, but it could still be heard, raw, in her voice. "He did not remember me when we met again, but be very certain I remembered him. That voice, once heard, is not soon forgotten. He now reeks of some alchemical substance, and my neighbors say he wears the robes of Thotharn. How very like him!"

Niall considered this. "I should take you to see my sergeant, but understand it is a very flimsy story," he warned her honestly. "You say you can identify him, but you are blind, and voices can be readily disguised. It's many a former captive who would go to any lengths for vengeance; you would not believe the false accusations we had the first year after we restored order to the land! To say nothing of the usual fights, killings, and common thefts."

Corielle considered that she did not want Niall knowing how she had acquired some of her tools that first year—damn the fair-ward for a sometime clairvoyant!—and said mildly, "You would not believe by what means I freed myself, Niall."

Niall smiled. "Knife, poison, cord, heavy object? Or did you just burn the place down around their ears? Come on, let's see the sergeant."

The chief of the fair-wards was a veteran of the plains wars, well on in years, who listened briefly as Niall said, "This is Corielle the jeweler, who has seen—" He corrected himself uneasily. "Who has identified a banished man, the wizard Lamok. Tell him, Cori."

Corielle settled herself on a bench along the wall and tilted her head toward him with all unconscious arrogance. "I am Corielle, once jeweler of Ingnoir, now merchant-artisan. When the wars drove my lady, Mareth of Ingnoir, and her lord Rumagh into exile, I stayed behind. My sister was great with child and would not risk the roads, and needed me."

Her voice grew rough. "Interlopers took the house of Ingnoir, and often invited this wizard Lamok to their table. Not only did the lord wear the skirts in the house, and concern himself with such matters as serving-maids stealing a crust of bread, but he would ask this Lamok to render judgment in such cases! At the time I had been stripped of tools and rank, and set to waiting tables—truly, this new broom swept very clean—and heard his voice and saw him often. Oh, yes, I know him very well."

"It was he who stripped you of your tools and made you a common drudge, eh?" the old sergeant challenged her.

Corielle shook her head. "That happened early, by the lordling's hand. It was cruel, but it was his right."

The older man touched her scar, less gently than Niall.

"How had you this?" he asked in the same half-accusing tone.

Hot anger swept over Corielle. "My sister was delivered, and she named the child Rumara, for the child was born to the name of Lord Rumagh. The interloper had her brought before him like a thieving laborer when this Lamok was here, and demanded to know the father of the child. Then this wizard, as gleeful as a nasty little boy, said, 'You are not this Rumagh's wife? Then you are a common whore, and shall be delivered to the king's brothels with all the others of your kind.' And it was done."

Her voice rapped out her rage. "She was no vagabond, but clothmistress in a great house; but it was done. And for what? For abiding by our customs and not theirs, before we ever knew them? I thought it was revenge; for what, I did not know." She found herself holding back old tears. "I tried to stop it, but the wizard's bullies carry whips, and I was one to their many, and was overpowered easily."

She blinked back the tears and said more softly, "The gods granted me a look at Lamok's mind today. I saw what may have been my sister, Lamok's cagebird, and now do wonder if the whole thing makes sudden sense."

The sergeant drew in a sharp breath. "You practice wizardry, mistress?"

"Her bird is her eyes, no more," Niall put in. "That the gods send her a sight at times is nothing out of the common, and I know her, sir; wizardry to her is only a means to have her sight, one way or another."

Softly his chief said, "Was it this bird that saw this wizard?"

"It was," Corielle answered.

The sergeant set down his pen. "Mistress, if I took this tale to any judge in the land, I would be laughed out of my office. A blind woman and her bird identify a banned man! A suspicion of wizardry yourself, and you know how closely we control the use of these arts. A woman with a grudge; not old, as you say, but as new as this morning, for half the fairground heard his remarks concerning you. I am sorry, but if you could deliver him to me, or find better evidence than this, I will be forced to act. Until then, good day and good business."

"May yours be as good," she said politely, then remembered what "good business" was in his trade and smiled.

All that day, sitting at her stand, she pondered the question of how to bring Lamok to justice, and whether or not that was Lirielle held captive in his room, and if so, how to free her. It seemed she was further from an answer than when she had been an unregarded drudge in a house held by strangers, for there she at least saw the wizard daily and could plant a knife in him when vengeance became more important than her life. She listened, and was alert for the alchemical smell that clung to Lamok's robes, but heard and smelled nothing.

At the end of the day she folded her stand and went, as she always did, to the outer section of the fairground where old Mother Kallille sold and trained her birds. Pawky flew ahead of her, circling the head of his first mistress before returning to the shoulder of his second, then flew back to greet the child Rumara. The woman who had taken in Corielle and her sister's child when they were fugitive and hungry greeted the jeweler with a hug and said, "Well, I see Pawky's in rare form today. What have you had him doing?"

Rumara shoved a honey cake into her aunt's hand. "Aunt,

Aunt, I touched a hunting bird's mind today and made him do what I wanted!"

"It's a fine apprentice you've given me," the old bird-mistress confirmed with a smile. "Now tell me the whole tale."

The telling of the tale lasted throughout their simple supper and well into their second cup of ale. Rumara jumped up and down at the mention of her mother. "We'll get some bravos and raid the wizard's palace and rescue her," she told the women.

Corielle shook her head. "Between us, we could not raise enough coins to buy one such man a drink, and coins they must have; it is their livelihood."

Rumara's face fell and she tried to argue. Old Kallille looked toward the Temple of the Three Lordly Ones and said, "I have heard that some priests are curious about the cult of Thotharn and about wizardry, and will even pay for information. Every priestess I know loathes the priests of Thotharn. They do not tell common merchants why."

Corielle thought of her day's earnings, much reduced by the time spent with the fair-wards away from her stand. Would that she could carry her wares with her and hawk them as she went! But that was strictly forbidden by the temple laws for the fair. "Could I borrow Rumara to watch my stand for the time it would take to see them?" she suggested.

"I could not lose that many years from her apprenticeship," the old woman said with dour wit. "Well, you know how it is with birds; once begun, you stay with the bird until you have him in your hand. I'm sorry, Cori, but I, too, have a living to make."

For a moment Corielle was tempted to let the pursuit of Lamok go by. Then her anger rose within her as she remembered his smirking pleasure at the many cruelties inflicted on the artisans, officials, and servants left behind in the house. It was he who had decreed that Rumara should be surnamed "the Bastard" and be called nothing else, and smug was his satisfaction at this torment of a small child.

She herself had suffered at his hands, beyond the whipmark, for the wizard had a horse-keeper who tried to show the world he could impose his will on any woman. In those days, Corielle still innocently cried to her lady, even to the interloper's wife, for justice; but the interloper was the master of his lady, and the wizard was master of the man. They asked Corielle but two questions. "Are you virtuous? Does this man threaten your virtue?"

The smirk on the wizard's face warned her not to answer as she wished, that her honor was in her own hands, not his, but that he did threaten her person. Instead she answered yes, truthfully, to both questions, and found herself in sudden horror handed over to the horse-keeper as his wife! Which among these people was a brutal bondage indeed. To disobey him, or seem to, meant a beating, and none would defend her; to kill him was to be burned alive. Not even by perfect obedience and walking in fear was she spared, for the horse-master was a cruel and suspicious man who, like his master, delighted in setting traps for the unwary.

But, said the wizard in satisfaction, her virtue had been saved!

Hers was not the only such story; she had seen how the wizard loved to play with people's lives. She could bring no great charges against him, to hang him, but if she saw him crawling on the ground, she would step on him like the poison roach he was.

Corielle sat shaking as the bitterness of those years came back. "I will go see those priests tomorrow, at first light," she said. "Rumara, I may not avenge your mother. But it will not be for lack of trying." She settled her ragged gown around her and began to plan what she was going to say.

She brought no bribe to the temple precinct. All she had was little enough, and she would not have it rejected in scorn. She walked by the gatekeeper with her usual proud arrogance; he almost let her get by. Then suddenly he bawled, "Here, here, mistress, just where do you think you're going?"

She turned a lofty blind stare in his direction. "I have information for one of the priests or priestesses concerning an old enemy of theirs."

Her ragged gown and proud bearing was nothing new in any marketplace since the wars, and his mouth twisted slightly in scorn. "I am their ear, madam, and what you would tell them, you may tell me."

A slight, amused murmur in the crowd of waiting petitioners told her what she had already suspected, that his price for conveying anything at all to his superiors would be far beyond what she could pay. On the other hand, she lost nothing but some time in telling her tale, as long as she did not believe him. Speaking as if she did, she began.

A burst of raucous laughter interrupted her story. "Your bird saw him, mistress? No doubt it can be induced to talk!" The gatekeeper laughed at his own wit. "Shall we take this bird's oath, and ask what he does at Ithkar Fair?"

Corielle flushed hot. "He is my eyes, and I see through him."

"Aha!" the gatekeeper exclaimed. "Wizardry! It could be that my masters would wish to speak to you after all, sorceress." He held out his hand suggestively.

"I have nothing to give you to save myself from a charge of sorcery," she snapped, her voice ringing clear. "I keep a trained bird like any falconer, and if you would imprison me, you must not only feed me, but my bird. Or would you roast him for your dinner table in lieu of a bribe?"

People did not talk that way to the gatekeeper of the Shrine of the Three Lordly Ones, but to judge from the murmur in the crowd, most fairgoers were glad somebody had!

An open window high in the wall of the shrine now fell shut with a crash of wooden shutters. Soft footsteps pattered down a stairway, and the crowd parted. Skirts rustled, and through the bird's eyes, Corielle saw an underpriest of the temple, a weedy youth with deference in his very walk. Well trained, she thought, as if he were one of Mother Kallille's cagebirds.

"You are Corielle, once of Ingnoir?" his voice came softly. She felt something pass before her face and snorted a little in disgust.

"I am," she said.

"And you say you have seen this Lamok. My master, Ynet, son of Komal, would have me hear your tale, to judge it for himself. He is . . . sworn to stay apart," the youth said nervously, "so I do this for him."

Like master, like man, Corielle thought, wondering why her heart did not leap at the thought of a priest hearing her tale so soon. But he questioned her in such detail that she knew at last somebody was taking her story seriously. Over and over again, the boy tried to ascertain just how much she had seen, or known at first hand. At last she sighed. "I know it is a very thin tale, Ynet's apprentice, but there it is."

Ynet's apprentice whistled thinly through his teeth. "You have no man and live alone," he said.

"Fear not," Corielle said boldly. "I have friends on the fairground, and a kinswoman"—the gods forfend he ever learn she was only eight years old!—"and a foster mother, and my stall neighbors know my name. I need no bodyguard. But it was good of you to think of that."

The boy's breath whistled through his teeth again. "You shall hear from my master soon," he said at last. "Meanwhile, just go about your business as if nothing were amiss, and my master shall see about . . . correcting your distress."

Then Corielle's heart did leap, and she reached for his hand. Not finding it, she shrugged in irritation. "Then thank you, lad," she said, "and thank your master, too, with all my heart." Pawky flying before her, she went back to her stall in triumph.

Three days went by with no word, and Corielle kept to her stall, anxiously awaiting anything concerning Lamok, or any occurrences that might involve wizardry. Niall said nothing had come to the attention of the fair-wards but added, "If it's priestly business, we'd not know in any event." With that she had to be satisfied.

Then, on the morning of the fourth day, when Corielle was returning from a brief visit to the fairground's edge, Daramil the baker rushed up to her. "Look what came to you by way of a temple serving-lad!" she cried, pressing two sheets of parchment and a small heavy bag into the jeweler's hand. The bag felt and sounded as if it contained coins. "I swear, he was just waiting for you to be out of the way before he came," the baker exclaimed.

Corielle felt the bag wonderingly and touched the parchment. "My daughter has a little learning," Daramil went on eagerly. "Shall I have her read it to you?"

Corielle smiled a little at that, certain that the baker's daughter had read it already, to everyone in sight! "Please do," she said.

"To the woman at the jeweler's stand," the letter began.

It grieves me to see a decent woman brought so low, so I have commissioned from you a work described on another page, to be finished at your discretion. Your payment will be twenty temple coins, from which you may buy whatever material you please. What is left, taken together with the value of the tools you use, should leave you a respectable *dot*. I have sent an advance so you can buy yourself a pretty dress and find yourself a man. May your quest be successful.

Ynet, son of Komal.

Corielle frowned as she puzzled over the wording of the letter. But its import was clear: he was financing her search, even to hiring a bravo to aid and protect her. As the realization sank in, joy spread over her face. She shouted, and leaped high in the air, and laughed. Then she thought to ask, "What is this work like that he has asked me to do?"

The baker's daughter rustled the parchment, then whistled. "It is like lacework, but in metal," she said in awe. "A pendant, two bracelets, and a pair of ear-bobs, all very delicate, and even the ear-wires are of the finest.''

"Metal lacework is only another technique," Corielle said joyously, still singing at the thought of having an ally. "I can use a silver-gold alloy; I will have to buy molds and wax.''

"Your patron spoke of a gown," the baker reproved her. "He seemed to consider it to be of first importance.''

Corielle sobered. Well, true enough, she looked like a beggar, and people valued her work at the worth of her gown and not her talent. She whistled for Pawky and sent him again to the bird-tent with the message, "Rumara, be my eyes.'' As he left, she said with a smile, "Strange, how the gods have given him the gift of speech, but not the wit to say anything of any worth.''

"I know some priests of Thotharn in the same case," the baker answered with a sniff.

As time went by and neither Rumara nor Pawky came, Corielle remembered that her niece had a hawk in hand to train and, unable to wait any longer, found her way with the aid of a stick to the tent of Ryeth the tailor. "I have a commission and a patron," she said, singing with the news, "and need a gown. An artisan's gown in the old style, utterly simple, for my work is to be its only ornament. Rare is the tailor who can make one, since the wars; can you?''

"And be delighted not to have to pay seamstresses to make and tack on all those frills and furbelows the conquerors' wives loved so," Ryeth said, a queer catch in her voice. "Besides, you call me *tailor*, not *sewing-woman*, so a tailor's work you shall have of me. Dark red goes with your coloring, but green with your bronzework; what do you say to a mix of colors?''

They were deep in measurements and fitting when a shrill, heartbroken cry of "Aunt!" split the air, and Rumara thrust her way into the tent, sobbing. "Oh, Aunt, where have you been? I have been looking all over for you," she accused, and laid a small feathered body, soft and still, in Corielle's hand. "Someone's murdered Pawky!" the child cried, and wept until the tailor handed her something on which to blow her nose.

"A cruel blow to strike," Corielle whispered, stunned, as she felt the arrow protruding from the little bird's back. "Very well." She got down from the tailor's stool. "We go hire that bravo now, with no more delay. Rumara, tell Niall the fair-ward. A bird's life may be nothing to the great ones, but violence is forbidden in this precinct." Vengeance sang in her voice. "You go lay the accusation before Niall; I will be at the warrior's wineshop."

It was not that easy, of course. Rumara had to know what she was doing ordering a gown, and how she had gotten the money. She must read the letter, for Corielle had seen to it she learned her letters. She must sniff at the design; "overfancy," and ask, "What's a *dot?*"

Corielle felt herself blush. "It is a gift of money to a man to be your man. My patron is telling me there should be enough left over for me to—"

"To get your bed warmed," the child said impatiently. Well, she had been reared on the fairground, and before that among drudges. Besides, she was right. Corielle, blind and impoverished, was still a woman with a woman's needs.

"Or a good meal in a wineshop," she said indifferently, knowing she did not fool Rumara but impelled to show some pride.

She stroked Pawky's feathered corpse again. "Poor little bird," she said with tears in her eyes. "Now how sorry I am I so often called you 'birdbrain.' "

It was not often that a woman came into the tent where the men who lived by the sword were drinking. Many looked up and choked; some of their rough speech died in midword. Those closest to the entrance, seeing she was blind, called out to her that she was in the wrong place. Others in back whispered and laughed, only because a woman was among them. The owner, a one-eyed veteran, hastened over. "How may the swordsmen of this place serve you, mistress, or do you seek elsewhere?"

"I need a swordsman," she said, uncertain how to go about this business. "To seek out an old enemy, see if my sister is held captive by him, and avenge the murder of a harmless bird, through whose eyes I last saw him."

A bold voice called out, "What do you offer in payment, mistress? We are poor men, with our own livings to earn."

"Name your fees," she said impatiently, "and I will tell you if I can meet them."

She barely remembered anything of the rest of the day but the noise and confusion, the clamoring voices, the smell of wine and man-sweat, and the nagging wish that she could read their faces. Some she dismissed readily as too expensive, or stupid, or cruel-seeming, or whining, or half-mad. Many could not be told from any other. The old bartender kept order; she thought she heard Niall the fair-ward in the back of the tent enforcing it, for which she blessed him.

Then, as if in counterpoint to her thoughts, came a soft and tired voice with the accent of the border holdings along

127

Galzar Pass. Just so had Lord Rumagh, border-born, spoken. "You are the jeweler with the bird," he said gently. "Murdered as an eyewitness to villainy, as so many are?"

"Just so," Corielle said, swallowing hard. "May I know your name, swordsman?"

"Rumal," he said in the local speech, the single name marking him as without house or clan. "And if you need a strong and handsome youth, I would not deceive you. But forty years on the battlefield have taught me something, I like to think, and old warriors come cheap. Mistress, I am in sore need of your commission, and besides, your bird's death angers me."

He could be telling her what she wanted to hear, to earn a few coins from her; somehow she didn't care. "How did you come to this, Rumal?" she asked instead.

He laughed a little bitterly. "Shall I tell you I was once lord of a great house? Or that I have had the chance, and would not, for my honor's sake? Na, what chances I had I threw away, for one reason or another. Tell me of this enemy, and of your sister's plight."

Some of the bravos started to drift back to their pursuits as they decided the strange, ragged woman had chosen her man. A few whispered that they made a good pair, for age and his enemies' blades had marked Rumal deeply. Corielle talked on, oblivious to all of this. At one point the mercenary started. "Lirielle," he whispered. "I once knew a Lirielle. We were lovers. Go on with your tale, mistress."

Without realizing it, Corielle found herself telling the mercenary all that had happened in the house of Ingnoir since the conquest and after. "And when our soldiers came through," she concluded, "I took Rumara and fled, leaving Dunca the horse-master dead with a house warrior's dagger in him, and made my way here. I tried to learn what had happened to Lirielle, but never found anyone who knew her, or had ever heard of her. I sang her spirit down to death, wept, and took her child to be my own, as I dared not before."

She could smell cooking and found herself suddenly hungry. "I have forgotten," she said. "It must be mealtime. Let me buy you whatever you please, and I will have the same."

The meal, when it came, was soldier's fare, a stew of beans and strong-flavored vegetables and roots, with tidbits of odd meats, all served with a heaping plate of coarse, flat cakes. She ate with a hearty appetite and puzzled over his concern for strange housefolk in those years. "I dared not," she answered a question, "because I did not trust Dunca around anything weaker than I was, least of all a maidenchild. He cultivated brutality as other men sharpen their swords."

She heard a snort from across the table. "I know the breed too well," he said in disgust, shoving plate and mug away. "It is nearly dark, my lady. May I escort you to your place of business?"

"I had not realized," she admitted, and rose. He gave her his arm so that she did not need sight to find it.

Mother Kallille and Rumara would be in bed. Corielle went straight to her stand and stood irresolute. "I sleep under the stand, and it is the only shelter I can offer," she said. "Nor would I have you misunderstand; I am not the sort of employer to ask you to earn your pay in bed; it is shelter. Unless you desire," she added painfully, because she suddenly found that she did.

The mercenary stood close by her. "Not for a crust of bread or a warm place to sleep," he agreed. "I talked of fee

129

before my fellows, not to seem cheap, but I came with you knowing—''

"Do not be fooled by an old gown," Corielle said tartly.

The soldier laughed. "But my lady, you ate that meal without complaint, and asked for more. Exquisite courtesy, by the gods!" His voice grew gentle. "But I do like you well, and think it has been overlong since either of us felt the touch of a lover's hand; to do this would be my pleasure."

"And mine, too," she said, and shook her head. "We must both be moon-mad."

The midnight stars were high in the sky when Corielle moved her hand from the soldier's face and said sleepily, "My lord."

Amusement in his voice, he whispered softly, "You are my employer; it is for me to call you *my lady*."

Just as softly she answered, "I will keep your secret, and never ask how you came to fall so low, but you should not have let me touch your face and hear your voice together. You are Rumagh, once Lord of Ingnoir. Tell me, does the Lady Mareth live?"

"She lives and is well. I will also tell you this," he said with honest regret. "I am still her sworn man, and can give nobody more than the crumbs from her table, Corielle. But what I do give will be honestly given."

She touched his hand in reassurance. "But how did you come to a mercenary's hiring hall?" she asked then.

Rumagh of Ingnoir stretched and collected his thoughts. "My lady thought the evils which had befallen us since we took back our land could not be explained by natural means. Too many crops failed among our friends; too many women and she-animals miscarried, as did Mareth herself. The old healer wandered in her mind; age, they called it, but I am no younger. Those so attacked were all the conqueror's enemies and our friends, and the priestesses called it wizardry. So I am here to seek a wizard." He laughed a little. "One bright spot in all this blight; the cheesemaker was delivered of a fine, fat daughter, also named Rumara."

"That, too, may be mischief," Corielle said suddenly. "You are not supposed to want any daughter, highborn or lowborn, nor any bastard, boy or girl. Your lady was supposed to make great trouble for mother, child, and you, and the cheesemaker is supposed to be in agony that her wickedness has found her out."

"What wickedness?" he demanded. "Taking a few cheeses home to her kin? But it does seem you know the mischief-maker's mind. Have you found the wizard I am here to seek?"

"His name is Lamok," she said, and began to tell him all she had learned about the wizard.

"Tomorrow I will ask about the arrow," Rumagh said, "and you about the man. Until then, let us ask the gods to send us a dream or sign in our sleep." He kissed her and was soon asleep himself.

They had breakfast with Kallille and Rumara, who were both full of questions. The mercenary answered them patiently and with good humor, so that when he left to recover bird and arrow from the fair-wards, the old woman said, "He'll do."

"He's all right," Rumara echoed, and tugged at her aunt's skirt. "Come on, Aunt! The birds have been waiting since sunup!"

131

"What?" Corielle asked, listening to the racket from the perches under the canvas. They did seem to be unusually upset. "What do they want?"

"To look you over," the child said, dragging her by the hand into the tent. "Just let them get to know you," Rumara ordered, "and they'll let you know."

It brought back the pain of losing Pawky again, and Corielle walked into the tent grieving for a scarlet little fellow with a hooked yellow beak spotted with green, a raucous voice, and a great greed for roasted, salted flower seeds. Around her the birds squawked, shrilled, and argued, one massive predator yawning his foul breath in her face. She walked among them, trying to banish Pawky's image by calling to mind the birds that were there. They calmed down, no longer upset, but as if conferring among themselves.

One in particular was making a great pest of himself, flying against her and around her face, brushing her with his wings, crowing, then flying off. He settled on her wrist and laughed at her. Trenchantly she said, "Bird, I don't think I like you."

"Not Pawky, not Pawky," the bird mocked.

"No," she said seriously, "I don't think that's all of it, although you're quite right, you know."

The tent-flap was brushed aside, and boots rustled against straw. "Very handsome," Rumagh approved. "Hello, bird. Do you have a moment, Cori?"

"I haven't touched minds with him yet," she said, sitting on a bale of straw. "What news?"

His foot against her bale, he laid Pawky's body in her hands. "Bury him," he said. "The fair-wards have the arrow. Its mate was seen in the quiver of a weedy, meeching youth in country clothing, the sort who might hide behind a skirt; he has not been seen again.''

Corielle, Pawky's body on her lap, listened to the rest of the description, coloring and pimples and walk and accent, and said, stunned, "I do know him, Rumagh, and he hides behind a skirt indeed; he is a temple lad and my patron's apprentice. Nobody will believe my testimony; how can we get the one who saw him inside the temple precinct to identify him?''

Rumagh drank from a bulging wineskin and offered a cup to Corielle. "The Lord of Ingnoir, whoever he be, is welcome wherever gods or gold is worshipped," he pointed out, "and what lord travels without a bodyguard? Even a masterless soldier. For that matter, what of his hawk-mistress? Come, my lady," he said, laughing. "There must be a gowner somewhere in this market!''

By midafternoon Corielle's long brown hair had been washed and dressed in the coiled braids of a tradeswoman who was her own mistress. She wore Ryeth's dark red gown, ornamented with her own work; Bird rode on her wrist, silent. A man with an up-country accent attended them as she and Rumagh, Lord of Ingnoir, dressed in his finest, called on the Shrine of the Three Lordly Ones.

The gatekeeper who had once bawled at Corielle, "Just where do you think you're going?" kicked back his chair to rise and say deferentially, "How may I serve you, my lord, mistress?''

Corielle heard a clank of coin in the gatekeeper's box as Rumagh ordered, "See if the Lady Elandel will see me, my good man.'' His good man bawled for a servant; footsteps pattered toward the inner shrine. As skirts rustled down the

133

stairs, Rumagh loudly dismissed the soldier, then said warmly, "Well, Elandel, the veil must make you ageless. Look at me, all raddled, and you as handsome as you were twenty years ago. May we talk privately? I'm afraid it is only matters of state," he apologized.

With Rumagh's own accent, the priestess answered, "Matters of state or gossip from Galzar, my ears are yours, Rumagh, despite the compliments." She led them upstairs to a room with comfortable chairs, a fireplace, and some sort of desk or table, then called for refreshments.

"To begin with," Rumagh said after they had tasted a cup of spiced brew, "my hawk-mistress has a nose for bad odors and an ear for voices, and . . ."

Corielle sniffed suddenly, her face a mask of shock. From the courtyard came the familiar hard, contemptuous voice, overlaid with false joviality, ". . . can hardly expect a slut who can scarce brush her own hair to be trusted to tend a fine mount like this, but . . ."

Rumagh shut the window and said, "How is it he rides a fine mount and not a priest's donkey? Compassion for his kind?"

The priestess stifled a laugh and said, "It is part of his business to spy on the priests of Thotharn, so he must be seen to ride like one; and, I fear, adopt their manners."

"How do you know he is not a priest of Thotharn in his heart, spying on you?" Corielle asked suddenly.

"A good question," the priestess admitted. "We watch such men closely. That is Ynet, son of Komal, and I gather that you know him."

Corielle held out the parchment. "Is this his hand?"

"His very hand," the priestess agreed. "But these are a

134

lady's ornaments, and Ynet lives alone like all Thotharn's highest priests, vowed to neither lady, mistress, nor kinswoman. But it is his taste. How did he come to commission such a work?''

Corielle laid a hand on Rumagh's wrist. ''I do not understand it, either,'' she said, frowning. ''Ever since I heard the voice of a proscribed wizard among Thotharn's priests, strange things have happened. An unknown priest commissions this after I have talked to his lad, then this very lad's own arrow is found in my bird's back—then I have a sight that this very wizard holds my sister captive, who ordered her dragged off to the king's brothels for her love for Lord Rumagh, but where?''

''Would you know the voice if you heard it again?'' the priestess asked, excitement carefully muted in her voice.

''I might,'' Corielle answered. ''Understand, I only heard it once. My lady, may I beg a favor? I am a jeweler; to do my work well, I must know whether white or yellow gold becomes this lady better. May I be taken to see her?''

Cautiously the priestess said, ''Where do you think she is, mistress? For Ynet lives alone.''

''Ynet must be seen to live alone,'' Corielle corrected.

A slight laugh escaped the priestess, and she rang a bell. ''Send me Devira, Ranet, and Jaleth,'' she said, and soon three women came in. Their voices came from somewhere above Lord Rumagh's head.

''Devira, you and Lord Rumagh look for his bodyguard, then bid Ynet's lad attend me. Ranet, Jaleth, attend this craftswoman and me; we are paying a call on Master Ynet's room.''

Shortly Corielle was led through a maze of rooms to a

135

door. The priestess knocked; slowly the door opened, and the priestess gasped. "By the Lords!" one of her guards exclaimed.

An apathetic voice said softly, "How may this slave serve you, my ladies?"

"Whose slave are you, and how did you come to this?" the priestess demanded, outraged. "And who are you, mistress?"

The woman sighed and through tears said, "I was Yarrol of Red Creek Farm. My master's name was Lamok, but now is Ynet, a priest of Thotharn . . . but who are you? There are no women among the priests of Thotharn! Has he been overthrown?" She began to weep noisily.

"Mistress," Corielle said gently, "have you ever heard your master speak of a Lirielle?"

Yarrol of Red Creek swallowed her tears. "He said she was his whore, and was now on the dungheap with all the other carrion, then beat me for asking; I am his whore now, but she was his before me." She shuddered deeply and broke down again.

Corielle put an arm around her. "How did you come to this?" she asked gently.

The woman shuddered again. "I had a lover; we had not yet talked of marriage. Lamok spied on our meetings and charged me with whoredom—with my own sweet Janek! —and told me it would either be the brothels or this. I hated him and chose the brothels, but you do not know"—she shuddered again—"you cannot know . . . I only regret I did not die sooner."

Corielle held out the parchment. "Ynet, or Lamok, asked me to make you this," she said, still gentle.

The woman laughed bitterly. "I was never to see it. He

boasted to me that he had bought you off with enough to garb yourself like a rich woman and set yourself up in a better life, and so you would, and never touch tool to metal.''

Corielle burst into unbelieving laughter. ''Hung with his own rope,'' she said, voicing everybody's thought. ''For I am not made in his mold, though he thinks everybody else is; nor are the rest of us. Mistress, I owe you all thanks, and the jewelry is yours by right. Or would you rather have the metal?''

''B-but Lamok . . .'' she stuttered.

There was a great roar from the courtyard, and the priest-ess smiled. ''Lamok is under guard, and your tale will see him hanged or exiled.'' As a petulant younger voice joined the chorus, she added, ''And so is the lad who murdered your bird, jeweler. We will want you both as witnesses, but when that is over, be free and rest easy, all of you.''

''So I am a lord's daughter after all, and you are a lord,'' Rumara said skeptically. ''Are you really my father?''

''I am,'' Rumagh said, ''but for the fortunes of war which parted us, and delivered you to the wizard's cruelty; and that will be no more. My lady will welcome you; we have only an old military hawk-master long past the work, and a good-hearted lad with no talent for it.''

''I think maybe I am for the marketplace and not the house,'' the child warned him.

''So be it; you have a good mistress in Kallille,'' Rumagh said cheerfully. ''And you, Corielle, are you of her mind?''

''It may be, after a season; I have been my own mistress too long,'' Corielle admitted.

"My lady knows several men who might want a wife," he suggested cautiously.

Corielle was blind, but her aim was good. Swinging her long stick like a fair-ward's quarterstaff, she belabored her lord about the head and shoulders until he cried for mercy. Then, laughing, they all set out for Ingnoir together.

ESMENE'S EYES

Ardath Mayhar

The litter lurched and swung between the horses. Esmene set her hands against the thinly padded walls to brace herself as the horses stumbled into and out of the ruts of the road. Rough passages were more common than smooth ones, even here, and the trip down from her mountain home beyond the steppes had been even worse. She knew that once the small caravan reached the broad Plain of the Ith her journey would be easier. The mountain tracks, the road across the steppes, and the very fact of travel at all had her crippled body sore within and without.

She had sworn never to subject herself to such discomfort again, three fairs ago, when last she had plied her trade at Ithkar. She had saved enough to see her through what could only be a short life, as well as her son into adulthood. There was money to buy the sacred herbs to burn at her husband's grave. There was no desire within her to return to the Fair of the Three Lordly Ones.

A hand tapped at the side of the litter, and she let down a sliding panel, through which a fine mist of rain whipped.

"You are well, Esmene?" came the anxious query from the man striding alongside.

She grunted an affirmative and rammed the panel up. Little did Horthgan care for her welfare, she guessed. He'd as little concern for her as she had for him. Spittle upon him! If he had not been a coward, her Haldorn would not lie in his cold mound of stones, cut to bits by a mountain cat. Brother or no, Horthgan had deserted his twin.

If only she, instead of that one, had been on the mountain with her man! But she had been carrying young Hal, unfit for climbing and tracking after predators. It had been, she was told at the time, a miracle worthy of the Three Lordly Ones that she had survived her infant's birth. And indeed, though that had crippled her, it had not harmed the child. He was a sturdy seven-year-old now, safe with his grandam.

Her prematurely lined face softened into a smile as she thought of her boy. Then it hardened again. No, Horthgan had been instructed to bring her, safe and well, to Ithkar, to the temple, and to the enigmatic priests and priestesses who guarded the secrets those long-ago visitors from the stars had left with them. She, perforce, must go, let her body pain as it would.

The litter dipped sidewise, and her box of silks and needles slid roughly against her knees. Just one more ache added to those that she had acquired in this unexplained journey. Though she knew it to be unjust, she held that, too, against Horthgan.

It was better down on the plain. There it was warm, and there was no rain. She opened the panels on either side of the litter and breathed in the green scents of the lowlands. There was the smell of water and mud and the things that live in both . . . the breath of the Ith, coming forth to greet her. She liked that scent and relished it, knowing that it would be lost in the stenches of the city, once they drew near.

This year those stinks were even worse than she had remembered, she found as they clopped down the way leading to the temple. There seemed more people, more beasts in the section of the fair set aside for the dealers in animals and their attendant matters. An unusual number of cooks and craftsmen seemed to be swarming about the middle section, where she had always set up her stall. She had had her own spot, and all had known it. There had been many a fine lady, many a wealthy merchant, many a vain priest who had come to her to purchase her fine needlework. But she supposed that after her absence from several fairs, her stall would be occupied.

To her surprise, Horthgan did not halt the litter horses at the great doorway. Instead he motioned to the rest of the craftsmen in the group to go their own ways. Then he went forward to lead the animals through the congested streets of the fair. They were approaching the temple itself, Esmene saw. It did not surprise her overmuch, but she felt her heart tighten in her chest.

She had seen those keepers of the temple at their best and their worst, in the years of her fairing. Most were cynical time-servers who hadn't a vestige of belief in those long-ago sky-travelers who had set their strange house here on the Plain of the Ith. It was that sort that had come to her for the furbishing of their garments and the making of exotic scarves

141

and shawls. Yet she had suspected that there were other, more earnest guardians of the old secrets. Once or twice she had heard tales of real miracles that had been performed in the temple, using those arts. Only those serious about such things would be able to make them work, she thought.

Now her brother-in-law was leading the horses into the forecourt of the temple. The litter jerked to a stop, and Esmene unlatched the door panel and swung her almost useless legs about until her feet hung above the cobbled paving. Giving a push with her hands, she dropped, to stand clutching the litter for support until her limbs consented to sustain her weight. She had felt her face go white with the pain, and Horthgan moved toward her, his hand out to help.

Before he reached her side, a quiet voice said, "Do not trouble yourself. We will bear the needlewoman as is needful, and we shall return her to the proper place when we are done talking. You may go about your affairs, Horthgan."

Then that same voice said, "Close your eyes, lady. We go a secret way, but we trust your honor, and we will not bind up your eyes."

She did as bidden, and quick hands buckled something like a belt about her waist.

"Do not be alarmed. This is the easiest way. You will find that you move without effort," said the voice. A hand grasped her arm above the elbow, another touched the thing at her waist, and she found to her startled surprise that she was lifted just clear of the cobbles. She could feel the uneven ones brush against the soles of her slippers, now and again, as she glided along. To one who watched, she knew that it must seem that she walked by herself, guided by the hand on her arm.

"Marvelous!" she whispered. "Magical indeed. I have found it in my heart to wonder if those long-ago secrets truly exist."

"They exist indeed," rejoined the voice. "Here we go left, then right again. Draw in your elbows."

It seemed a very long way, the more so as she could not see their route. But they stopped at last, and another touch at her waist brought her slippers into firm contact with a floor. Smooth panels of wood, she thought from the sound. She stood as quietly as she could on her protesting legs, while the belt was removed from her.

"You may open your eyes," someone said, but it was not that one who had brought her there.

When she did that, she found herself standing beside a low chair. The spot in which she and her companion stood was brightly lighted, the rest of the chamber in shadow. Because her eyes had been shut against the light for so long, she was able to tell that they were in a big round room with a domed roof. Then the light sent even that into dimness.

"Sit, Esmene. There is food here, and wine. Then we will talk."

She was famished, and she did full honor to the temple food. The wine dulled the ache of her hips and legs, and she turned, at last, to that other who sat, veiled and swathed in gray, in the one other chair that she could see in the pool of light.

Esmene said nothing. She had been brought for some purpose, and she knew that its nature would be revealed in good time. She folded her needle-pricked fingers in her lap and stared at the veiled face so near to her own. The veil wrinkled as if the face beneath might be smiling.

143

"You are dutiful, Esmene, to come at the cost of so much pain when those of the temple call." It was a woman's voice, she now was certain, and her companion's shape was frail and small-boned, far different from her strong mountain-bred frame.

"Though I have doubted, as all who think must do, I believe that some of those in the temple work for the good of our kind. You would not call for me if there were not a driving need," she answered.

There came a dry chuckle. "Some indeed! Fewer than is comfortable to think upon. But those of us who know the secrets, who guard the strange methods, are true to our teachings. And we have needs that none outside our tiny group can guess at." The head cocked to one side, as if the woman studied Esmene's expression.

"Have you met any of those who follow Thotharn, in past years, as you sat at your work in your stall?"

"More than one. An odd assortment indeed. There is something . . . wild and forbidding . . . about the feel I get from them, no matter how seemly their ways."

The veiled head nodded slowly. "You have a skill, Esmene. One that you seldom use, and that only after long thought and soul-searching. One connected with, yet independent of, your embroideries." It was not a question.

Esmene started, though she managed not to show it. She had thought her secret to be hers alone. "It . . . is not a thing of which I speak," she said huskily.

"Yet now is the time for speaking, for that is the skill of which we have need. Your old stall is set up for you. Your old clients have been told that you are here for one last fairing. We need your needle, Esmene, wedded to that talent

144

that allows you to stitch other things than beautiful patterns into the designs that you work into cloth.''

"How did you know of it?'' the woman asked. "I have never spoken to any of the matter, and I have used it only twice while here at the fair.''

"You know that the fair is monitored, that none may enhance his wares by magical means. The exercise of power, even a very small one, is detected by those whose task it is to keep surveillance over such things. The spark of magic that you stitched into those two items alerted the temple, and the matter was examined. But it was found that you had sewn healing into a headscarf for a child beset with pain . . . and that it did the thing you intended and relieved the young one of his misery. The other . . . that amused us all. The priest for whom you embroidered the cloak with ravens had been, we found, cheating the gem merchants whom he was sent to regulate. Your spell countered his own, and left him to do his business honestly. For that we were grateful, for it is difficult to oversee all that happens at such an event as this fair has become in the past four centuries.''

"And what do you need me to embroider for you?'' asked Esmene bluntly. "Have you more dishonest priests and priestesses?''

"Many. Oh, many indeed, but not for that did we bring you across the mountains. No, we need to spy upon a certain priest of Thotharn. We believe that he is engaged in evil practices among those who come to the fair, and we are sworn to protect all who come here. Yet he is sly and intelligent. No spy that we have sent has returned. Which may give you a notion of his kind.''

145

Esmene swallowed, her throat suddenly dry. "And how is it that you can make him come to me?"

"There is a woman. He is beguiled by her—to a certain extent. She will desire a scarf broidered with butterflies. He will, we are sure, come to you, for you are by far the greatest mistress of your craft in this generation. And the eyes in the butterflies' wings . . ." The voice trailed off as unseen eyes stared into Esmene's own.

"Will see. And I shall see what they see and tell it to you. But have you thought how difficult it may be for me to ply my trade convincingly and keep such a watch?"

"We have planned better than that. You will have a young apprentice, whom we will attune to your magical eyes. None notices apprentices. You may turn your own mind away from the work that you have done, for your strength is not now sufficient for such a dual endeavor."

Esmene sighed. "I will do it," she said. "But little do you know how such workings drain me of the little energy I have left to me. This will remove at least a year from the life I have remaining to me, and that is not much."

A thin white hand reached from the gray robes and pulled aside the veil. A pair of twinkling black eyes looked into hers, their glance seeming to renew her flagging strength.

"Think you that there will be no reward, Esmene? You would do this thing from faithfulness alone, but we would not have it so. You will be rewarded, believe me. I will not say how, but it will be with a thing that will give you joy."

When the veil was pulled back into place, the light went, and Esmene found herself sitting in darkness. Once more, hands set the belt at her waist, and she was wafted through halls, along streets, into echoing places and out of them.

When she was told again to open her eyes, she found herself beside the stall that had always been hers. The silks were already draped to make it a place of color and texture, and her ranks of needles were thrust into their velvet beds, waiting for her touch.

A fair young woman stood beside the worktable. She looked up as Esmene limped into the enclosure. "Ah, Esmene of the magical touch!" she said, coming forward to help the woman to her cushioned chair. "I am Nadesh, your apprentice. I shall be your swift feet and strong arms and busy hands. You shall be the skilled fingers and the knowing mind. That is suitable?"

Esmene smiled up at the eager young face above her. "Quite suitable. Has anyone come, as yet? Of course it is early, and the fair is not yet entirely set up. But I would have work to do to keep my mind from yearning toward my son."

Nadesh laughed. "Indeed, when it was noised about that Esmene once again graced the place, many came to make certain that it was true. And there, if I am not mistaken, comes one back now . . . see? The tall woman with red hair!"

It was, indeed, a customer, and she was followed by others until the table was filled with small orders upon which the two women might stitch while waiting for more. Esmene set the pattern upon the cloth and did the fine detail, leaving the filling-in of the patterns to Nadesh, and so the two completed much in the first day of their partnership. They were compatible, which was a comfort to the older woman, who found herself in much pain as a result of the journey.

Two days went by. The fair was now under way, most of the stalls filled in all its segments, the streets thronged with

147

incomers from the mountains and the lands to seaward and even from beyond the seas. Business was brisk, and only Esmene's sure touch and instant inspiration kept them from falling behind in filling the orders they received.

On the third day the priest of Thotharn came, accompanied by a pretty woman who seemed to have more hair than brain. She giggled and hesitated and flirted with her companion until Esmene was fit to burst with impatience, but the dark-skinned fellow seemed charmed by her and consented to anything that she chose.

"Then butterflies," she pouted. "Yes, I think butterflies— the big blue-and-gold ones with eyes in their wings—you know them?" she asked Esmene, who nodded. "And I need it by tomorrow, for we go to a celebration. Can you have it finished before sundown?"

"It will be done," promised the needlewoman, and the coquette took her escort's arm.

"We will come then." She giggled. "Oh, do make it wonderfully beautiful! I have been told that you work magic with your needle!"

At the word "magic," the tall man stiffened a bit, but it seemed completely innocent of meaning, and he relaxed and drew her away into the crowd.

Now the time had come for serious business, and Esmene went behind the curtain that divided the front of the stall from a private area, leaving Nadesh to talk with any who might come. There was work-space there, too, and another chair to ease her painful bones. She sat in it and drew a long piece of gauzy stuff from a bundle.

Closing her eyes for a moment, she visualized her design . . . seven great butterflies, dipping and swooping above a field of poppies. Then she took up a silver needle and pulled from her head a long black hair.

She could hear Nadesh laughing from the front of the stall, but she knew that she must concentrate her failing strength, now, without distraction. She closed her ears and her eyes, pulling herself away into those dark and secret places that she had sought only in time of need. The hair seemed to curl about her fingers as she held the needle. Something tingled in her hands and her head and her heart. Then she opened her eyes and went to work.

The scarf was a thing of utter beauty. So lifelike were the insects that one expected any of them to complete its flight and alight upon a golden or scarlet poppy. The stitchery was so fine that the work seemed painted upon the cloth, and the black-centered eyes on the wings of the butterflies stood out boldly. Nadesh exclaimed over it, even before it was done.

When the last minuscule stitch had been set and anchored, it was very near to the time promised for the scarf's delivery. Esmene fidgeted, worrying over the matter, until at last she turned to Nadesh.

"If the scarf goes with the woman, how will it aid in watching the man? No matter how taken he is with her, he will certainly not go everywhere with her, or she with him."

Nadesh shook her head. "Have no concern. Miralle is not the fool she appears to be, and she will manage to give him the scarf as a token of her undying affection. Just wait. You will see. . . ."

The two appeared among the crowd, moving toward the stall. Miralle was lovely, her hair powdered with golden dust, her hands a dazzle of gems that the priest had evidently

149

bought for her in the jewelsmiths' quarters. She bounced up to the stall and set her childish chin in her hand.

"Have you made me a lovely thing?" she asked. "Oh, show it to me. All have said that you do such magnificent work!"

Nadesh drew out the scarf and held it between her hands so that its glowing colors shimmered in the torchlight, and the butterflies seemed to move of their own volition. Even Esmene was charmed by it, though her hands had labored to make it.

"How marvelous!" shrilled the light voice. "Oh, Esbre, it is too much! You have been so generous with me, and you have bought nothing for yourself! Think how that would look draped across the back of your black cloak—dramatic! Dashing! You must take it for yourself, and by that you may see how much—how *very* much—I love you."

As by now a crowd of admiring people had been drawn to the spot by the loveliness of the scarf, the priest could see for himself the envious glances cast at it by both men and women. He flushed with pleasure and drew forth the coins in payment.

"It is, indeed, a marvelous bit of work, madame," he said. "Will your assistant stitch it to my cloak in the way most advantageous for displaying it?"

Nadesh took her needle and went out of the stall. Carefully, she stitched the scarf to the back of his black cloak, arranging it so that it showed to its best effect. The sighs of those who watched told the man that it was, indeed, attractive, and he offered extra payment for work done superlatively.

The two in the stall watched the hovering butterflies out of sight. Then Esmene turned to Nadesh. "Can you tell if you are properly attuned? I have never known that that could be

150

done, except through the maker. Do you see another set of images inside your skull?''

Nadesh frowned, leaning against the counter of the stall. ''I'm a bit dizzy—ah, it's his motion as he walks. Yes, I can see the crowd. I can see— How strange! I can see us and the stall, growing smaller and smaller, with figures passing between my vision and the spot where we stand. Yes, Esmene, the attunement worked.''

The next day Esmene was ill. Not mildly. It was as if the evocation of her magic had drained her as dry as a summer runnel. She could not lift her hand or feed herself. Yet the stall must stay open, or Esbre might become suspicious. So Nadesh plied her own needle, and to good effect, for she was skilled at such work. Esmene lay on cushions in the back of the stall, passing into and out of awareness.

This left her open and subject to the visions of those black eyes upon the black cloak. Her head swirled with passing shapes, with strange beasts in the section of the animal tenders, and with whispering conversations that she was too weak and ill to catch or to remember. She only hoped that Nadesh was young and strong enough to grasp and hold it all, as well as tending the stall.

On the third day, she was able to sit in her chair again, though she could embroider for a short time only. The images still wavered through her head, and now she realized that the whispers that had troubled her fevered state, as well as those that hissed through her deepest thought now, held treasonous things . . . and worse. The images she saw were filled with flickering torchlight, and though she turned her thought away, leaving the watching to Nadesh, she was drawn inexorably into one of those visions as she sat in her chair, needle in hand.

"Ahhh!" wailed Nadesh, though softly.

Esmene almost shrieked herself, for she was seeing Miralle, bound to a pillar, being slowly flayed. "Where!" she gasped to Nadesh. "Can you tell in which direction this abomination is taking place?"

Nadesh swung one hand vaguely outward, toward the outermost part of the fair, where the beasts were kept. Then her forehead furrowed, and Esmene knew that she was conveying the terrible vision to the temple.

Esmene felt herself falling, though she realized that she was still in her chair. Still, she was falling, as if into herself, down and down through whirlpools of darkness and dismay. And when the fall ended, the fair was gone. She was gone. Nothing remained except a grateful blackness.

When she woke, she knew instantly that time had elapsed. Perhaps a great deal of time. The air had held the feel of late summer when that vision had seized her. Now it was steamy, and she could smell ripe melons, which were only available in earlier midsummer. Her body felt strange, thinner, and when she raised her hands to look at them, she could see blue veins through their white fragility. No needle pricks scarred her fingers. Weeks had gone by, she did not doubt.

She sighed, and someone she had not seen before rose from a stool beside her couch. "Lady? You are awake?" came a gentle whisper.

"Yes. Have I been ill?"

"I cannot answer that, precisely. I will call Andrell. She will explain to you."

Esmene's heavy eyelids closed again, and she moved away

a bit—not altogether, as before, but to a place in which she could rest and keep watch simultaneously. The touch of a small, hard hand on her brow brought her to alertness again.

"So, you have consented to rejoin us. We have been troubled about you, daughter. But your weariness went deep, deep, and you needed to rest untroubled by your flesh. And while you rested, we gave you your reward."

Esmene blinked. "Oh. The reward. I cannot think what it might be. I have enough coin for my needs. I have my son and my husband's mother. I have Horthgan, if you can consider him worthy of mention. What could you give me as a reward?"

The gray-veiled head bowed, and the small hand swept aside the veiling, removing it entirely from the upper body of the woman who stood there. She was young. Unexpectedly, inexplicably young. The black eyes were still wells of energy, and the lips beneath them were smiling with childish delight.

"Firstly, let me inform you that your work with the scarf did its task exceedingly well. While we have not been able to uproot the worshippers of Thotharn, we have at least removed from activity the priest Esbre. He had sacrificed more than one to that enigmatic god. Miralle gave her life to bring him into our hands, and even now he is being . . . educated. From him we have learned of matters that will give us much aid in keeping watch over his kind. You earned that reward, Esmene."

"But what? What reward?" The woman felt the itch of curiosity growing within her.

"Oh, you are *slow*!" teased Andrell. "Stretch yourself, lazy Esmene. Thrust your feet down, move your legs. *Feel!*"

Startled, Esmene complied. And her long legs extended

themselves, toes pointing, stretching. With no pain. Weakness, yes, as was fitting when one had lain abed for weeks. But no *pain*!

"What . . . did you do?" she asked, moving herself about on the couch, testing out all the old problem spots. The grinding ache in her pelvis was gone. The sharp line of pain down her right hip to the foot. All of them had evaporated as she'd slept.

"The Three did, indeed, leave secrets for our use. In each generation, those chosen are trained to use them. Healing by means of opening the body and correcting matters within it was one of the most frightening of those, and yet by means of the techniques handed down to us from those far-traveling ones we have made many well who would have spent their lives in misery."

Esmene pushed herself into a sitting position, though her head whirled for a moment once she was upright. "You have made me whole again? Able to climb the mountains as I teach my son to hunt game and to track predators? Able to share the work of the gardens? That is a reward for which I have no words to thank you."

Andrell smiled, a bit sadly. "There are others who might benefit from our secrets, but they fear. You might have feared, also, if you had not been already unconscious. But now you can return home astride a horse instead of cooped in a stuffy litter. With Horthgan." She looked closely at Esmene as she said this.

"Horthgan! That coward!"

The priestess laid her hand upon Esmene's. "You have been bitter in your pain and helplessness. You lost a husband, the father of your child. Horthgan, through no fault of his, lost the one closest to him of any in all the world. We have examined the matter closely. Your man's brother was not at fault. How can one blame him for being in another place when the cat attacked his twin? He came as fast as feet could bear him, and he came too late. Can you imagine how that has rankled in his spirit in all the years since?

"He has done his best for you and your son, and you have rewarded him with harsh words and harsher thoughts. He has borne them patiently. Now, Esmene, you no longer have the excuse of your pain. Look with the eyes of a sane woman upon your brother-in-law, and make him your friend. Your son needs him. Your mother-in-law loves him deeply, for he is her only living son. You have ignorantly created unhappiness for others, lost as you were in your own. Grow up, Esmene. It is time!"

The woman on the couch lay back against the cushions. A crease grew between her brows as she thought.

Then, "I have been unjust?" she asked. "The blame that I have heaped upon poor Horthgan did not belong to him? I have been hurting all those I love by my hardhearted attitude?"

Andrell nodded.

"I will grow up," said Esmene. She stretched, once again, reveling in the free movements of her limbs against the smooth cloth of the couch. Her body, though light and weak, felt as if it might well become, once more, the strong instrument of her youth. She caught at Andrell's hand as the priestess stood to leave.

"Thank you, Priestess. Convey my gratitude to those others who work with you. And to Nadesh.

"I will come again to Ithkar. And next fairing, I will bring with me my son, if you should care to see him. My needle is at your disposal, always and in all ways.''

Andrell looked down at her, her small face thoughtful, the black eyes sparkling. ''I shall remember that, Esmene Haldornethe. I shall remember that indeed.'' Then she was gone, and Esmene slid back into sleep that was no longer the blackness resembling death, but a living thing and full of growing strength.

SWAMP DWELLER

André Norton

I am of Quintka blood no matter my mother. Shame-shorn
of skull, snow-pale of skin, her body crisscrossed by lash
scarring, her leg torn by hound's teeth, lying in a ditch, she
bore me, to hide me in leaves before death came. The Calling
was mine from the first breath I drew, as it is with all the
Kin, and Lari, free ranging that day, heard, pawing me free,
giving me the breast with her own current nurseling, before
loping back to Garner himself to show her new cubling.

Quintka I plainly was by my wide yellow eyes and silver
hair. Though my mother was of no race known to Garner, and
he was a far-traveled man.

The Kin paid her full death honors, for it was plain she had
fought for my life. Children are esteemed among the Kin,
who breed thinly, for all our toughness of body and quickness
of mind, gifts from Anthea, All Mother.

Thus did I foster with Kin and Second-Kin, close to Ort, Lari's cubling. Though he was quicker to find his feet and forge for himself. However, I mind-spoke all the beast ones, and tongue-spoke the Kin; thus all accepted me fully.

Before I passed my sixth winter I had my own team of trained ones, Ort as my seconding. I was able to meet the high demands of Garner, for he accepted only the best performers.

Because I was able so young, the clan prospered. Those not of the blood seemed bemused that beasts such as Orzens and fal, and quare, clever after their own fashion, head-topping me by bulk of bodies, would obey me. Many a lord paid good silver to have us entertain.

Nor had we any fears while traveling, such as troubled merchant caravans that must hire bravos to their protection. For .all men knew that the beasts who shared our covered wagons, or tramped the roads beside us were, in themselves, more formidable weapons than any men could hope to forge.

Once a year we came to Ithkar Fair—knowing that we would leave with well-filled pouches. For Garner's shows were in high demand. Lords, even the high ones of the temple, competed in hiring us.

However, it was not alone for that profit we came. There were dealers who brought rare and sometimes unknown beasts—strange and fearsome, or beautiful and appealing—from the steppes of the far north or by ships plying strange seas. These we sought, adding to our clan so.

Some we could not touch with the Calling, for they had been so mishandled in their capture or transport as to retreat far behind fear and hate, where the silent speech could not reach. Those were a sorrow and despair to us all. Though we ofttimes bought them out of pity, we could not make them friends and comrades. Rather did we carry them away from all that meant hurt and horror and sung them into peace and rest forever. This also being one of the duties Anthea, All Mother, required of us.

I was in my seventeenth year, perhaps too young and too aware of my own powers, when we came that memorable time to Ithkar. There was no mandate laid upon me to mate—even though the Kin was needful of new blood—but there were two who watched me.

Feeta's son by Garner—Wowern. Also there was Sim, who could bend any horse to his will, and whose riding was a marvel, as if youth and mount were of one flesh. Only to me my team was still the closer bond, and I felt no need to have it otherwise.

The fair-wards at the entrance hailed us as they might some lord, though we scattered no gold. From his high seat the wizard-of-the-gate, ready to make certain no dark magic entered, broke his grave mask with a smile, waved to Feeta, who also makes magic, but of a healing kind. Our weapons were few and Garner had them already sheathed and bundled, as well as the purse for our fee ready, so there was no waiting at the barrier.

We would pay a courtesy visit to the temple later, but, since we were not merchants dealing in good, we made only a silver offering. Now we pushed on into that section where there were beasts and hides, and all that had to do with living things. Our yearly place was ready for us—a fair-ward waiting, having kept that free for our coming. Him we knew, too, being Edgar, a man devoted to Feeta, who had cured his hound two seasons back. He tossed his staff in the air to pay us homage and called eager questions.

We all had our assigned tasks, so we moved with the speed of long practice, setting up the large tent for the showing, settling in our Second-Kin. They accepted that here they must keep to cages and picket lines, even though this was, in a manner, an insult to them. But they understood that outside the Kin they were not as clan brothers and sisters, but sometimes feared. I know that some, such as Ily, the mountain cat, and Somsa, the horned small dragon, were amused to play dangerous—giving shudders to those who came to view them.

I had finished my part of the communal tasks when Ort padded to me, squatting back on his powerful hindquarters, his taloned forepaws lightly clasped across his lighter belly fur. His domed head, with its upstanding crest of stiff, dark blue fur, was higher than mine when he reared thus.

"Sister-Kin . . ." The thoughts of beasts do not form words, but in the mind one easily translates. "There is wrong here. . . ."

I looked up quickly. His broad nostrils expanded, as if drawing in a scent that irked him. Our senses are less in many ways than those of the Second-Kin, and we learn early to depend upon what they can read by nose, eye, or ear.

"What wrong, Brother-Kin?"

Ort could not shrug as might one of my own species, but the impression of such a gesture reached me. There was as yet only simple uneasiness in his mind; he could not pin it to any source. Still I was alerted, knowing that if Ort had made such a judgment, others would also be searching. Their reports would come to those among the Kin with whom they felt the deepest bond.

The Calling we did not use except among ourselves and the Second-Kin—and that I dared not attempt now. But as I dressed for fairing, I tried to open myself to any fleeting impression. A vigorous combing fluffed out hair usually banded down, and I placed on midforehead the blue gem I had bought at this same fair last year, which adhered to one's flesh, giving forth a subtle perfume.

Ort still companied me. Mai, Erlia, and Nadi, the other girls, were in and out of our side tent. But there was no light chatter among us. The tree cat, that rode as often as was possible on Nadi's shoulder, switched its ringed tail back and forth, a sure sign of uneasiness, and Mai looked abstracted, as if she were listening to something afar. She was like Sim with horses, though also she had two Fos deer from the mountain valleys in her team.

It was Erlia who turned from the mirror to face the rest of us squarely.

"There is . . ." She hesitated for a moment with her head suddenly to one side, almost as if she had been hailed. Still facing so, she added, "There is darkness here—something new."

"A distress Calling?" suggested Mai, her face shadowed by concern. She faced that portion of the fairgrounds where dealers in beasts had their stands and where we had found those in pain and terror before. Erlia shook her head.

"No Calling—this rather would hide itself—" She brushed her hand across her face as if pushing aside an unseen curtain that she might sense the better.

She was right. Now it reached me. There are evil odors to

161

sicken one, and evil thoughts like dirty fingers to claw into the mind. This was neither, yet it *was* there, a whiff of filth, an insidious threat—something I had never met before. Nor had these, my kinswomen, for they all faced outward with a look of questing.

We pushed into the open, uneasy, needing some council from any who might know more. Ort snarled. The red glare of awakening anger came into his large-pupiled eyes, while the tree cat gave a yowl and flattened its ears.

Wowern, his trail clothing also changed, stood there, his hand resting on the head of his favorite companion, the vasa hound that he had bought at this same fair last year—then a slavering, fighting-mad thing who had needed long and patient handling to become as it now was. That, too, was head up, sniffing, as Wowern frowned, his hand seeking the short knife that was all fair custom allowed him as a weapon. As we joined him he glanced around.

"There is danger." The vasa lifted lip in such a snarl as I had not seen since Wowern had won its trust at long last.

"Where and what?" I asked. For I could not center fully on that tinge of evil. Sorcery? But such was forbidden, and there was every guard against it. Not only was there a witch or wizard by every gate to test against the import of such, but those priests who patrolled with the fair-wards at frequent intervals had their own ways of sniffing out dire trouble.

Wowern shook his head. "Only . . . it is here." He made answer, then added sharply, "Let us keep together. The Second-Kin"—once more his hand caressed the hound's head—"must remain here. Garner has already ordered it so, for Feeta urges caution. We may go to the dealers, but take all heed in our going."

I was not so pleased. All of us usually spread out and explored the fair on our own. Within the breast pocket of my overtunic I had my purse, and I had thoughts on what I wanted to see. Though first, of course, we would visit the dealers in beasts.

Heeding orders, we moved off as a group, Sim joining us. Nadi set the tree cat in its own cage, and Ort returned reluctantly to the tents. I felt the growth of uneasiness in him, his rising protest that I go without him.

There were other beast shows along the lane where our own camp had been set up. One was manned by the people from the steppes who specialize in the training of their small horses. Then there was a show of bright-winged birds, taught to sing in harmony, and at the far end, the place of Trasfor's clan—no bloodkin to us, yet of our own race. There we were hailed by one hurrying into our path.

Color glowed on Erlia's cheeks when he held out hands in a kinsman's welcome.

"Thasus!" she gave him greeting. I believed that this was something she wished and was sure would happen. By the light in his golden eyes, she was right.

"All is well?" He broke the gaze between the two of them, speaking to all of us as if we had parted only yesterday. "The All Mother has spread her cloak above you?"

Wowern laughed, giving Erlia a tiny push toward Thasus. "Over this one at least. You need have no fear for her, brother."

Erlia did not respond to his gentle attempt at teasing. Her head turned away and on her face lay again a shadow of distress. I had caught it, also, stronger, more determined— that echo of darkness and all evil.

163

This time it was as if I had actually picked up a foul scent—the kind that clung to swamps, places of death and decay ruled by tainted water. Then it was gone, and I wondered if I had only made a guess without foundation. There are those who sell reptiles and crawling things, yes. But they are set apart from our beasts and have their own corner. One which I, for one, did not spend time in exploring. Yet I was sure this was no stench of animal or of any living thing—

It was gone as quickly as it had come, leaving only that ever-present uneasiness. Still, I dropped a little behind and tried in a very cautious way—not really Calling—to pin upon that hint of evil.

"What is with you, Kara?" Wowern matched his stride to mine.

"I do not know." That was true, yet deep within me something stirred. I was certain that never before had this unknown touched me. Still . . .

Once again I caught that rank stench. It was stronger, so that I wavered—and, without being aware of what I did, steadied myself by a touch on Wowern's arm. He, in turn, started as might a horse suddenly reined in.

"What—" he began again as I swung halfway about to face an opening between two smaller stalls.

"This way!" As certain as if a Calling drew me, I pushed into that narrow opening, heedless whether the rest of the Kin followed or not.

Ahead was a second line of booths fronting another lane. From these came the chatter of smaller animals, squawks and screams of birds. This was the beginning of the area where merchants and not showmen ruled. Yet it was toward none of these that that trace of need—for need did lie beneath the overlayer of evil—drew me.

I entered the section I had always hitherto shunned—that portion of the mart where dealers in reptiles and scaled life gathered. Dragons I knew, yes, but they are warm-blooded in spite of the scaled bodies and in their way sometimes far more intelligent than my own species. But the crawlers, the fang-jawed, armor-plated creatures, were to me wholly alien.

"What—" Again Wowern broke my preoccupation. I threw out a hand, demanding silence.

The afternoon was nearly spent. Flares outside booths and stalls blazed up—adding their acrid odor—not enough to cover the ill smells of the wares. A deep, coughing bellow drowned out whatever protest my companion might have uttered. Whether the others of our company still followed I did not know nor care.

I stood before a tent perhaps a third the size of ours. But where the leather and stiff woven walls we favored were brilliantly colored, gay to the eye, these walls were uniformly a sickly gray, overcast with a yellow that made me think of decay and pustulant nastiness.

Over the tent-flap the light of a torch brought to life a device such as might be the mark of a noble house. However, even when one stared directly at this (it was as dull as tarnished and unkempt metal) it was difficult for the eye to follow its convolutions. This might be a secret seal only a mage could interpret.

Shivering, I looked away. There was an impression of dark shadow angling forth, as might the tentacle of an obscene creature questing for prey. Still, I must pass under, for what I sought lay within.

No merchant stood to solicit buyers. Nor was there any glow of lamp. What did issue as I walked slowly, more than half against my will, toward that dark opening was the effulgence of a swampland wherein lay evil and death.

There *was* light after all—a greenish gleam flaring as I passed the flap. I could see, fronting me, a short table of the folding sort, some lumpish stools, like frozen clots of mud. Around the walls of the tent were cages, and from them came a stealthy, restless rustling. Those within were alert . . . and dangerous.

I had no desire to walk along those cages, peer at their occupants. I had no wish to be here at all. Still, my body—or an inner part of me—would not allow me back into the open air. Out of the gloom, which pooled oddly in corners as if made up of tangible hangings, emerged a figure so muffled by a thickly folded robe, so encowled about the head, that I could not have said whether I fronted man or woman.

The green glow that filled the tent, except in those shadowed corners, appeared to draw in about the newcomer, forming an outline, yet not illuminating to any great extent. There was an answering glow of dullish light from the breast of the robe. A pendant rested there—gold, I thought, but dull. I could make out (as if it were purposefully expanding and drawing color just to catch my eyes) the shape of a head—beautiful but still evil. The eyes were half-covered with heavy lids, only I had the fancy that beneath was true sight, so I was being regarded by something reaching through the metal—regarded and measured.

"Lady." The voice from beneath the hood, shaped by lips I still could not see, was clear. "You would buy." It was not

166

a true question, rather a statement, as if any bargain we might make was already concluded.

Buy? What? I wanted nothing from any of those cages whose contents I still could not see. Buy? . . .

My gaze was pulled—away from the robe-hidden seller—until I looked over his or her left shoulder. There was one cage apart from the rest, a large one. And within it—

As one walks in one of those troubled dreams wherein one is compelled to a task one dreads, I moved forward, though I still had enough control over my shivering body to make a wide circle, not approaching either that table or the one who stood by it.

The cage was before me and here the shadows were thick curtains—the light did not reach. Nor could I discern any movement. Yet there was life there—that I knew.

I heard a sound from the merchant, out of my sight unless I turned my head. Did he speak or call? Certainly what he uttered was in no tongue I knew.

In the air above the cage appeared a ball of sickly yellow which cast light—no flame of any honest torch.

A creature crouched low upon the floor of the cage, so bent in upon itself that at first it was difficult to see any exact shape. Its skin was a dirty gray, like the tent walls, not scaled, but warty and wrinkled, hanging in folds. There were four limbs—for now it uncoiled to rise. When it reached its full height, it stood erect on hind limbs, its feet webbed and flat. It was taller than I, matching Wowern's inches.

There was a thick growth of ugly yellow wattles about the throat and a ragged comb-crest of the same upon its rounded head. The forelimbs reached forward as massively clawed digits closed about the bars of the cage, scratching along the

metal. There was no chin, rather a wide mouth like that of a
frog, above that a single slit, which must serve it as a nostril.
Only—the eyes . . .

In that hideous nightmare of a face they were so startling
that they brought a gasp from me, for they were a clear
green—like wondrous gems in an ugly and degrading setting.
Nor were the pupils slitted as one would expect in a reptile or
amphibian—but round, somehow as human as my own. Also
. . . in them lay intelligence—intelligence, and such pain as
was a knife thrust into me when our gaze locked.

What the creature was I could not tell. Certainly I had
never seen its like before. A flutter of movement to my left,
and the robed merchant moved closer. From one of those
long sleeves issued a hand as pale as that of any fine lady,
very slender and long of finger. This waved in a surprisingly
graceful gesture toward the still silent captive.

"A rare bargain, lady. You shall not see the like of this
perhaps again in your lifetime."

"What is it—and from where?" Wowern's voice was loud
and harsh. He moved in upon my right and I could sense his
growing uneasiness, his desire that we both be away from
this hidden-faced one and his or her strange wares.

"What is it?" the other repeated. "Ah. It is so rare we
have not yet put name to it. From where? The east."

Then I felt cold. All who roved knew what lay to the
east—that swampland so accursed that no one ventures into
it—about which all kinds of evil legends and tales have been
told for generations.

"A bargain," the merchant repeated when neither of us
made comment. "All know of the Quintka—that you delight
in your trained beasts—that you seek ever new ones to add to

your company. Here is one which will bring many flocking to see it. It is not stupid, I think you can train it well."

Those green eyes—how they demanded that I look upon them! That feeling of pain, of sorrow so deep that there were no words to express it—flowed from them to me.

"It is a monster!" Wowern caught my arm in a grip so tight that his nails near scored my flesh. I could sense fear rising in him—not for himself but for me. He strove to pull me back a step or two, meaning, I understood, to take me out of this place.

"Five silver bits, lady."

The caged creature made no sound; I felt rather than saw its compelling gaze shift a fraction. It looked now to the robed one, and within those green eyes was a flare of deep and abiding hatred. Within *me* arose an answer.

Those eyes, did they trouble me with some fleeting memory? How could they? This was an unknown monster. Yet at that moment this feeling of emotion was as much a true Calling as if mind-words passed. Our meeting was meant to be.

I brought out my purse. Wowern's hold on me tightened. He protested fiercely but I did not listen. Rather I jerked free, and, without the usual bargaining, I counted forth those bits. Not into that long-fingered graceful hand; rather, I turned and tossed them on the tabletop. I wanted no close contact with the merchant. Nor did I want to linger here, for it seemed those heavy shadows reached farther and farther, drawing out of the tainted air any hint of freshness, leaving me breathless.

"Loose—" I got out that part order, past a thickening of my throat, not sure that even a Quintka could control such a

169

creature. Still, when I met again those eyes so wrongly set in that hideous face, I was not afraid.

The robed one uttered a queer sound, almost as if he or she had choked down jeering laughter. There was no move to draw any bolt or bar locking that cage. Instead, the slender hand went to the pendant lying heavy on the robe, fingers closed tightly about that, hiding the beautiful, vile face from view.

There sped a puff of darkness from that hand—thrusting outward to the bars of the cage. The creature had retreated, standing with shoulders a little hunched. I smelled a sickly sweetness which made my head swim—though I stood well away from that black tongue.

It wreathed about the bars and they were gone. For a long moment the creature remained where it was. From all the other cages about uprose not only a frenzied rustling, as if the other captives aroused to demand their own freedom, but also gutteral grunts and croakings, hissings—

That thing I had so madly purchased shambled forward. I was aware, without turning my head, that the robed one moved even more quickly, retreating into a deeper core of shadow. That retreat pleased me, made me less aware of my own recklessness. Did this merchant fear the late captive? If so, no such fear was mine. For the first time I spoke to the monster, using the same firm tone I would with any new addition to my team.

"Come!"

Come it did—treading deliberately on hind legs as if that came naturally, its taloned paw-hands swinging at its sides. I turned, sure within myself that where I went it would follow.

However, once outside that tent I paused, for whatever

compulsion had gripped me faded. Also, I realized that I could not return to our own place openly. Even though the twilight gathered in, this creature padding at my heels, as if he were a well-trained tree cat, was far too obvious and startling. Though it was often the custom for one of the Quintka to parade a member of his or her personal team through the fair lanes as an inducement for a show, none of us had ever so displayed a creature like unto this.

Wowern wore his trainer's cloak hooked at the throat, thrown back over his shoulders. I had not brought mine. The feeling that we must attract as little attention as possible made me turn to him. There was no mistaking the frown on his face, the stubborn set of his chin.

"Wowern . . ." It irritated me to ask any favor; still, I was pressured into an appeal. "Your cloak?"

His scowl was black, his hand at the buckle of that garment, as if to defend himself against my snatching it from him. Behind him the monster stood quietly, his eyes no longer on me, for his bewattled head was raised as he stared at the device above the tent-flap door.

At that moment I swayed. What reached me was akin to a sharp blow in the face, a blast of raw hatred so deep—so intense—as to be as sharp as a danger Calling! Wowern must also have been struck by it. Hand to knife hilt, slightly crouching, he swung half-about, ready to defend himself. Only there was no attack, just the creature, its arms still dangling loosely at its sides, staring upward.

His eyes narrowed, his scowl fading into something else, an intentness of feature as if he strained to listen, Wowern surveyed that other. Then, with his left hand, for he still kept grip upon the knife, he snapped open cloak buckle and swiftly spun the folds of cloth about the creature in such a skillful fashion that its head was covered as well as its body to the thick and warty-skinned thighs.

"Come!" He gave the order now. Again he seized upon my arm with a grasp I could not withstand, propelling me forward to the opening of the same narrow side lane that had brought us here, taking no note of the muffled creature, as if he were entirely certain it would follow. Thus we came back to the place of the Kin, Wowern choosing our path, which lay amid such pockets of shadow as he could find. I allowed him this leadership, for I was in a turmoil within myself.

I realized that we two had been alone. The others of our company must have gone on when I had been seized by the need to hunt out the dismal, shadowed tent. Which was good—for the moment, I could have made no real explanation of why I had done what I did.

Ort met me at the edge of our stand, his head forward, voicing that anxious, half-growling sound he always used when I left him. Sighting what accompanied us, he snarled, lifting lip to show gleaming teeth, his claws well extended as he brought up both paws in the familiar stance of challenge. Before I could send a mind-message, his growl, which had risen to a battle cry, was cut off short. I saw his nostrils expand, though since we had left that foul tent I had not been aware of any odor from the creature.

Now Ort fell back, not as one afraid, rather as one puzzled, confronted by a mystery. I picked up the bewilderment which dampened his anger, confused him to a point I had never witnessed before.

"Brother-Kin," I mind-reached him. Though the muffled monster betrayed no sign of anger, I wanted no trouble. Ort

172

had never been jealous of any of my team. He knew well that he was my seconding, that between the two of us there was a close bond which no other could hope to break. "Brother-Kin, this is one who . . ." I hesitated and then plunged on, because I was as sure as if it had been told me that I spoke the truth. "Has been ill-used—"

Ort shuffled his huge hind paws; his eyes were still on the creature as now Wowern caught his cloak by the edge and whipped it away from that ugly body, plainly revealed in the torchlight.

The monster made no sound, but its bright eyes were fast on Ort. I saw my Brother-Kin blink.

"Sister . . ." There was an oddness in Ort's sending. "This one—" His thought closed down so that I caught nothing more for a long moment. Then he came into my mind more clearly. "This one is welcome."

The stranger might be welcome to Ort, but with Garner and the rest of the clan it was a different matter. I was told that I had far overstepped the bonds of permissiveness, taking upon myself rights none had dared before. I think that Garner would have speedily dispatched my monster to his former master and cage, save that Feeta, who had been silently staring at my purchase, broke into his tirade. The rest of the clan had also been facing me accusingly, as if, for the first time in my life, they judged me no Kin at all.

"Look to Ort," Feeta's voice arose, "to Ily, Somsa—" She pointed to each of the Second-Kin as she spoke.

We stood in that lesser tent where our smaller teammates were caged, or leashed, according to fair custom. What she made us aware of was the silence of all those four-footed

173

ones, the fact that they regarded the newcomer round-eyed—
and that they had broken mind-link with us.

Garner paused in midword, to stare from one to another of
those seconding our teams. I felt his thought, striving to
establish linkage. The flush of anger faded from his face. In
its place came a shadow of concern, which deepened as he
beat against stubbornly held barriers.

Feeta took a short pace forward, raising her right hand so
that her forefinger touched the forehead of the monster at a
point between its brilliant eyes. Then she spoke to me alone,
as if all there were only the three of us—healer, monster,
and I.

"Kara . . ."

I knew what she summoned me to do. In spite of the deep
respect and obedience she could always claim from me, I
wanted to refuse. Such a choice was denied me. Was it the
power of those green eyes that drew me, or the weight of
Feeta's will down-beating mine? I could not have said as I
went to her, taking her place as she moved aside. My hand
came up that my finger, in turn, filled the place where hers
had touched.

There was a sick whirling, almost as if the world about me
was rent by forces beyond my reckoning. Also, I sensed once
more that overshadow of faint memory out of nowhere. This
was like being caught in a vast, sticky web—utterly foul,
utterly evil, threatening every clean and decent thought and
impulse. Entrapped I was, and there could be no loosing of
that bond. No! There was also resistance, near beaten under,
still not destroyed.

The net was not mine. That much I learned in a breath or

two of time. Just as that stubborn, near despairing resistance was not born from any strength within *me!*

Danger—a murky vision of thick darkness, within which crawled unseen perils all so obscenely alien to my kind as to make the very imagining of them fearsome. Danger—a tool, a weapon launched, set to strike—but a tool that could turn in the user's hand, a weapon whose edge might well cut the wielder.

"What threatens us?" I demanded aloud, even as I also hurled that thoughtwise, threading it into that wattled head through my touch.

I felt Feeta catch my free hand, hold it in a tight grip between both of hers. From the creature came a pulsating flow—sometimes sharp and clear, sometimes fading, as if the one who sent it must fight for every fraction of warning.

Evil, dark, strong, rising like a wave— There lurked within that darkness the beautiful face of the pendant. It leered, slavered, anticipated—was arrogantly sure of victory. I heard a gasp from Feeta—a single word of recognition.

"Thotharn!"

Her naming made my vision steady, become clearer. Names are potent things, and to call them aloud, our wise people tell us, can act as a focus point for power.

Thotharn I might not know, though of him I had heard, uneasy whispering for the most part, passed from one traveler to another as veiled warnings. There were the Three Lordly Ones upon whose threshold Ithkar stood, there were other presences within our world which my kind recognized and paid homage to—did not *we* look to the All Mother? But Thotharn was the dark, all that man feared the most, shifting westward from swamplands into which no man, save he be outlawed and damned, dared stray.

It is an old, old land—the swamp country. We who tread the roads collect tales upon tales. It is said there was once a mighty nation in the east—greater than any existing today, when small lordlings hold their own patches of land jealously and fight short, bitter wars over the ownership of a field or some inflated pride. The north was ravaged when I was a small child, by the rise of a conqueror who sought to bring diverse holdings under one rule. But he was slain, and his patchwork of a kingdom died with him, by blood and iron.

Only in the east was no tale of a lordling with ambition. No—there was far more, a rulership that impressed itself on all the land and under which men lived in a measure of peace, no lord daring then to raise sword against his neighbor. There came an end, and tradition said this end was born of evil, nourished in evil, dying evilly, even before the Three Lordly Ones came to us. With the breaking of this power the land fell into the depths of night for a space. All manner of foulness raved and ravaged unchecked. Was Thotharn a part of that? Who knows now? But in these past few years rumor spread again his name—first in whispers, and then openly.

Thotharn's priests walked our roads. They did not preach aloud, as did the friars or the wise ones who serve All Mother, striving thus to better the lives of listeners. Nor did they shut themselves into a single temple pile and impress their weight of service demands as did those who outwardly acclaim the Three Lordly Ones. They simply walked, and were . . . while from them spread an unease and then a drawing—

From the creature I touched flared red rage, strong enough

to burn my mind. Thotharn—yes! That name awakened this emotion. But it was *against* the dread lord of shadows that that blaze was aroused. Whatever this creature might be, he was no hand of the east.

No hand. It caught at my turn of thought, seized upon it, hurled it back to me, changed after a fashion. Obey the will of Thotharn—no, not that, ever! When I acknowledged that fraction of half appeal, that need to make clear what lay inside the other's brain and heart, there was a swell of triumph through the sending—a quick flare like a shout of "Yes, yes!"

I spoke aloud again. Perhaps some part of me wanted to do so, that I make very sure of what I learned.

"They believe you serve them? . . ."

Again a burst of agreement. There is this about mind-send: a man may cloak his values and his desires when he uses words, but there can be no hiding of the truth while sending. Any barrier becomes in itself a warning and injects suspicion. That this hideous thing out of the swampland could hide from me in thought was not to be believed. But, knowing this, why then would any follower of Thotharn—such as the robed merchant must surely be—thrust upon a Quintka possessing sending powers a creature so easily read?

That thought, also, was picked up. The churning within the other became chaotic in eagerness to answer. Thoughts were so intermingled, came so swiftly, that I could not sort one from the other. I heard far off, as if she were now removed from me, though still our hands were locked, a gasped moan from Feeta. I guessed that it was only our linkage, her power and mine together, that made this exchange possible at all.

There were scraps of information—that the robed one of Thotharn knew of the Quintka, had marked them because of their far traveling, the fact that they were readily welcome in lords' keeps, even the temples—that the people who gathered for our showings were many in all parts of the land. Where a wandering priest or priestess of suspect learning could not freely go, one linked with us might penetrate. However, the swamplanders did not truly know the Quintka. They accepted us as trainers of beasts, not realizing that, to us in our own circles, there was no Kin and beast—two things forever separated—rather there was Kin and Second-Kin linked by bonds they did not dream existed.

This one had been prepared (the plan had been a long time in the making—and it was their first such) to be sent out as a link between their great ones, who did not leave the swamp, and the world they coveted so strongly. The first—there would be others. The robed one I had dealt with—I learned in that half-broken communication with my purchase—had believed *I* was under the influence of Thotharn's subtle scents and pressures when I bought it—that when I left, already I was a part, too!

"Why do you betray so easily your masters?" I strove to find some flaw in this flood of explanation. "You were made for what you do, yet now you freely tell us that you are a thing designed to be all treachery and betrayal—"

"Made!" Again a flare of intense anger—so painfully projected into my mind that I flinched and near dropped my finger contact. "Made!"

In that bitter repetition I understood. This thing, in spite of all its grotesque ugliness, was near mad from the usage it had received. It had lain under Thotharn's yoke without hope—

178

now it took the first opportunity to strike back, even though any blow it might deliver could not be a direct one. Perhaps it also had not realized the Quintka had their own defenses.

It was even as I caught this that there dropped a sudden curtain of silence. But not before, it seemed to me, a whiff of foul air blew between me and this purchase of mine. The green eyes half closed, then opened fully. In them I read appeal—an agony of appeal.

Feeta loosed her grip, caught at my wrist, jerking me back from that touch which had brought us such knowledge.

"What is it?" I rounded upon her.

"*They* are questing—they might learn," she half spat at me. Never had I seen her so aroused. "Is that not so? Blink your eyes if I speak the truth!" She spoke directly to the creature.

Lids fell over those green eyes, rested so for a breath as if to make very sure that we would understand, then arose again.

I heard a swift, deep-drawn breath from Garner where he stood, feet a little apart, as one about to face an enemy charge. Feeta spoke without turning her eyes from the swamp thing.

"You mind-heard?"

Garner bared his teeth as Ort might do. "I heard. So these crawlers in the muck would think to so use *us!*"

"To plan is not to do." I did not know from whence those words came to me but I spoke them, before I addressed the swamp dweller.

"These you serve, do they have a way of setting a watch upon you? Blink in answer!"

Again, deliberately those eyes closed and reopened.

179

"Do they know of our linkage? Blink twice if this is not so." I waited, cold gathering within me, fearing one answer, but hoping for another. That came—two measured blinks.

"So . . ." Garner expelled breath in a mighty puff. He dropped a hand on Feeta's shoulder and drew her to him. The tie between them was so old and deep that I did not wonder he had been able to link with her during that exchange. "Now what do we do?"

I had one answer, though whether he would accept it or not I could not tell. "To return this would arouse their suspicions, lead them to other plans."

He snorted. "Think you that I do not understand that?" He regarded the creature measuringly. Then he made his decision.

"This one is yours, Kara. Upon you rests the burden."

Which, of course, was only fair.

Garner and the others left me with the self-confessed spy of evil. Only Second-Kin—Ort, the rest of the beasts— remained. They continued to watch the stranger with unrelenting stares.

We had no cage large enough to accommodate the being, and somehow it did not seem fitting to set a rope loop about its neck, tether it with the four-footed ones. Where was I to keep it? Soon would come time for the night shows, and it should be under cover before our patrons came to look at the animals as was the regular custom.

Ort answered the problem with action that surprised me greatly. He padded to the baskets of act trappings set along one side of the tent, came back to me, a wadding of cloth in his forepaws. I shook out a cape with a hood, old and worn, which had been used to top and protect the stored "costumes" our teams wore. It was a human garment and the folds appeared adequate to cover the creature.

Wowern had already taken back his cloak; now I flung this musty-smelling length about the thing's shoulders, fastened the rusty throat buckle. To my astonishment the creature, as if it were indeed a man and not grotesque beast, used its forepaws to pull the hood up over its misshapen head, well forward so that its ugliness was completely hidden. I could almost believe that I fronted a man—not a monster.

Ort chirped, one of those sounds my human throat could not equal. Our disguised one swung about, stumping after my seconding, out of the tent and into the shadows beyond. With an exclamation I hurried after.

Ort apparently had no such thing as escape in mind, nor did the other, who was certainly powerful enough to leave if it wished, deviate from the path shown it. Rather, it squatted down at the end of the row where our mounts were tied, concealed behind the bales of hay now stacked as a back wall. In those shadows the dull gray of the cloak was hidden, one would not have known that anything sheltered there.

The horses and ponies had stirred uneasily at first, but Ort paced down their line, giving voice to that soothing throat hum which he had used many times over to reassure nervous beasts. They accepted this newcomer because of his championship.

I hurried to change clothing, catching up some cold food to eat between the doffing of one robe, the donning of another, the fastening of buckles, the setting of sham jewels about my throat, wrists, and in hair strings. Nadi and Erlia were already prepared and on their way to lead forth their teams, but Mai stood before our mirror applying a thicker red to her lips.

181

"What do you plan to do?" she asked bluntly. "To carry with us a spy—even though it seems to have no liking for its true master—that is to endanger all of us. Why do you bring this upon us, Kara?" There was no softness in her voice, rather hostility in the eyes that met mine within the mirror.

"I—I had no choice." To me that was truth. I had clearly been drawn to the merchant's booth; once there I had been enspelled. . . . Enspelled? I shivered, the cold was well within me now and I could not rid myself of it.

"No choice?" She was both scornful and angry. "This is foolishness. Would you say you are englamored by this bestial ugliness out of the dark? Ha, Kara, you cannot expect the rest of us to risk its presence."

She swept away and I knew that she gave a truthful warning. Those of the clan would not long accept—even at Garner's and Feeta's bidding, if I could depend upon that— this addition to our party. I did not want it, either. I—

Yet I had paid that silver without a question. Unless . . . Again I shivered and stood very still, my hands clasped tightly on the handle of my team leader's wand. Unless there was something in *me* which that robed one had been able to touch, to tame to his or her will, even as I lead my team! If that were so, then what flaw lay inside me that evil could reach out so easily and twist to its own usage? At that moment I knew fear so sharp it made me waver where I stood, throw out a hand to the edge of the mirror table and hold fast, for it seemed that the very earth moved under my feet.

I heard the thump of drums in the show tent. Habit set me into motion without thought. Nadi was dancing with her long-legged birds now—next I must be ready with my marchers. I staggered a little, still under the touch of that fear. Ort awaited me, his hand drum slung about his thick neck. Behind him, in an ordered row, were Oger, Ossan, Obo, Orn—just as they had been for months and years. Tall all of them, their talons displayed in order to astound the audiences, their bush combs aloft, and their long necks twining back and forth to the beat of the drums.

Nadi's music faded. She would be issuing from the other side of our stage. I breathed deeply twice, steadying my nerves—putting out of my mind with determination all except that which was immediately before me—the need to give my part of the show.

We had finished the first appearance of the evening and Garner was talking to several who wore the shoulder ribbons and house marks of lords, making arrangements for private performances. Those would be steady for us all during the two ten-days we were in Ithkar. However, another stood in the lesser light just at the edge of the torch beams as if waiting his or her turn at bargaining. Enveloped in a cloak, it might well be a woman—and of that I was sure when a hand bearing a ring-bracelet came out of hiding to draw closer the cloak. She made no effort to push forward until Garner had finished and the others were gone. I saw her speak and Garner raise his head, stare across the crowded yard between our tents where fairgoers came to see closer our teammates. He looked at me, nodded, and I could not escape that silent order.

So I went to join him and the other. Her gem-backed hand touched her hood, pushing it back a little. I saw a face, deeper brown in color—some southern-born lady, I thought. Her features were thin and sharp, with an impatient line between her straight brows. No beauty—but one who was obeyed when it pleased her to give orders.

"Speak with this one." Garner was also impatient. "What we know is her doing." He left abruptly. The lady regarded me as I would a beast unknown—curious, perhaps. However, there was a sting in that survey. I lifted my chin and eyed her as boldly back.

"You made a purchase." She spoke abruptly. There was a slurring in her speech new to me. "It was one not meant for you."

"I was asked a price and I paid. The merchant seemed satisfied," I returned. This might be the answer to our problem. If she wanted the swamp dweller, then let her have him. But I would not strike any bargain until I knew more. At this moment it seemed to me that I saw between the two of us those wide green eyes.

"Paugh!" Her lips moved then as if she would spit, as might any common fair drab, highborn though she seemed. "That merchant exceeded his instructions. I have come"—a second hand appeared from beneath her robe, in it a purse weighing heavy by the look—"to buy what is rightfully mine. Where is he?"

"Safe enough." I made no move to take that purse. The hand holding it had come fully under the light and on the forefinger I saw the ring—the same smiling face of the merchant's pendant formed its bezel.

"Summon him." She moved a little, almost as if she wanted to be well away from us. "Summon him at once!"

Had they then learned, these followers of Thotharn, that the swamp creature had betrayed their purpose, and so were eager to reclaim him? What would be his fate at their hands? I knew that Garner would report to the temple all we had learned. These could reclaim the creature, slay it, and deny all. What proof would we have then that they had tried to move so against the peace of Ithkar?

"I—" Fear I had known, even disgust, when I had made that purchase; still, I would betray no living thing. For the Quintka might not deny refuge to the Second-Kin. Second-Kin—a swamp creature out of the dark land? Yet Ort and the others had made it welcome after their own fashion, and their instincts I trusted.

"Summon him!" Her order was sharp; she waved the bag back and forth so it gave out a clink of metal. It must be well filled with coin. "I give you four—five times what you paid. He is mine—bring him hither!"

I heard the guttural throat sound from Ort and looked over my shoulder. My Brother-Kin led a cloaked shape into the open, the swamp creature. Still, Ort lifted his lips a little, showing fangs, and I knew that what he did was not in obedience to such as she who stood with me, nor even to me. He moved for himself—and perhaps another.

Those who had come to see the animals had passed along—I heard the boom of a gong signaling the second part of our performance and the thud of hooves as the horses moved out into the circular space beyond. We were alone now—the four of us.

"Ran . . ." Her voice was far different from that with which she had addressed me. "Ran, I came as I had promised—freedom!" She swung up the purse to give forth again that clinking.

I saw a warty paw in the open, tugging at the hood so it fell free upon his broad shoulders. His nightmare face was clear. She bit her lip and could not suppress the shadow of distaste, near of loathing. She is not, the thought flashed into my head, as good an actress as she believes.

"Take it!" Again she shoved the bag in my direction.

I put my hands behind my back as the green eyes turned toward me. I could not pick up any clear mind-speech, and I dared not touch him to establish linkage. But somehow I felt again that blaze of red rage—not for me, but for this woman.

"I will not," I said firmly. Though I could not find any true reason why—except those eyes.

"You shall!" She thrust her head forward and her hood fell away, her eyes bored into me. Then I saw her gaze change a fraction; she caught her breath. "No . . ." Her voice was a half whisper. "Not that—the blood—"

I am no voice of the All Mother, I wear no robe of the Three Lordly Ones—I am no shaman of any tribe. Still, there awoke in me then something that I had sensed twice before this day—an ancient knowledge. Nor was that of the Quintka. Partly of their blood I might be—yet who knew what other strain my dead mother had granted me?

What I did came in that moment as natural as breathing—I brought forth both hands as I took two quick steps toward my monster. He pawed at the buckle of his cloak and that fell away from him, leaving his nightmare body bare. My hands fell to his shoulders, the roughness of his skin was harsh under mine. He had to bend a little from his height. All that filled the world now were his green eyes—and in them was a flashing light of eagerness, of hope reborn, of pain now fading—

"By the thorn and by the tree,
By the moon and by the sea,
By the truth and by the right,
By the touch and by the sight,
Let that which is twisted,
Straightened be.
That the imprisoned go free!"

I pressed my lips to the slimy cold of his toad mouth. Fighting revulsion—pushing it utterly from me.

When I drew back I cried aloud—words that had no meaning, yet were of power—and I felt that power fill me until I could hold no more. My fingers crooked, bit into his odious flesh. I tore with my nails— The skin parted, as might rotted cloth. As cloak so old that nothing was left but tatters, that skin gave to my frantic hands, rent, and fell away.

No monster, but a man—a true man—as I shredded from him that foul overcovering. I heard a shriek behind me—a keening that arose and arose. Then the man I had freed flung out one arm, to set me behind him, confronting the woman. She had her beringed hand up, held close to her lips, ugly and open, as she mouthed words across the surface of that head-set ring. Frantically she spilled forth spells. His hand shot out, caught hers. He twisted her finger, pulled free the ring, flung it to the ground.

There was a barking cry from Ort. One of his ponderous hind feet swept between the two at ground level, stamped that circlet into the beaten earth.

The woman wailed, then spat in truth, before she fled. Where the ring had been pounded there arose a small thread

187

of smoke. Ort leaned forward and spat in turn, full upon the thread, setting it into nothingness.

"So be it!" A deep voice.

A well-muscled arm swooped, fingers caught up the cloak, once more twisting it about a bare body, but this time a human body. "So be it."

"You are a man—" The power that had filled me vanished as quickly as it had come. I was left with only amazement and a need to understand.

.He nodded. Gone from him was all but the eyes—those were rightly his, marking him even through the foulness of the spell. "I am Ran Den Fur—a fool who went where no man ventured, and by my folly I learned. Now . . ." He gazed about him. I saw the cloak move as he drew a deep breath, as if inhaling new life to rid him of the old. "I shall live again—and perhaps I have put folly behind me."

He looked at me with the same intentness as when he had tried to link earlier.

"I have much to thank you for, lady. We shall have time—now—even in the shadow of Thotharn, we still have time."

QAZIA AND A FERRET-FETCH

Judith Sampson

Qazia seldom had a slack moment in her duties as tavern-mistress of the Joyous Goblet, but on this night she took time to gaze about her dark-beamed, torchlit, smoky-cornered tavern, thinking with quiet satisfaction, My family has run this place well for a hundred years. We have better served the pilgrims than the priests in the temple not too far away.

Caravanners wrestled with the tavern goblet-wenches or brawled among themselves with goad-knives. A sprinkling of omen-rovers hawked love-drafts, juggled gyro-balls, or cast plot-lines from the hands of any who wished to know their fate. The tavern's beam-dancer collected lovesick stares and ration-silvers in equal amounts, while the man with the trained lixus made it beg for tidbit-coppers.

Her glance suddenly riveted upon a man seated in an alcove. He reposed with the powerful ease of a skilled warrior,

189

but wore the garb of a song-weaver, resting his battered but well-crafted song-loom in the curve of his left arm.

As she made her way to the alcove, she saw that his golden eyes had the fixed stare of blindness, and where his skin was unscarred, it was deeply browned. His garments and boots, grayed nondescript by constant travel, almost concealed his refined, durable form that moved like a jessed jerfalcon.

Qazia tried to sit noiseless on the bench beside him, but his head tilted in her direction and he swung the song-loom into his lap. In a soft, unruffled voice he asked, "Who sits with Hoel?"

"Your tavern-mistress. Have a goblet?"

"My thanks, but excellent as your vintages are, they are not what I wish tonight. I await your pleasure to weave a song."

Although certain he had never been in the Joyous Goblet before, Qazia only said, "Now's fine. I'll quiet this mob." Rising to her full height, she set lean, muscular hands on her hips, whistled like a lixus screech, and the uproar ceased. Her blue-black hair and green eyes caught gold torch highlights as she announced:

"Give ear to song-weaver Hoel!"

Even the beam-dancer stopped her gyrations as Hoel felt his way to an open space where he could best be heard. Tucking the song-loom under his left arm, he ran his fingers over weft and warp in an opening tonal thread. In the fading hiss of that musical sword-blow, Hoel's voice burgeoned forth the first set of verses.

Qazia watched as her tavern crowd savored the adventures of "Ryddeg's Son," who escaped the lesser enemies of his house, earned knighthood, and tried to attack the wizard-thane, Chond of Grimkeep.

But Ryddeg's son proved easy prey for Chond. Song-loom thread-chords punctuated the air like spellstabs as Hoel chanted of the young knight's capture, imprisonment, and torture by Chond's sorcery.

Caravanners wept into their goblets, and the goblet-wenches joined in. Hoel's blind face lost some of its mask-calm, darkening as he conveyed the despair of his trapped hero.

An uneasy rustle of movement among the omen-rovers, coupled with the odd glances they threw at Hoel, brought Qazia out of her enjoyment, but she had no idea why Hoel's ballad had upset them.

He let the song-loom sound alone, plucking out isolated harmonies that told plainly of damp darkness, sliding of chains, dwindling of body and soul in endless isolation.

As the last notes faded, Hoel's fingers stroked a marching air; he sang again:

> "Chond is a powerful wizard
> But his spell-strength will not last.
> Ryddeg's son defies him,
> Despite enchantments vast.
>
> One day a simple charm
> Faded from Chond's brain.
> This forgetting of one spell
> Released the young knight's chains.

191

With his hands he freed himself,
And squeezed out of his cell.
Of all those in the wizard's gripe,
He alone escaped to tell.''

A mournful theme shimmered from the song-loom, and a great sigh arose from Hoel's audience as he continued:

"One does not escape Chond
Without paying baneful price.
Behind in Grimkeep dungeons,
Ryddeg's son left his eyes.

How can he fight the wizard
Without eyes to see?
But he has vowed to avenge his sire
Faithfully.

Ryddeg's son is friendless
And faces a masterful foe.
In that young knight's place,
What would you do?''

Hoel stilled the last unresolved thread-tone with a quick muffling press of his right palm. In a weighted silence he seated himself by Qazia; then, pent-up crowd noise burst like a shattering melasvino jar.

"A fine song," Qazia told Hoel. "Now will you guzzle?"

Although he refused a second time, Qazia did not leave him. To her he looked drained and off guard. She bristled at the way the omen-rovers extended their hands in the antihex sign of the bull's horned fingers each time they neared Hoel. At last she could no longer refrain from asking, in a casual voice, "Song-weaver, how do you know so much about Chond of Grimkeep?"

A joyless smile flickered across his blind face. "I was his guest for five years."

At his words the omen-rovers and caravanners began to mutter and look about with uneasy eyes. Some of the goblet-wenches whimpered.

Qella, Qazia's senior goblet-wench, hurried over to whisper, "Tavern-mistress, I can't handle the girls much longer. They're too frightened to serve and won't wrestle a single customer!"

"Pour everyone a stiff dose of comawine. Yes, the customers, too. Say it's on the house. Then have the girls start a veil-shedding dance. Between the wine and the bare bodies it won't take long to calm them all. Go on now, start serving!"

"My apologies," said Hoel. "I did not mean to ruin tonight's business. Let me absorb a small part of your losses by ordering a double ration of oblivabsinth."

"You can have it free if you'll enlighten me on certain points," Qazia replied. "What's the name of Ryddeg's son? How does one escape a place like Grimkeep?"

"Ryddeg's son must go unnamed, lest Chond hear he escaped. It is as my song says: when Chond forgets a spell, which happens once in five years, that is the time to escape from his clutch." His head cocked to one side, Hoel paused, then smiled. "Do I hear a jug of oblivabsinth being opened?"

"Yes. Before Qella brings it, answer one last question. How do you know my tavern so well when I'm sure you've never come here?"

193

Hoel responded. "Who does not know the Joyous Goblet and its famous tavern-mistress? Boy and man, I've come here often."

Qazia cast him a sharp look. "You're Ryddeg's son!"

Nodding assent, Hoel slipped the song-loom to the floor behind his legs and accepted his two goblets of oblivabsinth. Draining his double order in two long gulps, he pulled his cloak about him and leaned back to sleep. Though his blind face was slack with fatigue, he spoke distinctly. "If Chond sends one of his wights after me, cooperate."

Qazia made a soothing noise. But as Hoel slumped into heavy slumber, she saw how he resembled a gaunt, maimed lixus, weary of running from pursuit by hunting volvers. She knew she had to save his life.

A few deft signals, and Qazia had ordered Qella and the lesser goblet-wenches to conceal Hoel inside the huge aging-barrel for Jerezian wine which was stored in the cask-shed. Her women obeyed with only a few scared looks at the sleeping song-weaver.

"Hearmo, get your carcass over here!" roared Chond, wizard-thane of Grimkeep.

His half-man, half-weasel ferret-fetch bounded to dungeon cell 974 where the wizard stood scowling at an open door.

"Rabbit-brain! Hoel's slipped your soul-chains!" Chond scolded. "Breakbone knows where he is now! And you let him out!"

Belly-up in submission, Hearmo peered at his glowering master. "Master mine, it's you who loses a spell every five years."

"Doesn't mean for you to be careless, too," grumbled

Chond, but he did not hit the ferret-fetch. Only his red eyes, irritated sparks in the expanse of his black, coarse-furred face, surged with power.

"Shall I hunt for Hoel, master?"

Chond nodded, growling deep-throated as an urso.

On his feet at once, Hearmo raced to the end of the dungeon corridor and vaulted his sleek, nimble black-silver-haired body out a window slit.

From her position by the half-open door cut into the barrel, Qazia watched Hoel stir in his sleep. A look of pain crossed his face; he stiffened awake, his blind eyes blinking rapidly despite no use for such an action. As he sat up, his blanket slid down, and she had to stifle her gasp at the slave-fetter marks that scarred his throat, wrists, and ankles.

Hoel held one arm across himself and asked, "Who's there?"

When he heard her identify herself, he relaxed, muttering, "Thank wound-healer! I thought I was back in Grimkeep."

"None of Chond's wights showed," Qazia assured him.

"Then I'd best leave before they do," answered Hoel, groping for his bundled garments.

A little later she led him back to the tavern, handed him a chunk of carradbread and his song-loom, and steered him toward the main door to the road.

As Hoel put out his free hand to touch the doorframe, Chond's supple, black-silver-furred ferret-fetch materialized on the threshold, purring, "Ah, here you are, dear soul-prisoner! I've spent all night tracing your path. Chond didn't know you were gone for a year."

Hoel's face went gray; he let go Qazia's arm and tried to

break past Hearmo, who caught the song-weaver's ankles in a whisk of firmly looped tail. Hoel dropped to the floor with a choked cry. Tightening his tail-grip of the man's ankles, Hearmo addressed Qazia. "My thanks, tavern-mistress. You hid my master's property well indeed."

Even as the ferret-fetch spoke, Qazia snatched a stool and brought it down hard on the creature's head.

Both Hoel and the Chond wight crumpled, but Qazia did not stop to ponder. She freed Hoel and tied the ferret-fetch up in its own tail, then called Qella in from the kitchen and ordered, "Force a jugful of oblivabsinth into the Chond wight and watch him like a lixus stalking prey. I'm going for Virmith. His forge should have what we need to foil Chond."

When Qazia returned with Virmith the blacksmith, bearing a set of silver fetters, a distraught Qella greeted them, wailing, "I gave the oblivabsinth to the Chond wight, just as you told me, but the song-weaver keeled over, too!"

Hoel and Hearmo both shifted groggily on the floor. Virmith rushed over, snapped the silver fetters on the ferret-fetch, and stood back, grinning.

But the song-weaver and the Chond wight cried out and writhed in unison, their bodies shuddering equally in the silver's grasp.

"See?" sobbed Qella. "Why're they both reacting?"

Virmith gaped and scratched his head, but Qazia squatted by Hoel to ask, "Is this weasel-piss of Chond hexing you?"

Between slow rasps of breath the song-weaver groaned, "Soul-fettered to Hearmo, one of Chond's banes. Harm Hearmo, hurts me." Face drained of color, body shaking, he broke into low screams, such as a trapped lixus makes.

196

Grabbing the ferret-fetch by the scruff of its neck, Qazia demanded, "Stop making Hoel hurt!"

"Can't help it," whimpered Hearmo. "Silver takes away my control."

"I'll make him stop!" bellowed Virmith. "See this hammer, Chond wight? It's twenty vekils' weight, enough to dent your skull good!"

"Don't try it," Hearmo shot back, "Chond knows I'm here."

"Does he?" retorted Qazia. "Well, this time he's outsmarted himself. If he tries to get either you or Hoel back, we'll kill you both."

In the silence that was broken only by Hoel's weakening screams, Qella fled to the kitchen, hands over her ears.

"What now?" said Virmith. "We can't stay stalemate forever. Sooner or later someone'll have to back down."

Qazia's eyes flashed. "I won't turn Hoel over to that wizard-fiend!"

"Please," gasped Hoel, "bargain with Chond! He'll accept Hearmo for me."

"Both of them will just seize you somewhere else!" she snapped. "No! I can't let that happen, either!"

"Decide fast," put in Hearmo. "Silver can't kill me, but Hoel's not immortal."

Suddenly Qella burst toward them from the kitchen. "Help! Help! An urso's coming down the chimney!"

Hearmo grinned. "My master's come to make up your minds for you."

Chond's black-robed, bearish form, with its spark-red eyes and black-bristled snout, stalked into the tavern's main room.

197

Qazia and Virmith did not recoil; the smith flourished his hammer in a protective swipe.

With a snarl, Chond reached for his ferret-fetch, then drew off at the sight of the silver fetters. When the wizard grabbed for Hoel, Virmith's hammer blocked him.

Chond's eyes flared. He ran his blue urso tongue in and out between his red tusks, then spat a spell. Morning dayshine winked out as an electric green haze infiltrated the Joyous Goblet.

Virmith stood solid, but Qella sighed and collapsed, lying too still for Qazia's peace of mind.

Steel in my thigh-dagger ought to combat Chond's bane, thought the tavern-mistress. She whipped her blade from under her skirt.

In the acid green glare her dagger began to throb a brilliant wine red. Blade held before her as a shield, Qazia confronted Chond and forced him to retreat a few more steps. He barked a second incantation; the tavern heaved like a storm-driven sail.

Hard put to keep her footing, Qazia hung on to her dagger and shook it in Chond's hairy face. Reflected in the wizard's fiery eyes, she saw Virmith, untroubled by the buck-leaping tavern, still guarding Hoel and Hearmo. She had barely registered this glimpse when she stumbled against Hoel's song-loom.

A dissonant roar bounced from the loom-strings. All the tavern crockery shattered, benches and tables split. As Chond took breath for a third bane, the song-loom's discord smashed into him, knocked his wind from him, and threw him on his knees.

Dayshine burned away the green-lightning fog, and the

198

Joyous Goblet settled on its foundations again. Qella snapped awake and scrambled behind Qazia, who still thrust her wine-shimmering dagger protectively out.

"Master," shouted Hearmo, "we're neutralized!"

"So I have learned," Chond agreed, rising to his feet. "Mouse-brain! Why didn't you warn me this place was shielded?"

"It isn't!" protested the ferret-fetch. "Qazia knows by instinct which metals to use against us."

Qazia began to laugh. A few minutes later Qella and Virmith joined in. But Hoel remained a feebly breathing huddle on the floor.

Hearmo's weasel-whiskers twitched in a grimace, and the ferret-fetch tried in vain to lift one link of silver chain in a paw. "Master, you'll have to bargain. These people won't release me, and they'll kill Hoel rather than give him to you."

After a long glare at Qazia's wine-flashing blade, Chond gruffed, "Well, vomit-mopper, what do you want?"

"I'll trade your wight for Hoel!"

"Urrr!" muttered the wizard. "Give up Ryddeg's brat, he'll have more chance to kill me. But if give up Hearmo, lose half my powers. Either way bad choice. Urrr!"

His mumbles were indecipherable, but all awaited his decision. Qazia and Virmith maintained their guard; Qella relaxed enough to emerge from the shelter of Qazia's skirts. But Hoel's breathing grew more shallow, and he began to resemble a freshly dead corpse. Hearmo strained forward as far as the silver fetters allowed, trying to follow Chond's thoughts.

At last the wizard nodded sharply. "Done. But only on condition that you free my ferret-fetch yourself."

"Oh, no!" retorted Qazia. "I don't intend to be jumped! Virmith, you unlock Chond's wight."

Scowling, and in slow motion, the smith unshackled Hearmo.

Scampering at once to Chond's side, the ferret-fetch shrilled, "Thank you, most gracious master!"

Hoel moaned at the sudden restoration of movement and air to his stifled lungs, flexed his cramped arms and legs, and felt for an object to orient himself. His fingers blundered against the frame of his song-loom. By the time he started tuning the warp and weft, he was on his feet.

"Play a war song, quick," whispered Qazia.

Under the cover of a loud rendition of "Gyrech's March," Hoel asked, "Why'd you want a song?"

"Song-loom sound seems to nullify Chond's spell-casting."

"If I'd known that, I'd have avenged my father long ago."

"I discovered it by accident just now. Chond didn't know it, either."

Neither wizard nor ferret-fetch paid attention to the other persons in the room. Hearmo kept trying to perch on Chond's shoulder, and the wizard brushed his creature off every time. Finally, Chond growled, "Stop clutching me, ant-brain! I saved your hide because you're more valuable than you know. Now get off, and let me think!"

"That's it!" Qazia hissed in Hoel's ear. "Chond can't attack us because the silver chains weakened his wight, and because Virmith and I carry naked steel. The ferrety wight probably contains a good part of Chond's powers."

Qella whimpered, "Chond's scheming!"

200

"Just let him try!" reassured Virmith, with a threatening feint of hammer.

"Only one way to stop Chond permanently," Qazia whispered to Hoel. "Make his wight desert him. We must convince the wight Chond doesn't really love it. Can you improvise a taunt?"

Hoel's hands poised over the song-loom and a snickering trill of thread-chords launched his jeer:

> "Chond made a ferret wight
> And Hearmo was its name.
> Chond gave to Hearmo
> Half his black spells' bane.
> Yah!
>
> Hearmo thought Chond loved it.
> Chond cared only for Hearmo's power to witch.
> If Hearmo ever finds that out,
> Chond's magic strength will be in doubt.
> Yah!"

As the mocking melody dimmed, Hearmo tugged at Chond's robe, arguing in an urgent yammer.

Hoel listened, his song-loom tight in the curve of his arm, while Qazia, Qella, and Virmith watched the wight quarrel with Chond.

The wizard snatched the ferret-fetch by its neck scruff, shook it a few times, and thundered, "Yes, you have half of my powers inside your weasel-shape! But if you don't stop pestering me, I'll turn you back to burnt ermine fur, and create a more docile fetch!"

201

Hearmo screeched, squirmed around in Chond's grasp, and bit Chond's right thumb at the root, almost severing it. Chond jerked his bitten hand and lost his hold on Hearmo's neck.

Hearmo slashed at Chond with all four sets of claws, jumped clear, and landed on Qazia's shoulder, chittering, "You thinged me, Chond, like you tried to thing Hoel! I'll never give you back your powers, never! I renounce you! You're a ratling! I shred you and eat you!"

Even as the bane tumbled from the ferret-fetch's mouth, Chond of Grimkeep shrank from urso wizard-thane to a corpulent black rat that struggled to get its legs under itself to run. Hearmo swooped down from Qazia's shoulder, broke the rat's spine with a single crunch of jaws, and swallowed the former wizard whole.

"Bravo, ferret wight, that's the best deed you've done since Chond made you!" cried Virmith, setting his hammer at ease on the floor.

Hearmo ran his tongue around his mouth, brushed whiskers, and asked, "Tavern-mistress, may I have a goblet of your strongest Jerezian? Chond's aftertaste is very bad."

"You ate Chond of Grimkeep?" Hoel exclaimed. "How my father must be laughing, wherever his soul is!" He struck up his ballad again:

"The wizard-thane of Grimkeep
    Is bested now at last.
His ferret-fetch turned on him,
    Devoured him with powers vast."

"A round of Jerezian for all, Qella!" cried Qazia.

"Aye, tavern-mistress. May I fetch the ferret wight a

double ration, since he saved the Joyous Goblet?'' Qazia nodded.

With a shrug, the ferret-fetch protested, ''I just got mad at Chond. He wouldn't thank me for serving him like a good fetch. I'm glad I ate him; it's the first real meal I've had since I was made.''

Hoel stilled his song-loom and chuckled.

Virmith the smith held out his goblet of Jerezian and declared, ''May evil always lose its tongue!''

Clinking her goblet to his, Qazia responded to his toast, ''May bad ends always be well sung!''

FOR LOVERS ONLY

Roger C. Schlobin

The sweat ran down from his armpit in a chilling tickle. When he rose from his knees later, it would mix with his hair shirt and be this chilly morning's reminder of his sacrilege and crimes. Thotharn and lust! Did those stupid priests really believe he wore the horrible scourge next to his skin because he was penitent? False bastards—they'd wear one only to appear saintly when they were run over by a cart or assassinated by a lord in the Shrine of the Three Lordly Ones. Fools! They would lie beneath the wheels below everyone's notice, and what mighty lord could be bothered with a priest?

Brother Jerome hunched further into his pain, knowing from experience that his bent frame would conceal the gold candlestick tied to his chest. His brethren called him "the Huncher" because of his odd kneeling. He almost didn't suppress a chuckle. They teased but thought him impossibly devout. In their blind, false piety, they never guessed that he had for many mornings now been prayerfully wrapped around piece after piece of soft gold stolen from the temple's dusty treasure vault. Even the fearful sweat that constantly glazed the center of his tonsure was thought the product of his intense devotion and prayer.

Fools, thought Jerome. Pious, unsuspecting dolts. Even the high priest, with his supposed grand education and pompous pronouncements, had been fooled.

Just the other morning, the high priest had condescended to speak to him. "Ah, Brother Jerome, up before everyone again. Pacing the halls like a curled saint, praying, praying, praying. You must be kinder to yourself. Straighten your shoulders, your back. Those we worship have no need of red-eyed and stooped servants." Jerome felt a wave of goodwill stab through him. That damned badge. He fought the feeling down. Long ago he'd learned to resist the high priest's hypnotic Lordly Ones amulet. Silence and deadly purpose were his defense. Let him and the others think that their sanctimonious posturings and pat conclusions were omnipotent: "Ah 'tis the devote Jerome, mumbling his way through the rolls of the Songs of Summoning, stalking the halls, bent with his eyes on his dirty toenails."

Damn their laughter. Damn the high priest; his rewards would come anyway. For too long he'd indulged in the spices, wool, jewels, and fur that wandered up and down the Ith. The fat pig would learn when the next noble visited for a token Holy Ten-day appearance that the purest of the precious gold was gone, his storeroom shelves marked with dust-free shapes and empty cases. Jerome had so wanted to stand straight for the bloody ass. What fun it would have been to watch the false beatitude drop from his fat face when he saw a temple treasure outlined beneath his robe! Jerome had even wished, as he'd lain each night on his pallet hating, that he could be there when the high priest opened the door and saw his losses; but by then the Ithkar Fair would be over, the lustful fleeced, and he on his way to take care of *her!*

Devotions over, Jerome rose carefully, straightening only at the knees, to leave the bare resident chapel with the other priests. Despite the high priest's stern presence, there were the usual whispers and muffled chuckles as they made their ways back to their cells for the morning's hour of solitary meditation. Being careful to avoid the spaces between the ill-fitted flagstones and the worn curves on the stairs, Jerome made his way along the too familiar route to his only private place. It wouldn't do to stumble now, not when he was so close to his goal. He again chuckled to himself when he realized that if he fell, he'd clank when he hit, a topheavy thief with a golden breast.

He did pause in the soft breeze of late summer to look out through the arched windows of the cloister across the rolling green hills. In the distance he could see the preparations for the fair. Dominating it all was the undeniable majesty of the Shrine of the Three Lordly Ones. The silver Ith, its filth hidden by sun and distance, ribboned the far boundary. The skeletons of the rising tents, soon to capture more colors than the rainbow; the permanent, more spacious stalls of the guilds, even the gray edifice of the stoneworkers' hall of statuary. Wagons of traveling players already ringed the shrine and turned it into a giant pinwheel. Off to the side a young boy and girl performed tricks on a galloping pony; the distance made them look like centaurs. Jerome even thought he saw the spinning flashes of the axes thrown by a juggler practicing his art and the sharp flashes of the controlled fire of a trained dragon. He looked for one wagon in particular and was both angered and relieved when he couldn't find it.

" 'Tis a beautiful sight, is it not, Jerome?" remarked Brother Sadmust, the heal-all.

Jerome brushed by. "Eh, Sadmust, I must, I must, go to my cell . . . my prayers, the souls of sinners, my soul, my brethren. I will come by after the fair, after all the responsibilities of so many visiting souls are done."

"My pardon, I did not mean to keep you, but the high priest and I are . . ." Sadmust's words echoed along the vaulted corridor; Jerome was already picking his careful way toward his cell. Sadmust stared at the departing back: a strange man, unquestionably devout, but disquietingly different from the monastery's usual population. And that poor, sad back. How cruel that the priests mocked his piety before all. It would not be a happy fair for him. Sadmust nearly followed but thought better. Still, he must have another chat with the high priest about Jerome. Try to convince him that Jerome's piety deserved to be treated as more than a comical curiosity.

Jerome leaned his back against the door to his cell. Gods, it was good to straighten up. Almost inadvertently a groan escaped his lips; he repeated it. Oddly, it helped ease the poisoned stomach he had endured since she'd left him for the ragtag guardian-wizard. "Ooooww." He let it escape slowly. Better, a bit better, though never gone. He retched as he did most mornings and had to hold his hands above his head to stop from puking. Let them listen and marvel again at his agony for the world's pain. This was his pain, his to keep, to hold, to nurture. *Sweet pain, sweet moan. Cursèd woman, soft, beautiful woman, firm breasts, warm quilts, wonderful hunger, caring—* Stop, fool! Again she had seduced the revelry from him. Again he clenched his teeth against the love that crept within him without cause, without reason. He must deny her, he must survive. *Reason?* spoke something within him; *Purpose?* it asked again.

Jerome spoke again to his constant haunter. "It will pass; I will be healed; it will be better; I will one day be free of her. There will be payment. . . ." From a deep, secret place within him, there rose a sardonic chuckle, and Jerome snapped his head sharply back and forth to rid himself of his own voice, to rid himself of the feeling that he would never be whole again.

"I will be healed, but not by the butcher of a barber in the town with his faded red-and-white pole, nor by that meddling Sadmust. That fool of a heal-all; he doesn't even believe in bleeding. If there was blasphemy, that Sadmust was in it up to his nostrils. No humors, what a turd! All I'll need is enough money to be bled by an expert. All that ails me is too much black bile. A balanced system, microcosm matching macrocosm—then I'll be free of her and the pain."

For the moment, he was almost free of his stomach and his aching back had begun to stretch out. . . . *She used to rub it—* Stop! He ripped his robe and hair shirt over his head in one motion. Lords! He nearly dropped the Y-shaped rod, that noise would be hard to explain. He rubbed his blood-streaked chest with grease he'd taken from the kitchen. It provided little relief, but its smell did contribute to his reputation as a denier of the flesh.

As his hands flashed in practiced motions over his chest,

under his arms, and as far around his back as he could reach (he shuddered to think what his back must look like), his eyes swept the all-too-familiar cell. The short, thin slit of a window with its cracked wooden shutter. He had to spill water on it in the winter to ice it tight. The crude copy of the Three Lordly Ones' badge above the pallet, its top clumsily carved off center. Across from the pallet was a small, wooden shrine covered with white cloth and topped with an earthenware singing cup and a fat candle. A small, three-legged stool beside a large wooden washing bowl and chamber pot completed Jerome's meager holdings.

Again he drew a moment's humor from his cleverness. All looked exactly as it should; it was the same as all the other cells that marched the east wall. Seemingly stoic and barren, it hid far more than anyone could suspect. The shrine, ah, the shrine, that was the real triumph.

Jerome allowed himself the brief luxury of stretching out on the pallet. The soft yielding of mildewed straw concealed its real contents. Now he had to twist his mouth into his shoulder to conceal his almost hysterical glee at the high priest's vanity. The perfect peacock, so fastidious. Had he ever worn the same vestments twice? The smug fart would be astounded if he ever went back into those cedar chests he has stacked in the crypt. Beneath one layer of vestments was the straw from the pallet.

One vestment at a time, Jerome had smuggled the varicolored robes back to his cell. For weeks he'd had to hide his pin-pricked fingers, curled into his palms or thrust into his sleeves. Fortunately, saying the scratches on his fingers had their disguising effect, and it had contributed mightily to his pious reputation. But slowly and surely the tent had grown

210

under his fumbling, thimbleless fingers, the tent that would rise above his masterpiece and attract all the rich and greedy simpletons at the fair. For nights he'd trembled with the fear of intrusion when its rainbow colors had been spread all over the cell, draped from ceiling to floor. His silver-hilted knife, the last remnant of his nobility, flashed through the costly fabrics, ready to be turned upon even an innocent visitor. He wished the tent was bigger, but it would be impressive enough with its precious threads, that was most important. His black velvet robes and conical cape, shaped from four vestments from the Eulogy for the Departure of the Three, would be wonderful dramatic contrast.

"Enough preening, clever devil, a morning's work lies ahead."

Crossing to the shrine, Jerome eased it away from the wall. Umm, it was getting heavy; there had to be fifty cubits of gold wire by now. Once he had angled it out, he paused to admire the carefully carved wooden Egg and wheel; its bulk filled two-thirds of the hollow shrine. Ah, 'twas his own little lordly Egg. Briefly he admired the curve of wheel and the Thotharian and Lordly Ones symbols that covered it. Sadmust and the high priest would shudder to see some of those signs, but Jerome knew they were only part of the larger sham that was all there was to life. Inadvertently, he'd once hummed one of the Songs of Shaping as he carved. Suddenly, the runes had seemed to crawl about the Egg. Fear prevented any further humming. Besides, it had surely been a trick of his tired eyes.

All those days wandering about his father's estates, ignored as only a third son could be, had paid off. His once expansive and insatiable curiosity feeding as he watched the

211

hands of the master carver, the smith, the weaver; those moments stolen in the library of the keep's resident wizard as he read the old manuscripts; his fascination holding the indecipherable symbols in his mind. Recalling them for his Egg. "An idle woman's fetish," they had called his fascination with reading. His father's and older brothers' continual riding or sword clanking were the true manly arts.

Again a chuckle briefly escaped Jerome's pursed lips. Even when he was with Dulcesans . . . *She had so delighted in the new things that you wanted so much to show—* Stop!

He still saw and remembered things. Little did any of them know the uses he would turn all of it to, little since the day he'd denied the position on the Ithkar Board of Trade his father had bought for him. What could they have ever suspected when he'd run, cursing and heartbroken, from their scorn, to be found weeks later half-starved and raving on the steps of the temple on the hill. What could the priests have known of the bosom serpent that they'd taken in and succored that night!

Jerome reached into the shrine; his hand curled around the familiar oiled handle of his most precious tool. The chisel had once been one of the prized possessions of Brother Hoosh, the carpenter; its fine metal gleamed in the candlelight despite the constant dampness. When the tip had been notched by an inept and presumptuous acolyte, Hoosh had thrown it in the corner in an impious rage. Only Jerome had remembered, and when his scheme had emerged on that fateful night almost five months ago, he had returned and found it.

Easing himself down on the low stool and pulling the colorless blanket from the pallet about his raw shoulders, he

212

set the wash basin between his feet. Taking the soft gold Y-shaped rod, he began to push the chisel along its length. Fine gold curls rose from each stroke to fall into the basin with dull, repetitive thunks. Once a young acolyte had overheard the noises on his way to the scullery and fortunately had asked Jerome what they were. He'd remarked that they were probably his prayerful breast-beating. Another piece of the gossip surrounding the reclusive, devoted Jerome. . . . That dark chuckle slipped out again.

The Y-shaped rod, despite its branching, was easier than the singing cups. For the longest time, he had fretted over the jewels that had had to be scraped off and were useless to his plan. However, this year's spring planting had solved that problem. He would be long gone by the time Sadmust noticed the gaps in his herb garden and longer still before some priest would think he'd turned up another Lordly Ones treasure come next spring.

Jerome's hand and chisel moved in hypnotic regularity as he stroked the rod toward nothingness and as the basin filled with golden locks. Despite the rigid control and relished revenge that kept Dulcesans out of his mind amid the day-to-day tasks, his sour gut and the thoughtless monotony of his task allowed his mind to slip unguarded into the past, to harken to that deep, secret voice he so desperately tried to ignore.

It had been one of those crisp, sharp days that made autumn a season of clarity and cleansing. The harsh winds of winter that would blow through the unmortared seams between the stones of his father's keep and move the tapestries as if wraiths hugged the walls were still in the distant future.

That morning he had learned from his mother of the position on the board of trade. It was to have been his father's surprise at dinner, but his mother never could keep secrets from her youngest and most precious son. He had only one thought: to tell Dulcesans of his joy. Finally he would have a purpose, a place. She, widowed early and able to inherit her husband's small wealth, property, and business, was one of the few, favored single women in Jerome's world. Despite her youth, she had prospered in the small shop. Jerome had always been uneasy with her skill and presence, but his love shadowed that even when she spoke of things he didn't understand. All he could do was offer support. He'd had to content himself with giving her the small figurines his clever hands shaped with a skill beyond his years, and she did joy and laugh in the stories he culled from the old books. Whenever they met, he always had a bag of something for her and one of his great pleasures was to watch her explore its confines for the little treasures he'd collected.

He'd sent her a missive the night before asking that she contact him today. He'd had no word, and despite his deep respect he tended to worry. She was the light of his small, trusting life and he feared for her living alone. Had he been more astute, less devoted, less mindlessly impassioned, Jerome would have been forewarned. More and more, his ardent attentions had been treated by Dulcesans as impositions, his messages unanswered, her promises of words and meetings unfulfilled. He had excused her with the stresses and preoccupations of the shop and her increasing devotion to matters mercantile. *Fool, half a man, fool,* the inner voice hissed.

But that day had too much blinding ecstasy for him to

think of his forebodings. He danced more than ran. Bumping people on the street, his tabard flying about his head, he spun, he laughed till all thought him mad as he pirouetted his way through the narrow streets to the shop's back door. Finally, he had something of his own to offer. They would go to the city; they would share all moments.

Had Jerome's normally sharp eye not been consumed with tears of joy, he would have noticed. The brazier that burned outside the door with the remains of skewered meats was the same as the small, intimate feasts they had shared before, and he had hoped to have today. *Used fool.* The shrouded wagon, emblazoned with the sign of Compo, the guardian-wizard, should have told it all. *Worthless fool.* When she rushed out the door to meet him, to stand between him and the shop, he should have known. Her gaze was cold, chill for a stranger; a blouse he had bought for her on a rare trip to the city was shaped tight to her breasts. *Empty fool.*

"I have news; I had expected word this morning," Jerome offered, his heart dying as he finally took in the obvious signs about him.

"I never said when today. There is company. I will send word this afternoon." There was no love in her voice. His insides iced further.

"Is everything all right?" Jerome hoped his honest concern would warm her. It didn't.

Abruptly: "Until then."

"Until." No kiss, just a retreating back.

There was no word that afternoon. He waited without hope where he could see any messenger entering the keep. Later in the afternoon, when his loutish, oldest brother had made an offhand remark about Dulcesans's long afternoon's lingering with a guardian-wizard, it had been too much. Little remained in Jerome's memory of what he screamed at his father, his family, of the spit that flew unbidden from his mouth, whipped by his frenzy across his chin. *Fool. Loon.* All that remained was the poison-without-balm that filled his stomach, and he began to stoop and moan as he ran from the keep.

He spent the first night curled in a stand of willows, too crippled to move, too stricken to will anything. Cursed with the taunting voice that became his constant companion: *Seed spilled upon emptiness. Void. Caring, dreams, tossed among the rotting vegetables. Love crushed, barren.*

Some reason returned the second night. And his pearl ring, a gift from his mother, bought him a bath and a meal at a small inn on the trade road on the outskirts of town. The grease-spattered innkeeper thought himself a clever fellow to receive so much for so little. Jerome didn't care. The ale and the bird did nothing for his pain. Nor did he notice the looks his soft moans and soiled finery drew from the other patrons.

Yet, in those who believe too truly to survive among people, hope and love are difficult to kill. As the evening moved on, Jerome began to distrust his own eyes and his brother's words. She had told him just five nights before that she loved only him, that the future bound them together. They had been together so long, shared so much preciousness. *Simperer.* He crept back to her, woke her. He was greeted with a blast of hate and summoned ugliness that his basic good nature could not stand against. *Empty, riven fool.*

"Don't touch me!"

No one ever knew how much time passed from then until

the priests found the wretched bundle curled about its stomach, failing moans rising from it. *Fool.*

"Bong. Bong. Bong."

Ah, she had done it again. Would the pain never kill the love? Jerome struggled toward waking, uncurling himself from the ball of his nightmare-ridden sleep.

"Bong. . . ."

Must, must, more gold for the stupid . . .

"Bong. . . ."

Priests' blood! The call to morning tasks! Must hide this stuff. The shrine . . .

"Jerome, Jerome, are you ill? Jerome, come to the door."

That infernal meddler Sadmust. Jerome breathed deeply, trying to compose himself, hands over his head fighting down the ever-present nausea. "Yes, Sadmust, I am coming. Just lost in the tragedy of the sinful, the sick. I'll be right out."

"Ah, Jerome, we will lose you yet to your piety. Hurry, the pots and pans wait for no one." Sadmust chuckled.

Jerome breathed deeply as he heard Sadmust's footsteps fade away. He had no time to put the hair shirt back on, and by now it was so cut and curried for his special purposes that he hadn't planned to wear it much longer. It was only moments later, the cell once again looking depressingly barren, that he noticed that he'd cut himself with the chisel while he'd slept. A thin stream of blood ran across his groin and down the inside of his thigh. Again that sardonic chuckle from deep within him: *Jerome, the True Believer.*

*   *   *

As Jerome went out to the kitchen, he hoped that the yellowed square of linen would stop the bleeding of the small cut. What he really needed was a leech, but the gold dust on the chisel would be the best of all healing agents. He wanted to avoid Sadmust at all costs. He had begun to believe that the man was sincere in his concern despite his rejections of proper healing and alchemical lore. Probably hadn't even read *The Ruby Tablets of Semreh the Thrice Mighty*. The man was beginning to appeal to Jerome. For his bitter purposes, he could afford no human emotion, no kindness. It weakened him. As he got closer to the smoking kitchen, he did reflect for a moment that the fellowship of the quiet, withdrawn priests had had its moments. Even the high priest's usually inept attempts at humor had almost drawn laughter from Jerome. That discussion last night, that we were due for the kitchen to burn down again. What was it that he had said . . . ah, yes: "If a master goes down with his ship, shouldn't the cook go up with his kitchen?" That look on poor Brother Hubert's face. Surely their cook understood that wood construction, chimneys, and flying fat made kitchens very perishable. Why, every day a kitchen was burning somewhere.

Jerome's faint smile vanished as he entered the kitchen. Thank Thotharn, that smelly Hubert was gone and delivering the high priest's breakfast. Quickly he drew a small bag from beneath his robe and emptied the fine, white sand into the proper trough. His poor hands had further suffered from the pot scrubbing, but he'd needed the sand to finish his beautiful, false Egg. Only two more days of this! One night of making glowing curls; the second night off to the fair to set his trap. Oh, that Compo would show as advertised! That she, the whore, would be with him! Argh, the pain again!

218

*   *   *

Jerome woke to the noises of the setting of the fair. He stretched from his usual cramped posture. Why, the pain was less this morning! No doubt in anticipation of today's rewards. He rose to his feet and admired his handiwork. He had managed to find a small spot at the outskirts where all the grass hadn't been turned to the fair's characteristic mud. The morning's light streamed through the tent's multicolored panels, casting rainbows over his smoothly polished Egg, highlighting its wheel, catching the silver of the knife, as they perched upon the converted shrine. His disappearance from the monastery had been uneventful, the only minor delay the reopening of his wound when he had struggled with the gold-laden Egg. Fortunately, he had not worn the soft black robes; the bloodstains on his priest's habit were inconsequential. He cared little whether or not they noticed his absence: Brother Jerome was dead! Long Live Jason the alchemist! *Clever devil.* Jerome chuckled, stifled it, and then realized that he never need conceal his glee again. "For once, my personal succubus, you are right. 'Clever devil' indeed!" Crumpling his forged permit for this space, he paused for a moment to admire his handiwork of last night; the next-to-last act in his little comedy. The sign read:

**FOR LOVERS ONLY
THE GOLDEN FLEECE
HAIR INTO GOLD
JASON THE GENEROUS**

Enough! The pleasure of the day must be readied. Reaching beneath the white samite cloth with its silver-and-gold threads, he removed the hair shirt from the shrine. Its stiff fibers had been combed into luxuriant locks; woven throughout were the precious colored threads from the high priest's ravaged vestments. It caught the light and sparkled as if by magic.

First, the robe. Jerome preened as its soft nap caressed his abused flesh. *Soft hands, trusting hands, sliding hands—* Stop! Quickly he threw his hands above his head, fearing to spoil all his efforts. The bitch again. Soon his belly and mind would be free of her! When the spasms eased, he finished arranging the black robe, drawing it about him with a silver rope that a Lordly Ones talisman had swung from just as recently as last night. Part of the hair shirt was fitted to his head, covering his tonsure and rolling down around his ears and onto his shoulders. He pulled the remaining piece to his face, knowing the plaster he'd gotten from that dumb Sadmust would hold it in place. He laughed aloud as he recalled the days he'd shuffled about the monastery with a piece of hair stuck to him somewhere, waiting until he was alone to jump up and down to see if he could dislodge it. Already the world was a better place.

As he moved to the tent-flap, he wished he had a looking glass, but he had practiced too long for anything to be amiss. Throwing the canvas aside, making sure it slapped loudly, he paused before Jason made his grand entrance into the Ithkar Fair. Then, slowly, with paced dignity, he stepped into the light. The cacophony of animal cries and crafts at work continued for a moment, then began to still as his dark-shrouded figure was noticed. The couper across the way paused as he bent an iron hoop about a tube; the woman next to him advertising her act as she paced lost control of her small flight of acrobatic, dwarf wyverns; the fortune-teller stilled the cloth that caressed his crystal; the sausage-maker hawking his wares here at the fringe of the fair slapped as at a drop of hot fat on his wrist but never dropped his eyes. A small group of apprentices—the printers' guild from their stained hands—nearly fell over themselves as their leader stopped suddenly to stare. Jerome permitted himself no outward show of joy as both merchants and passersby stared transfixed at his ominous and majestic presence. Lifting his head only slightly, he turned slowly, letting the light creep in under his cowl to catch the brilliant threads in his beard. Setting the sign down on its pedestal, he returned to the tent, dropping the flap, hearing it slither closed behind him. He had the fools now, only a matter of time before they were lined up hand in hand. Lovers were fools!

Slowly, the noise rose up again around the tent. But now it had a more agitated tone: "A new wonder. Never seen before. Hair into gold. Crazy."

Through the gauze shadow-panel sewn into the flap, Jerome watched as a small crowd of couples began to gather. Ratty-looking lot. Guildsmen, freedmen, journeymen mostly. Men threadbare; women pock-marked. By Thotharn, the times wore the common folk down quickly. As they moved and milled, Jerome caught a scab here; rotted teeth there; a crooked leg, broken and never healed properly. A priest passed, lingering to satisfy his curiosity, to listen to the whispered conversations. He'll be back with a woman, thought Jerome. Disgusting what's happened to the priesthood these days!

221

Jerome didn't have to wait too long. A couple separated itself from the small crowd. The woman reached forward to scratch at the flap.

Reaching forward with both hands, he threw the flaps apart and stepped into the sun before her nails made contact. The crowd stepped back quickly at his sudden, seemingly omniscient appearance.

His cowl thrown back, his lidded eyes peering out from his curls, Jerome spoke, "My children, how may I serve you?"

"M'lord Jason . . ." It was the girl who spoke; Jerome could not help but notice that her full breasts strained against her farmers' poor finery, that her gums had drawn back from her few teeth. Ripe, ugly cow!

"M'lord, the kind priest, he read us your sign. Do you really turn hair into gold?"

"Only for those truly in love, my child." Jerome had seen the bumpkin's callused hands moving against her as they had stood in the crowd. Knuckles brushed along a thigh. Fingers creeping from waist to ass. Let her think his lust is love.

"Oh, m'lord, Phillip and I are to be married at the first planting. I will help his mother; his father will give mine wool; the farms will be joined; we . . ." Phillip's bump and scowl made it clear that such jabberings were common.

"Ah, my children, it is clear even to such an old tooth as I that your union is foretold in the stars. A moment and then I will serve you." Jerome turned and lifted the tent's cunning front to each side, revealing the gleaming Egg on its samite throne. The crowd sighed, almost moaned in wonder; Jerome's stomach twitched, but he caught himself before it bent him.

"Now, my fine swain, all I need is a lock of your beloved's fine golden tresses." Jerome wondered if anyone could think of that sun-bleached straw as "golden," but the lout seemed oblivious to the irony.

"Why, just help y'rself, m'lord."

"Nay, Master Phillip, for the spell to work only your hands may touch the lady's tresses." Jerome laid the silver-hilted belt knife in his hands, noticing the third finger was missing. The way the bumpkin hefted it Jerome wondered if he would be around at the next planting, perhaps preferring a more lucrative, if short-lived, career along the dark stretches of the Three Lordly Ones' Highway. Reaching up, Phillip crudely grasped a lock, exacting a small gasp from the girl. From the way she gazed at him, Jerome wondered if she was one of those who liked the pain—*Small bites along the neck, sweet pain noises, grasping tighter*— Stop! Jerome was jerked back from his revelry as the farmer offered the stiff bunch of hair.

"Nay again, strong Phillip, we will have no hint of sleight of hand here. You will put it in the Egg." His sleeve flared as he swung his arm to regard the Egg. The crowd gathered closer. Jerome removed the small fitted lid, revealing an inner wheel marked by a silver hook. The hours that had gone into those workings: the guide that would slip the hair off, the hidden bin the hook would pass through to snare the gold wool, the spring that kept the gold's level just high enough. Reaching forward, Phillip stuffed the hair into the cavity.

"Carefully, my son, be sure that it's wrapped all around the silver. Otherwise, it will not all be transformed." Sure that the lock was properly entwined, Jerome replaced the lid. "Now, my children, this only I can do."

Jerome had given much thought to this phase and had decided that he need not fear the superstitious mind rot of the various cabalistic and arcane tongues. He sang as he moved the wheel through its full rotation, allowing himself a rising crescendo as he finished and whisked the top off the Egg: "Come, children, take the product of your deep love!"

Phillip nearly fell over the farm girl in his greed, but she got to the Egg first and the squeal of her glee echoed up and down the rows of the fair. Hastily repeating, "Thank ye, m'lord," they quickly backed into the group, struggling with each other for possession of the warm gold as many shoved and peered to see. Jerome chuckled inwardly at their premarital struggle and wondered if the assertive Phillip had not gotten more than he bargained for. Oddly, as they moved away, it suddenly seemed as if they genuinely began to try to force the gold on each other. Compassion? Generosity? No, probably just the wrong perspective.

Jerome lacked for no customers. His skin crawled with fevered pins as the crowd's mutterings brought him the news he had prayed to the dark gods for: "Almost as good as Compo, that one." "Better, m'thinks, though Compo has that fetching wench at his elbow." *They've come to do you again.* Jerome forced down the inner voice and the gore that rose again to the tender back of his throat. Now was the time to bring the full wisdom of his plot to the fore.

Cleverly, he made sure to serve those couples who arranged a temporary union at the edge of the crowd as well as those who appeared genuinely in love. Let him gain a quick reputation as a fool: he had love to appeal to the empty-headed Dulcesans; now he had stupidity to appeal to the jaded Compo. Finally, as the sun rose to its highest, he had to plead weariness to escape the many who pressed forward for his gifts. Weariness was only a small part: he had to reload the gold and compose himself for the visit he hoped Compo and Dulcesans would take after the guardian-wizard's afternoon show of chicanery.

As he rested in the closed tent and kept his eyes on the shadow-panel, Jerome deepened his hate and purpose. He must not yield to her again. *Believer.* She had lied and toyed too often. *Gull.* Now let her feel the force of his anger. Once I have destroyed the pompous pride of that swaggering bumpkin, a mere diviner gone crazy over the worship of innocent women, I will take her in my arms— No! No! No! I will leave her with her stupidity and ruined magician. Will this eating pain never destroy the love?

Jerome was never sure how long he waited. Small groups gathered and called for the wonder-worker Jason. Couples lingered silently for an indeterminate time. Yet none were the victims he loathed and desired. *Love, hate, fear, purpose; goodness how you twirl about, false priest; argh, that poisoned gut again.* Jerome remained steadfast, all controlled and buried for the play to come.

There they are! There they are! Jerome almost screamed it aloud. Easy, easy, let them get a bit past. Make it look like nothing. Make them think there is no special attention. By the Three, they've stopped right in front.

"Oh, Compo, he's not open. I did so want to have our love affirmed by a golden tress." Jerome listened with sink-

225

ing hopes to her caressing voice. The things he'd done for that voice, for those hands. He grew sicker as he watched the wizard's hands move on her, encouraging her consuming wanting. *Wanting, wanting, wanting, fool.* Her voice became just a droning blur of "I"'s. He could stand no more and burst from the tent, catching his composure only as their heads snapped toward him in shock.

Jerome stood with his arms raised above his head, his voice carrying up and down the lanes. "I feel the presence of a great love, a great union here at the fair. It is the undying love of Guelph and Semwai, the tragic union of Regort and Yelwee, born again in this place of merriment and wonder. Who is it that stands before me?"

"Why, my lord Jason, it is only I, Dulcesans, a humble widow, but I bring with me my dearest friend, Compo the Magnificent, the greatest guardian-wizard in all the kingdom." Her face bore a look of apparent wonder, but Jerome knew better: Hussy!

Compo showed a leer or a sneer; Jerome wasn't sure which. He was just deeply relieved that they didn't recognize him.

Looking out over the crowd, Jerome was pleased to see a number of priests from the monastery among its numbers. Even Sadmust gazed curiously at the black figure before the varicolored tent. Ah, a fellow practitioner of the art. There was no better audience than another adept! Jerome reached back for the silver knife and thought for a moment how easy it would be to finish it all immediately. Two quick slashes and a slow fall into the blade reversed. *Do it, do it.* No, too much planning to behave like a footpad now.

Jerome froze halfway in his reach when he heard Compo's sarcastic tone: "A fellow adept?" He wondered if he could reach the knife before anything else happened: No, I am too far, he too close.

"Compo, Compo, my golden hair; don't offend him." Dulcesans's soft tones again pierced through Jerome.

"Softly, my dear." Sharper again, "Softly, my dear," as she moved to speak again. "There is more here than meets the mortal eye." Jerome stood frozen before Compo's darkling eyes and vibrant voice.

This . . . this was not the plan. *Fool*.

"So, my seeming Jason, you turn hair into gold. . . ." Compo spoke loudly for the crowd as he stepped by Jerome to the Egg. The wizard reached out to the wheel; Jerome could only stand, his head lolling over his shoulder as he watched for the inevitable. Compo reached out one long finger and flipped the lid to the ground. Quickly he gave the wheel a sharp, strong spin. Gold wool cascaded into the air, catching in the couple's hair, striking Jerome's face. "Where is the hair for this, Jason?" Compo stilled the crowd with a sharp gesture as it moved toward the gold that was scattered about the tent and muddy aisle. "Ah, my dear Jason, there is yet another way to turn hair into gold." He leisurely moved back to the front of the tent. Jerome began to hunch forward as the poison rose in him again and slid uncontrollably over his lip. The group was still. Dulcesans quiet, fearful. She cringed away from Compo as his voice took on an even darker, more arcane resonance. He chanted in a language so ancient that no one could understand. From the way it moved through the marrow, no one cared to understand.

Jerome felt the beard pulling his head to his chest, felt the wig begin to slip to the side. "No . . . No . . ." The texture of the hair changed; it felt smooth and cold against his sweating tonsure, his dripping face. The wig fell to the ground with an embedding thud.

"Gold . . . His hair . . . to gold." The murmurings moved through the crowd. "Why, it's the Huncher; it's Jerome." "Oh Jerome." Sadmust's cry rose above the crowd as he moved quickly to the falling priest. The heal-all had to fight his way by too many to reach Jerome before he hit the ground chin first, dragged by the golden beard that refused to break free. By the time Sadmust reached him, a black bile had begun to foam over Jerome's lip, staining the fleece. Tears rushed from his eyes, deep retching was all he could add to his hand as it stretched toward Dulcesans. For a moment she appeared to yield, but Compo smoothly snaked his arm about her, his hand caressing her hip.

"My Dulcesans, ignore that offal. 'Jason,' indeed, clown more like. Imagine, my precious, trying to deceive our perceptions. Why, someone of your sensitivities should never be troubled by such as that!" Compo's tones slid across the woman; her eyes rose to his face in that adoring, self-indulgent look Jerome knew only too well.

Sadmust could do little as Jerome's head strained to watch the departing pair. He struggled unsuccessfully to free the golden beard and was startled when he heard a new sound begin to issue from Jerome's soiled lips. Quickly he moved to try to free what sounded like a swallowed tongue but realized that it was distorted laughter that rose from the wretched bundle in his arms. Jerome was managing a twisted smile, and Sadmust followed his eyes to the couple, Compo comforting, she leaning into the curve of his body. He looked quickly enough to see that Jerome's sacrilegious and ignorant spell-making had been potent in spite of his disbelief.

Compo was in love.

DRAGON'S HORN

J. W. Schutz

Tonya of Clan Sarg tossed a damp strand of her butter-colored hair off her forehead and carefully snapped the whip an inch above the right ear of the ox.

"Come, Lightning," she said, "I know you can do better than that."

Lightning, the ox, acknowledged her voice, if not the whip, by rolling an eye in her direction, but if he increased his pace, it was imperceptibly.

Beside her on the driver's seat of the great lumbering wagon, Tonya's betrothed, Driss, chuckled. "Lightning's not impressed," he said.

"He'd better be," Tonya replied. "If we don't hurry a bit, we'll not be at the fairgrounds in time to claim Father's good big place for the stage and the audience."

"Tonya, you worry too much. We'll pay off your debt and

get free of Lord Caum, really we will, even if I have to win a purse at the quarterstaff bouts.''

"You'll do nothing of the kind! Do you think I want to marry a man with his nose smashed flat and no teeth in his head? I'd rather be Caum's slave. Besides, I need you for the voice of Prince.''

"Is that all you need me for?''

"Of course not, silly!'' Tonya leaned over and kissed him. "Speaking of voices, though, we still haven't found anyone—that we can afford, at least—to speak for King, Village Girl, and Dragon. Dragon is the most important.''

"I could do Village Girl.'' The voice of a child came from inside the wagon and was followed by the appearance of his head at the curtain behind the driver's seat.

"Yes, perhaps you could, Vallo,'' Tonya said. "When you aren't doing Little Dog. That still leaves us King and Dragon.''

"Your brother's becoming ambitious,'' Driss said. "He'll be wanting to do Lord next.''

"Not until his voice changes,'' Tonya replied.

"I'm hungry,'' Vallo said plaintively.

"We'll eat when we come to the ford,'' Tonya said.

"Which we're coming to now,'' Driss said. "I can see a crowd on the road ahead waiting to cross. There must have been some rain upstream.''

The crowd thickened rapidly as Tonya's doll-wagon approached the ford. Rain-softened ground churned up by many wagons quickly became clinging brown mud, and Lightning began to complain.

"Looks like Vallo's not the only hungry one,'' Driss observed. "We'll need some fodder for the beast. I'll see what I can find if you two will fix us all a bit of lunch in the back of the wagon.''

As Driss trotted off into the crowd Tonya eased the wagon into the end of the line, put Vallo on the driver's seat with instructions to keep the ox moving as the line shortened, and prepared a lunch of bread, cheese, sliced apples, and buttermilk. This done, she installed herself on the tailgate, swinging her slim legs, to wait for Driss.

She had been there but a moment when a sturdy-looking peasant in a valet's vest approached and made a clumsy courtly bow.

"The day's greetings, my lady," he said in a singularly deep voice.

"And to you greetings," Tonya replied. "Although 'my lady' is too high a title for me. What is your business?"

"Alas, I have none at the moment. I am thinking that you and the child may need a strong helping hand at the ford and perhaps a man's protection on the road to Ithkar. For a copper or two and a bit of that bread and cheese I offer my service."

"A man's protection I have," Tonya said, nodding in the direction of the approaching Driss, who bore a huge armload of dry hay. "Yet if you need work, I may employ you if two coppers a day and food would suit you. How are you called?"

"Borg, ma'am. But two coppers is somewhat little."

"Little is what I have—in great quantities. You may pick up a bit more in tips, however, if you come with us."

"Tips?"

"Yes, tips. This is a doll show, as the paintings on the wagons show. I may use you to show the patrons to their seats. Let me hear you growl."

"Growl, ma'am?"

"Quite. Growl."

With a puzzled look Borg gave a deep and quite convincing growl. Driss, who was standing by, exchanged a look with Tonya.

"Fine for a bear," Driss said. "You're a dragon, however."

"I am?" Borg's look of stupid astonishment was so comic that none of the three travelers could restrain their laughter. Vallo insisted that Borg growl again, which he did with a good will.

Driss and Tonya explained what they would require Borg to do and tested him with a few simple lines and cues which he picked up quickly enough.

"You'll do, I think," Tonya said at last. "Two coppers, then, meals, and a place to sleep under the wagon. Done?"

"Done!" Borg agreed.

Tonya served out slabs of bread and cheese, buttermilk and dried apple slices as the wagon moved slowly to the head of the line. When they had finished she showed Borg a couple of the dolls; exquisite things, two hand's-spread high, carved from a soft white and flexible wood grown on the banks of mountain streams and painted and dressed with such microscopic detail that from a little distance they appeared to live. She also brought out Dragon, whose voice Borg was to be.

"Fierce-looking beastie, ain't he?" Borg said.

Dragon was indeed a fine, fierce beastie. He was over three and a half feet long, covered with silvery scales that had once belonged to a large ocean fish, and had a sharp ridge like the teeth of a saw down the length of his back. When a certain string was pulled, he could open his mouth and snap his jaws with a loud crack, displaying a long red flannel tongue which would flicker like a flame. Being heavier than the other dolls, his head and most of his body was hollow. Near the end of his nose was affixed a long horn of white boar's tusk ivory.

"I understand that your dolls are made to act a play," Borg said, "but how are they moved? Except for Dragon, as you call him, I can see no strings."

Vallo laughed scornfully. "Strings are for puppets. Our dolls move like real people. They are moved by spells!"

"Spells? Did you say spells?" An old man with a white beard down to his belt hobbled forth from the small crowd that had gathered to gawk at the dolls. He leaned heavily on a gnarled staff and was dressed in a somewhat battered peaked hat and a black robe embroidered with lines of strange symbols. The hem of the garment swept the ground and was slightly tattered and streaked with mud at the bottom. "I, madam, am Omz, the magician. I specialize in spells. It is my hobby. If you would be kind enough to give me space in your wagon as far as the Ithkar Fair, I could certify your spells at the gate. Otherwise they might not let you in, you know."

"No problem there," Tonya said. "My father has taken these dolls to the fair before and the spells are known to be harmless. You may ride in the wagon, however, at least to the gate, for I see you are lame."

"Lame? A small matter, young woman, a slight inconvenience. I have an excellent spell to cure it when I can find the time."

"And when the weather turns dry," Borg, the valet, observed.

"That, too," Omz replied. "Dry weather is, of course,

235

one of the conditions. As for your kind offer, young lass (or is it wife?), I accept with great pleasure."

"It's lass. And will you accept a bit of bread and cheese?"

"Thank you."

"Eat them quickly, then, old man. We're at the ford and things must be stowed," Driss said.

"Omz, sir. Omz. Never address a magician as 'old man.' "

"Sorry. Omz, of course. Get up on the driver's seat with me now. One of your spells may help Lightning if he should stumble."

Lightning showed little signs of stumbling as he started into the water. As the wagon approached the middle of the stream, however, things became more difficult and the force of the rain-swollen water began to move them sideways and to give the wagon a downstream tilt.

Driss shouted encouragement to the ox; Tonya, Vallo, and Borg threw their weight to the upstream side; and Omz, the magician, began to chant a spell in a high womanish voice and to wave his staff in cabalistic passes. The spell, if that was what it was, had no appreciable effect other than to make it difficult for Driss to handle the lines to the ox's horns. Finally Driss jumped down, tied a rope to the wagon-bed, and called Borg to help him pull. With the two men and the ox doing their utmost, the wagon was at last safely on the other side.

The wagon had been so deeply in the water during the crossing that some of the supplies had gotten wet. Fortunately the water had not reached the dolls or the food supplies which Tonya had stowed away in a tightly closed box. Among the items that were sodden was Dragon, who lived (during transportation) on the lowest shelf inside the wagon.

His ivory horn had come unglued and some of his scales had fallen off. Tonya examined the damage and, although she was mildly annoyed, set about immediately to making repairs, regluing the horn and the scales and setting Dragon and the other damp items on the tailgate to dry.

"Now if only it wouldn't rain," she said. "Better yet, if we could persuade the sun to come out. I don't suppose you could do anything about that, Omz?"

"On the contrary, dear lady," Omz replied. "It happens that I have a most excellent spell to prevent rain."

"Learned from a brother magician in the southern desert region, no doubt," Borg said.

Tonya frowned. "Don't be unkind, Borg," she said. "Go ahead, Omz, if you will. Even if your spell isn't strong enough, I'm sure it will do no harm."

After a momentary hesitation Omz picked up the hem of his robe, pulled a bit of the cloth around from the rear, and examined it thoughtfully for a long moment. Vallo, who was watching him with round eyes, could not resist a question.

"What are you doing now, Omz?" he said. "Is that a part of the spell, pulling your clothes about like that?"

"In a way, it is, young sir. Come closer and I'll tell you a secret."

Vallo approached and Omz leaned down and whispered in his ear.

"I may not look it, young Vallo," he whispered, "but I am over four hundred years old and I know so many spells that I sometimes forget some of the lesser ones. So I had them embroidered on my robe where I can read them to refresh my memory. You see?"

"Oh."

Omz's whisper had been perfectly audible to Driss and Tonya, who were only two paces away. They grinned at each other but said nothing. Omz, after a few moments more of studying the robe, pointed his staff dramatically at the spot in the sky where the sun was dimly visible and began to recite curious words in a high sweet voice. Nothing immediate happened, of course, and Omz glanced upward doubtfully a few times, then lowered his staff and climbed painfully onto the driver's seat of the wagon.

After a long moment of embarrassed silence Tonya spoke to the old man.

"Not even the best of spells works every time, Omz," she said kindly. "You have a beautiful voice, though. It occurs to me that you might be able to help us with the doll show for certain bits of dialogue. Of course I can't offer to pay such a salary as a magician might command. Would the same terms as I have offered Borg suit you? You might find the work amusing, you know."

"True," Omz said, looking slightly more cheerful. "I would have to take off some mornings, however, to discuss certain magic matters with some of my colleagues at the fair."

"Quite all right. We work mostly in the afternoons and evenings in any case. Are we agreed, then?"

"Of course, dear lady."

As they were speaking, Lightning the ox was plodding steadily onward and the sky had begun to clear. At Omz's last words the sun broke through bright and warm and cast a shaft of light directly upon the tailgate of the wagon. Omz broke into what could only be described as a grin, showing all of his several teeth.

"Takes a little time sometimes," he said with a fruity chuckle.

Omz's "spell" lasted the rest of the afternoon, during which time the road became more and more crowded with fairgoers. Jugglers, dancers, animal trainers, merchants of wares strange and wonderful, and sellers of sweetmeats pressed in from every side. Vallo took it all in with mounting excitement, begging Tonya every half mile or so for a copper to buy honey cakes or hot fried tarts.

"You'll spend all of our profits before we even reach the gates," Tonya told him, giving him a handful of walnuts. "Here, take these and open them carefully. With five little tufts of wool glued in the right places on the edges of half a shell you can make toy turtles. You might even sell a couple for enough to buy something sweet for that ever-empty tummy of yours."

This enterprise, although financially unsuccessful, kept him busy until they arrived at the gates to the fair. At the gates they fell into line to wait for the customary inspection and the issuance of their fair permits. The shadows were beginning to lengthen when they reached the head of the line. The fair-ward questioned Driss as to the nature of their show, and when he learned that Tonya was their proprietor and that the manipulation of the dolls required spells, he called the wizard-of-the-gate from his silken tent to complete the inspection.

The wizard-of-the-gate was an imposing old gentleman in somber but rich robes who recognized Tonya and greeted her by name.

"Where's your old rogue of a father, my dear? Too drunk to come himself this year?"

"Father died last winter," Tonya said.

"Forgive me," the wizard said. "He was in good health when I saw him last. An essentially good man, he was, if inclined too much to gamble."

"He went out in a blizzard to feed Lightning, our ox, and was lost between the barn and the house. We found him frozen in the courtyard in the morning."

"Sad, sad. Still, not too painful a way to die, I'm told. Your doll show is much the same as last year's, I take it?"

"Yes, sir."

"No new spells?"

"One or two."

"Show them to me."

Tonya took a beautifully crafted little chest of blood-red wood from under the seat of the wagon and opened it with a whispered word. Nested inside, each in a tiny tube labeled with the name of a doll, were rolled scrolls of thin parchment no larger than a thumbnail. On each of them was penned in blue ink a few cabalistic signs and a word or two. Tonya selected one of the dolls, inserted one of the rolled scrolls in a tiny cavity under the doll's hair, and spoke behind her hand.

"My profound respects, my lord wizard," she said.

The doll gestured with her tiny hands, her face appeared to smile, and when the speech ended she made a deep, graceful curtsy.

The wizard-of-the-gate smiled and bowed solemnly in return. "Is this one of the new ones?" he said.

"Yes, sir. Father had the spell improved so that she moves her lips when I speak for her. It usually can't be seen from the audience, I'm afraid." She removed the scroll from the doll's head and handed it to the wizard, who examined it and shot a glance at Omz.

"Not one of yours, I'm certain."

"No, Lofty One," Omz replied with his eyes cast down.

The wizard-of-the-gate examined a few of the other scrolls, pulled the string that made Dragon snap his jaws, allowed a bright spark to travel from his finger to the tip of Dragon's horn, and waved them on.

It was full dark when they were at last installed at Tonya's father's customary place, and they were obliged to set up their equipment by the light of fish-oil flares. In this they were not alone. The entire fairground glittered with a thousand such lights.

Driss lowered one side of the wagon and rested it upon trestles to make a small stage. The interior of the wagon was hidden by a painted curtain which made the backdrop. Stakes were set out which later would support a canvas fence to contain the morrow's audience. While this was going on, Tonya placed the doll, Snow Princess, on the stage and began telling passersby, "The Enchanted Doll Show begins tomorrow at noon. One copper for children, three for their parents, and four for those grown-ups whose hearts are still young." In response to these words Snow Princess waved and threw kisses to the children and curtsied politely to their mothers. At the end of each such invitation, Dragon popped out from behind the curtain and rumbled in Borg's deepest possible voice, "At noon, remember. Don't be late!" and snapped his jaws.

When it grew late and bystanders were few, Tonya and Vallo retired behind the curtain inside the wagon. Driss fed Lightning, then rolled in a blanket under the wagon. Omz

241

was given the space between the driver's seat and the dashboard and gratefully accepted one of Tonya's blankets. Borg was given a blanket but did not make immediate use of it. He disappeared and returned later to take his place beside Driss, smelling suspiciously like the inside of a wine barrel. Several times during the night pairs of fair-wards passed and repassed, swinging their long, bronze-shod quarterstaves.

Although Borg and Omz were missing for most of the morning, Driss and Tonya were able by good management and much hard work to have the show ready by noon as promised. Borg showed up late enough to avoid most of the physical exertion but at least quickly learned the few lines he was required to speak. Omz, on the other hand, returned earlier but spent a considerable part of his time muttering to himself behind the wagon and making passes in the air. A pair of passing fair-wards suspiciously observed him at this activity for a time but, since nothing whatever seemed to occur because of Omz's words and gestures, continued on their rounds without comment.

The show itself was a simple one, involving a dragon, who appeared to subsist entirely on a diet of virgins (in an historic era when virgins were fairly common); an overlord, who found this state of affairs not only unseemly but also bad for business; a princess, who had the misfortune to be captured by the dragon and tied to a stake for later consumption; a bold prince, who rescued the princess and converted the dragon to vegetarianism; a little dog for even more comic relief; and various maidens and townspeople.

It was not expected that the noon show would be heavily attended and it was not. But by the time of the evening performance word had gotten about concerning the charm and miniature perfection of the dolls, the ferocity of the dragon and the amusing antics of the little dog, and the last show of the day completely filled the space inside the canvas fence. Borg's deep and powerful roars and Omz's surprisingly melodious and varied voices added not a little to the play's attraction.

It was late when the last show of the evening was over and Tonya counted up the receipts. There was a goodly bag of coppers and even one shining piece of silver. She showed it to Driss.

"A few more of these and we might make it," she said. "We can't count on many pieces of silver, though, and unless we can pack in more admissions it will be a close thing by the end of the fair. Do you think we could enlarge the space for the audience?"

"We'd need more canvas to surround a bigger space," Driss said.

"There's the awning over the first six rows. You could use that. I'll help you pick apart the seams."

"Suppose it should rain?"

"If it rains," Tonya said, "no one will come at all. We could just fold up the stage and wait for the next day."

"It's risky," Driss said.

"We'll just have to take the risk against the chance to have a bigger crowd."

"You sound just like your father, Tonya. You aren't becoming a gambler, are you?"

"Father gambled on races and dice. This is different. This is betting on the weather. Farmers do it all the time. You've nothing against farmers, I hope?"

"While we're hoping, let's just hope it doesn't rain."

"It mustn't rain."

"You worry too much, Tonya. I promise you it won't rain. We'll use Omz's sunshine spell if necessary."

Tonya giggled. "I'd rather trust your promise than Omz's spells." Then, becoming serious, she added, "You shouldn't make fun of the old man, Driss. One of these days he'll surprise us."

"Sometimes I'm afraid he will," Driss said.

"What do you mean?"

"I don't know. He's a little . . . odd, you know. I hope, in his well-meaning way, he doesn't get us in some sort of trouble."

"Look who's worrying now. Go feed Lightning and I'll prepare us a good hot supper."

While Driss took care of closing down the show for the night, Tonya put away the coppers in the bottom of the blood-red chest, locking it with a whispered word. Next she fixed a spicy stew over the flame of one of the flares and called the men to supper.

The next morning the awning was sacrificed to make an addition to the screen surrounding the places of the audience. The result was at least ten more seats and they were well occupied during the day and evening performances.

They continued to be filled for the next several days, but then the attendance began to drop off. Many of the people in the immediate neighborhood had seen the show—some of them two or even three times—but the receipts for the sixth and seventh days were lower than on the first.

At the end of the seventh day Driss found Tonya sitting on the wagon's tailgate, her legs dangling, counting the coppers for the third time. She showed him some figures on a slate.

"If this keeps up, I won't be able to pay, even if I work as a seamstress or something after the fair until Midwinter Moon. Oh, Driss, what shall we do?"

Driss jumped up on the wagon beside her and put her head against his shoulder. "Please don't worry so, dear. We'll think of something. Suppose Borg and I go about in the mornings to tell people about the show?"

"Borg often isn't here in the mornings and I have the impression he'd keep more people away than he coaxed in. Besides I need you here. Neither Omz nor Vallo is strong enough to do your work."

Driss was silent for a long moment.

"Tonya," he said, "do you remember the merchant who paid in silver that first day to admit him and his family?"

"Yes, of course. What about him?"

"His name is Bothro. He's as wealthy as a flea with his own private dog and he has just dozens of children. Surely among all this horde of little Bothros there must be at least one who was born during fair month. He laughed and enjoyed the dolls like a child himself, if you remember."

"Hmm. Yes. Although he frowned rather fiercely when Village Girl was turned down by Dragon as inedible."

"We could leave that part out," Driss said.

"Just for Bothro? Everyone else seemed to think it was hilarious."

"Yes, Tonya. Just for Bothro. What I'm thinking is that if we could find out the birthday of one of the children, we could offer to do the show privately for his or her party on that date. Bothro could invite all of his friends and their children as well and we could charge him an arm or a leg or two."

"We'd have to in order to make up for moving the wagon and missing the proceeds from the other shows of the day. Do you think you could get him to pay enough for that?"

"I'm sure of it. I'll bet we could earn three days' receipts."

"Look who's gambling now!"

"All right, I'm a gambler, too. Shall we try it?"

"I'll think about it," Tonya said.

"While you're thinking, I'll find out who has a birthday this month."

Omz, who had been straining to hear the two young people's conversation, hobbled up, leaning on his staff.

"Did I hear someone say 'birthday'? I have a little spell—a trifling thing, really—which brings health and prosperity for an entire year if worked on a birthday. May I offer it to you on the birthday in question?"

"Of course, Omz," Tonya said with a smile. "But it's neither my birthday nor Driss's. We could certainly use all the prosperity we can get, if you think it would still work under those circumstances."

"I'll have to look that up," Omz said, and began pulling his robe this way and that to squint at the lettering on it.

Tonya and Driss darted each other a secret smile and Driss went off to feed Lightning and secure the stage for the night while Tonya prepared the evening meal.

After supper Vallo timidly asked if he could have a very special dessert.

"What sort of dessert, dear?" Tonya asked him.

"One of those pink ices the sweetmeat man sells. He says the snow to make it comes from our mountains."

"I was a bit afraid the sweetmeat seller's stall was too near. Things like that cost money, you know."

246

"But I've been working for a whole ten-day, Tonya, and you pay Omz and Borg two coppers a day. I heard you tell them. Aren't I worth one copper a whole ten-day?"

"The lad has a point," Driss said.

"All right," Tonya said. "But what will you put your pink ice in? The man doesn't give cups away, you know."

"I could use one of your little bone cups."

"They're very old and thin. Promise you'll be careful with it if I let you have one?"

Vallo promised, was given his copper, and dashed off at flank speed to the sweetmeat stall. To give him credit, he ate his pink snow with unusual care and neatness. Later, when Tonya was cleaning up the supper things, she took up the cup and almost dropped it because of its unexpected temperature. She wiped the moisture from it and placed it on a shelf. A moment later she found it still moist and was obliged to wipe it a second time.

"I declare, it's too humid to sleep tonight. I do hope it won't rain tomorrow." Smiling to herself, she added, "Driss promised me it wouldn't, so perhaps it won't."

Driss's promise held good the following day, but attendance at the day's shows still showed signs of falling off. The count of coppers that night almost made her regret Vallo's copper for the ice.

The next day in midmorning Driss returned from a foray into the temple precinct with a wide grin on his face and gave Tonya a sudden bear hug.

"Driss, what in the world has come over you?" Tonya said. "Have you discovered a silver mine?"

"Mm. Sort of."

"Whatever do you mean?"

247

"I discovered that one of the infant Bothros does indeed have a birthday. Better yet, it falls on ten-day next. And best of all, Father Bothro has agreed to pay us twenty-five silver pieces for the show!"

"Wonderful!" Tonya almost shouted and hugged Driss around the waist. "On the start of a ten-day people are at the temple much of the day, so we lose very little by moving the wagon. But however did you get your merchant prince or princely merchant to pay so much? Why, you and Omz can almost let it rain for the rest of our stay! How did you do it?"

"By exerting my manly charm upon Mama Bothro, that's how. She considers me a fine, handsome young man. She said so."

"I'm not sure I like that. What's she look like?"

"Remember Lightning when he was a week old? She weighs about the same and has the same highly intelligent look. Tonya, let's all eat a pink snow tonight!"

Borg had returned from the tavern quarter at the same time as Driss's excited homecoming and had heard most of this happy exchange. He maintained his usual phlegmatic expression throughout and shortly after made a second trip to a nearby tavern, returning only just in time for the day's first performance.

The remaining days before the private showing retained a heavy burden of humidity, and there was a slight chill in the air at night. To encourage a larger attendance Tonya had Driss place half a dozen braziers filled with glowing coals around the edges of the seating area. This helped a bit, but trade was still falling off and Tonya worried about it as she and Driss counted the day's receipts.

"If this goes on, we may have to find another rich

merchant,'' she said, ''and after ten-day—tomorrow—there
will be only a few more days to the end of the fair. We may
even have to sell some of the dolls, and I'd almost rather
work off the debt in Lord Caum's castle than do that.''

On the evening of the special performance, which was to
take place in the courtyard of Bothro's estate, the weather
was still damp and slightly chill. The children who assembled
for the show were bundled up and even the adults wore
cloaks or woolen shawls. Borg and Omz appeared only moments before the play was to begin and both had found heavy
capes somewhere. Omz looked almost ill. Fortunately the
audience was slow in settling down and the dolls were able to
make their first appearance without any annoying delay.

Never had the dolls performed as well as for the youngest
Bothro's birthday. Snow Princess was lovely and her enhanced spell allowed her sweet smile to be seen even in the
farthest rows. Never had Dragon's roar been louder or deeper,
and Little Dog was so convincingly doglike that he even
(quite naturally and unexpectedly) lifted one tiny hind leg at a
property gatepost.

The birthday child was entranced and she squirmed forward until her chin was almost on the edge of the stage. She
squealed in mock fright each time Dragon snapped his jaws,
and in the final battle she implored valiant Prince not to kill
him too cruelly. As if in appreciation, Dragon turned toward
her for his final roar and, as he did, a huge blue-white cloud
of smoke erupted from his open mouth straight into the
child's face.

Her screams were real this time and were followed at once
by a violent fit of coughing and a torrent of tears.

What happened next was utter pandemonium. With leonine

249

roars, Mother Bothro charged up and gathered her child to her bosom, than began screaming unladylike imprecations in all directions. Every other child in the audience began to bellow and every parent present added his or her voice to the uproar, some condemning the proprietors of the doll show, some threatening Bothro with the utmost rigors of the fair-court. Driss and Tonya thrust dismayed faces from behind the stage backdrop. Borg made a hasty dash for elsewhere but was quickly brought back by a Bothro footman, who held him firmly by the ear. Vallo, delighted with the event, sent Little Dog capering and barking lustily from one end of the stage to the other. The birthday child divided her time equally between shrieks and fits of coughing.

Mention, here and there, of the fair-court brought Merchant Bothro's captain of industry side to the fore and he dispatched several servants in search of fair-wards, who promptly appeared and roughly restored order. When the gathering was reasonably quiet, Bothro leveled a shaking finger at Tonya.

"I charge this woman and her crew with the use of unauthorized magic to attack my children and to ruin my reputation with my friends and business associates! Lock them up. They shall appear before the court no later than tomorrow morning to answer for their crimes."

Madame Bothro, being a practical woman, was the first to regain her poise. "Bothro, dear, I hardly think the court will take up the matter so soon. Besides, I have my seamstress coming in the morning. I shall have to send for a physician to look at Cyndia. There's no telling what these horrid people have done to her."

"The court will take up the case when I demand it," the

red-faced Bothro insisted. "I count for something in this country, I'll have you know. For the rest, send for your physician at once, if you will, and your seamstress will simply have to await your pleasure. Consider our position, woman!"

Locking up the doll show and its personnel was somewhat of a problem with space during the fair at a premium, but it was solved by sending for a temple wizard, who put a restraining spell on everyone and everything, including the ox, Lightning.

Despite Bothro's self-proclaimed importance, the court would not consent to considering the case until late the following afternoon. Under the spell, which limited their movements to less than three yards from the wagon, the five people (and Lightning, the least concerned) found the unavailability of fresh food and water and the humid overcast weather added considerably to their fears and general discomfort. Tonya's efforts to get to the bottom of the matter of the cloud of smoke did nothing to clear the air. The obvious suspect in the question of unauthorized spells was, of course, Omz.

"How could you have done this to us?" Tonya demanded. "You certainly must have known that even if you hadn't blown whatever it was in that wretched child's face, any magic which wasn't passed might cost me everything we've earned. And, believe me, the earnings are more important to me than you could possibly know. Now why did you?"

"I am, after all, a magician, dear lady. I meant only to add a bit of luster to the performance. If friend Borg hadn't clumsily turned Dragon in the wrong direction, no harm would have been done."

251

There was something strangely wrong in Omz's expression when he said these words. His dignity for the first time seemed false. Moreover his face was gray and he looked ill. Tonya silently considered him and thoughtfully turned away.

Court was convened at last and wagon and crew were returned to the fairgrounds to be tried there. The case was conducted briskly. Omz was the first to stand before the magistrate.

"You, sir, profess to be a magician?"

"A poor one, noble sir."

"If so, you are free to practice your trade—within reason, mind you—but surely you must have known that by embellishing a fair attraction with unauthorized magic you put the proprietor of the said attraction in danger of losing both profits and goods? Was this done with malice?"

"Oh, no, sir. Certainly not."

"Then why did you do it?"

"I was carried away by the interest of the play—which is a most excellent one, noble sir."

"Then, lest you get 'carried away' in matters more serious, I hereby divest you of any right to practice magic anywhere or for any purpose from this day forward," the magistrate said sternly. He then turned to Tonya.

"Now then, you, young woman. Stand before me and state your name and condition."

"Tonya of Clan Sarg, sir. Unwed."

"Clan Sarg, eh? I had occasion to know your father. A rogue, perhaps, but harmless. Why is he not here?"

"He died in last winter's great storm, sir."

"Hmm. I see. He left you his dolls, then. Aught else?"

"His debts, sir, as is the custom."

252

"A heavy burden, no doubt. Still, I must deal with you according to the law. Did you hire this . . . this magician with a thought of increasing the attractions of your play? In particular, did you order him to do what Merchant Bothro claims was done? Let me warn you; the court will deal most severely if you lie."

"I will not lie, sir. I employed Omz not for his magic but for his voice. Most suitable for King, sir, and even beautiful for other of my doll characters." As she said this she looked as kindly as she was able at Omz, but the old man would not meet her eye.

"Very well. I will now question you, valet. What is your name, man?"

While the magistrate was interrogating Borg, Tonya retired to the shadow of the wagon and joined Driss and her brother, Vallo. Omz stood some distance apart. Tonya examined the old man speculatively.

"Driss," she whispered, "I do believe Omz is relieved that he can no longer claim magicianship. None of his spells have ever worked."

"Except the one that got us in trouble," Driss said.

"I'm not sure he worked that one," Tonya replied.

"Who, then? Borg?"

"No. I think no one. I think there was no spell at all, but just a trick. A well-meaning one, perhaps. If I can make Omz admit that he can do no spells and that none was done, we are saved."

"You can't. Remember the warning against lies."

"I think—I know I can. Vallo, get me Dragon's horn. Quickly. now. Twist it off the knob on his nose. Be careful not to break the thin walls."

Vallo did as he was instructed and Tonya gave him two coppers, one of her little handkerchiefs, and sent him off to the sweetmeat seller with a warning to run as fast as his legs would carry him. He returned, panting, just as the magistrate released Borg, and handed Dragon's horn to his sister. Tonya wiped the horn on the hem of her skirt and stepped up to face the magistrate.

"Noble sir!" she said.

"What is it, child?"

"What is the punishment for him who lies to the court?"

"It varies from a sound whipping to being hanged up by the thumbs for a day. Why? Have you lied?"

"No, sir. But I believe I have discovered one who has. May I question the magician—former magician, I mean—Omz?"

"You may, but I warn you, I'll not permit pointless squabbling. Come forward, Omz."

"I am no liar, honored sir," said Omz, his chin (a slightly trembling chin) held defiantly.

"That we shall see. Come forward. You may now proceed, Tonya of Sarg."

Tonya rubbed the horn on her skirt, then held it under Omz's nose. "You have heard us talk of the importance of Dragon's horn, have you not? What you have perhaps not heard is that when my father first placed it on Dragon's nose, he said, 'Our Dragon now has a nose for lies. If we are endangered by any lie, his horn will break out in a cold sweat.' Answer this, now: Did you produce that puff of smoke by one of your spells?"

Omz cast an anxious glance at the magistrate.

"I did. Yes. It was a very small and simple spell, Tonya, noble sir. I meant no harm."

Tonya held the horn close to the old man for a long moment, then turned and showed it to the magistrate and again to Omz. The smooth ivory of the horn was beaded with tiny drops of moisture. "What you did, Omz, was not magic at all, but a trick, was it not? Beware a second lie!"

"It was a trick," Omz said in a low, trembling voice. "Borg showed me how to do it. He said it would convince you that I really was a magician and that you would be pleased. He gave me this hollow reed with bits of leaf in it that he got from a sailor. He put a small coal to one end and I was to suck on the reed, then blow through the hole that makes Dragon's tongue flutter. It made me quite ill."

At almost the first words of this confession, Borg made a dash for freedom but was quickly brought back by a fairward. More questions were put, Dragon's horn was shaken under Borg's nose as well, and the whole story came out.

Borg was in Lord Caum's employ. He knew that if Tonya could not repay to Caum her father's drinking and gaming debts, Tonya would become the lord's slave—and more. Lord Caum had promised him, Borg, ten silver pieces if he would help to bring this state of affairs about. Therefore, in Borg's eyes at least, Lord Caum was to blame and he, Borg, should not be punished. The noble magistrate retired to his tent for a few minutes to consider this wealth of evidence. When he returned he lined up all parties, including Bothro and his spouse, before him.

"Merchant Bothro," he said. "Is your daughter ill or has she suffered aught but a small fright?" He cast a pointed look at the horn which Tonya still held by her side.

"No, noble sir, but—"

"Enough. Tonya of Sarg shall reduce her price for the entertainment by one silver piece for this small mishap."

"But . . . but . . . but . . ." Bothro was becoming very red. His wife pulled at his sleeve. "Let be, Bothro," she said. "You'll only make yourself ridiculous. Consider our position!"

The magistrate waved them both away and pointed a finger at Omz.

"You, sirrah, have been relieved of magic that you never had. As further punishment for a lie before this court you are sentenced to one year of domestic service to Mistress Tonya of Sarg. How say you?"

"Thank you, most noble sir!"

"Hmp! I thought you might. Now you, Master Borg . . ." The glare the magistrate fixed on the unfortunate valet was much more severe. "Yours shall be the task of informing your master, the good Lord Caum, that his claim on the debts of Clan Sarg has been declared null and void because of the manner in which he has tried to collect. If I do not hear that you have done so before this month is out, you shall have twenty stout lashes. How say you?"

"Pity, noble sir!" Borg whined. "Lord Caum is a fearful hard man!"

"I had guessed as much. Be off with you." The magistrate now turned to Tonya.

"As you are no doubt aware, the court cannot hold you for magic which was naught but a trick. Your debts are canceled, your goods are your own, the money you have earned has no liens against it but the appetite of this small boy, your brother, who seems to be continually eating something."

"May we go, then?"

"No, you may not. You have performed unauthorized magic yourself before this very court! What did you expect I might do about that?"

"Why, nothing, Your Excellency."

"Well! Impudent as you are pretty! Did I not see you cause a bit of ivory to sweat when lies were told?"

"Yes, Excellence, but not by magic or spells."

"How then? And take care of lies yourself."

Tonya upended Dragon's horn, pulled out the handkerchief that had plugged it, and a thin, sticky pink liquid drained out of it. "You see, sir, it is only a pink ice which Vallo bought from the sweetmeats stall. So cold is it that, in this weather, dew forms on its container just as it forms on grass in the morning. See, I wipe it dry and hold it before you and even now it perspires. Surely you have told me no lies?"

His Excellency the noble magistrate, the powerful fair-judge, was silent for two heartbeats, then blasted forth such roars of laughter that several fair-wards came running to see what the commotion might be. When at last his mirth was under control, he wiped his eyes and told Tonya, Driss, Vallo, and Omz that they might go.

"I will not only not punish you," he said, "I will even thank you for the amusement. I may even use your unmagic spell one of these days when examining a witness!"

Later, on the road to the high steppes after the fair, Tonya said something of the sort to Driss.

"Do you love me greatly?" she said. "Beware Dragon's unmagic horn before you answer!"

HOMECOMING

Susan M. Shwartz

You're a dream-singer, Andriu told himself. What you sing manifests itself as life. If you don't want to cough, you won't. But an instinct deeper than magic warned him that even a dream-singing bard, a renegade from two priesthoods, wasn't immune to lung fever. Think of something else. That interminable ballad that the Rhos liked, the one with the refrain, "That passed; this will, too." All the way upstream that refrain, manifested by his special gift, had eased the ship past snags, rapids, and bandits. Somewhere during the trip, as he was earning his passage with his dream-songs (and off duty, with songs a lot less holy), the unseasonably early frosts had sneaked into his lungs. He had known that that might happen, but he had wanted to get home to Ithkar more than he had wanted to fret about his health.

Another cough started to scratch its way up from beneath

259

his ribs. He could tell that this was going to be one of the racking ones that made him spit up blood. Certainly he could go to one of the temple heal-alls, if he wanted to be identified straightaway as the boy who had run off fifteen years ago. He didn't know what the punishment was for that.

Just a few more minutes and you can cough, he told himself. Just not now. Not during the Appeal to the Dayspring, the most solemn moment of the Feast of the Comforter, the Lady and Mother among the Three Lordly Ones. As the high priestess abased herself before the Lady's image, Lord Father Demetrios, most senior of Ithkar's priests and a dream-singer himself, led the choir from the altar. He bore a fragrant torch and wore festival robes—silver gleaming beneath an open cope. No dream-singer, with his ability to shape reality from song, could preside at this rite. While transformation was involved in it, it was the faith of the worshippers that must transform the metal wreath of offering into something alive and fruitful.

Lord Xuthen, the temple's chief patron this year, came forward to present the wreath. He was a lean, disdainful-looking man with black hair and a silvered beard, and wore gem-embroidered silk that shone green in some lights, gray in others. Though he had almost a scholar's aloofness, he swept a glare across the congregation. His eyes paused at Andriu, swept on to a thin man and woman standing beside a child with a withered arm, past them, and over toward a girl dressed in the free-flowing fashion of Rhos women rather than in the stiff garments Ithkar ladies wore. Her wealth of blond hair was braided and fell against a massive necklace and earrings of amber only slightly less ruddy than the autumnal colors of her gown and surcoat.

Andriu had always had no respect for time and place. Now the bard in him awoke.

> A girl stood in a scarlet gown.
> Could you but touch it,
> Its cloth made a whispering sound.
> Eia!

You're here to pray, not to hatch up verses. Won't you ever learn? Andriu flushed with shame as well as fever. If he didn't learn now, he would have little time left in which to do so. Gracious Lady, Comforter, I believe! Belief had never been his problem. He had believed, had trusted too wholly. And so, when he had seen that underpriest bribe the guard to the female students' dorter, he had been too disillusioned to accuse the man. He'd had no belief left in him to think that Father Demetrios would listen to him. Instead, he'd run away. . . .

Now Andriu fixed his eyes on the magnificent wreath of offering in Lord Xuthen's hands: stalks of carved malachite, grain-heads of topaz and amber that glistened with a dew of freshwater pearls. "Be it Thy will, Lady and Comforter, that our faith make this wreath blossom!" the lord prayed.

"Blossom, flourish, grow for us!" All the congregation's hope and anguish were in that chant.

Tears formed in Andriu's eyes. He had forsworn his own initiation as a novice priest in this temple. Probably he had broken the old dream-singer's heart by running away into the west. And his behavior there had been worse. Since, like an imbecile, he'd assumed that he still ought to be a priest of some sort, he had joined the austere order of Cerdic Revived.

261

Susan M. Shwartz

"Let the wreath blossom!" Lord Xuthen cried for the
second time. The priestess moaned. The blond Rhos girl's
face was so pale it looked greenish. Like Andriu, she kept
raising a kerchief to her lips. The father of the sick boy
placed an arm about his shoulders. It wasn't going to work
this year. Only the noble's exultation shone forth undimmed
as he confronted the statue of the Comforter.

Andriu had to admit that his career as a priest of Cerdic
Revived had been conspicuous, albeit brief. Privately, he was
of the opinion that Cerdic had been a dream-singer. Look at
that one tale of the bannocks and flatfish. Who else but a
dream-singer could manifest so much food with but a chanted
blessing? When Andriu, in an excess of devotion as he
assisted the almoner, had tried it, he had earned a reprimand
and a long fast. Faint with hunger, he had attempted to
lighten his mood with a song. He had been too dizzy to
remember not to use the special resonances that distinguished
dream-singing from ordinary music. And during a highly
impassioned version of "Corisande Storm-lover," the lady
had revealed herself—literally, except for a few cloudy veils
and a sultry haze of lightning—before the entire community.
That episode had set him on his way as a bard, ribald ballads
in taverns a specialty.

He still had a fondness for the absurd, the inappropriate, or
the doomed to failure. It made him chuckle now, though this
was no time for laughter, and provoked a cough.

"So be Thy will," intoned Lord Xuthen. The priestess
began a lament, and the congregation sobbed. Xuthen set the
wreath down at the statue's base. He didn't look especially
distraught.

As the kerchief over Andriu's mouth grew warm and wet

262

from his coughing, he darted for the courtyard. The cool air
and river smells shocked him back to alertness. Near as the
temple court was to the river, there was a fountain in it.
Andriu dipped a cleanish corner of his ragged cloth into the
rippling water and dabbed at his face. That was when he
heard the gagging and heaving of someone vomiting. He was
surprised to see that it was the woman who wore Rhos dress.
She leaned against a pillar and shook with her spasms.

When she wasn't so ill, Andriu decided, she was probably
lovely. Her complexion was clear, her features (what he had
seen of them in the temple) well marked, her mouth generous.
Unlike the Corisandes and Melusines of his ballads, she was
but of medium height and her body, as much of it as he could
discern beneath her long garments, was pleasingly rounded.
The way her braids tumbled down her back made him think
of fields at harvesttime.

Seeing Andriu, the woman started. But the lure of clean
water was too tempting and she approached the fountain.
Andriu took the cup chained nearby, filled it, and poured the
Three Libations. He held it out to her in silence. She wiped
her mouth again, then drank thirstily.

"There's blood on your face," she observed. She held out
her kerchief. Andriu leaned over to look at himself in the
water. Like many natives of Ithkar, he was pale, except for
the hectic, unhealthy color flaming above his hollow cheeks.
His eyes were gray and too bright. His dark hair was strag-
gling onto his shoulders again because he could not spare a
half-silver for the barber.

When the woman shook her head at his attempt to return
her kerchief, he smiled. He was about to ask her name when

263

she rose and turned in alarm. "I must go back inside. . . . Sweet Lady, what if they missed me!"

"Vassilika!"

Apparently someone had missed her. Two women wearing the dress of well-off maidens of the city, one blue-green, the other brown and cream, came toward her. Their closely pinned hair under tiny caps, their dark eyes, and their pointed chins characterized them as natives of Ithkar, the daughters, possibly, of a well-off merchant. A certain stubbornness about the mouths of all three women marked them out as close kin.

"Were you just sick again, sister?"

"The fish I ate this morning was spoiled, I think," said the blond woman.

"Father sent you to market to buy it. Why would you buy bad fish?" accused the girl in blue-green.

"You're always the one who gets to go. It's not fair. And Mother says that no good will come out of Father's letting you keep to your Rhos mother's free and easy ways—"

"I think it already has," the woman in blue-green cut in slyly.

Andriu dodged behind the fountain. Quickly, as he'd learned to during his life as a strolling bard, he was adding up the clues. It sounded like a ballad, didn't it? A marriage between an Ithkar merchant and the daughter of one of the Rhos traders . . . Perhaps this Vassilika was all that survived of a first, youthful marriage. Then a second marriage to a lady of Ithkar, who envied her stepdaughter's freedom. . . .

Well, this Vassilika looked quite capable of giving a fine accounting of herself. Andriu settled down for an enjoyable harangue. He was surprised and disappointed when Vassilika seemed to wilt.

"Cyntha, Dorastrea, please, tell no one." She held out her hands for theirs, but both girls clasped their own hands almost tauntingly behind their backs.

"This year, Lord Xuthen said he wanted the temple laws—all the laws—strictly enforced," said Cyntha, in the brown and cream.

Vassilika recoiled. "Do you know what some of those laws do to women?"

"You're the one who reads," Dorastrea reminded her in the high, discontented tones of a child bringing up an old grievance.

"Father would have taught you. Or *I* would. . . ."

"You're too busy being sick in the mornings now."

Andriu winced. If Xuthen (who had always been somewhat of a scholar) had revived the laws of Priest Draco II, called the Vindictive, Vassilika was right to shudder. Half-mad and a confirmed woman-hater, Draco had decreed that a woman found pregnant without husband or suitor should be exposed, branded publicly, have her head shaved, and be cast out in her shift, just as if she had used evil magic to assassinate someone!

"I'm not . . . not what you're implying," Vassilika protested earnestly. "You couldn't accuse me. Think of how our father would feel, learning that one of his own girls had turned on me. It would break his heart. You criticize my behavior, but I ask you, is breaking a father's pride and heart proper conduct?"

Seeing the other two exchange sidelong glances, Vassilika smiled. "Look, Dorastrea," she said, her fingers caressing

265

her amber necklace. "You've always loved my necklace. When you were little, you used to beg me to let you wear it. And you, Cyntha, with your long neck and white skin, don't you think that my ear-bobs would suit you? Come now. Take the trinkets, please do—and not a word to anyone. I've just been a little sick, and I hate fuss. You know how I hate fuss when I don't feel well."

"Girls!" All three women turned toward the begowned and becoiffed matron whose assured voice summoned them. The two younger immediately walked off, their heads close together as they talked excitedly.

"In a moment!" cried Vassilika. "Please." The "please," Andriu noted, sounded like an afterthought. As her sisters disappeared, she sighed.

Andriu knew little enough of girls of this class. But he had seen quite enough of the women in taverns to know that greed would only chase spite out of their heads for so long.

Well, what was it to him? A rich girl got caught: it probably happened all the time. Then his cough tore free. If his muscles hadn't been those of a singer and active man, he might have broken something.

"Still here!" Vassilika cried. She looked frightened and annoyed. Nevertheless, she fished in her belt-pouch and offered him one of the sweet candies women used to soothe children or sweeten their breath. "This should ease your throat," she said. "You must see a heal-all."

"I can't," Andriu whispered painfully. The candy tasted good. "Why don't you?"

Her eyes grew round, and a smile trembled on her lips. Andriu wanted to smile, too. So she had caught his stray thought, that they both could hardly be avoiding the heal-alls for the same reason! Most people never understood his jokes, much less anticipated them. "Sweet Dayspring," he said, chuckling, "what a wonder that would be, wouldn't it? I can't see a heal-all because I used to be a novice at the temple. My name's Andriu, by the way."

What an imbecile he was to tell her! She sank down onto the rim of the fountain beside him, and he was glad.

"Tell me, freelady Vassilika, what will you use to bribe your sisters with next?"

Vassilika laughed a little wryly. "I'd been wondering that, too. Do you have any suggestions?"

Her courage brought more warmth to his heart than a mug of spiced wine. For fifteen years he had been running away, living only for himself, day to day, as the birds—who sang, too—lived. He was near the end of the race. Perhaps before he died, he could do something for someone besides singing. Why not for this lady?

"Where's the father?" he whispered, wincing at the blunt way the question came out. The great gong rang; services would be ending shortly.

Vassilika's face twisted. How could any man in his right mind abandon someone like her?

"I want to help you, freelady," he said quickly, "but . . ." Fair-wards and worshippers were emerging from the temple.

"I can't tell you now. Meet me at Sohrab's cookshop at twilight," she hissed.

Andriu forced himself to nod casually and then to saunter off, the very image of a considerate man who had stopped to assist a lady. The fair-wards barely glanced at him. If only he weren't a renegade! He could offer her an honorable escape.

267

As he left the temple precincts, a chill quivered across his shadow on the polished flagstones and sped up from it into his vitals. Only the sweet Vassilika had given him prevented him from coughing. He glanced about wildly. Within a nearby scribe's booth . . . someone wished him ill, had sensed his pain and confusion and reveled in it. His enemy . . . there stood Lord Xuthen, watching him. He bowed and offered an assiduously practiced innocent look to the noble. At first Xuthen's eyes swept over him the way icy water drenches a man who falls overboard. Then Andriu felt as if every last frailty and pain in his body had been cataloged and savored.

At least Xuthen hadn't denounced him. Weak with relief as well as fear, Andriu leaned against a wall. Xuthen turned away, moving deeper into the scribe's stall. Its proprietor emerged and bowed to him as if to a master. He wore a medallion and offered one to Xuthen. On each the mask of Thotharn glowered out at him.

A shawl flung over her hair, Vassilika was waiting at Sohrab's. She was eating bannocks dipped in honey, crisp-roasted fowl wings pungent with the exotic spices that had made the outlander's shop popular, and drinking something that steamed and made Andriu wish for money to spare. She passed him a mug and received change from the urchin at the counter.

Andriu shared her meal. Then they walked slowly on, an unlikely pair: he in his out-at-the-elbows tunic and chausses, his boots scraped white at the toes; she in her good, heavy robes. Flaming cressets lit each cookstall, supplemented by the lamps and cooking fires. The flames glinted off the fair-wards' polished helmets and struck rainbows from the

268

gemmed wristlets and pendants of the richer pilgrims. No one that Andriu could see wore Thotharn's mask. That did not reassure him. That anyone assumed the mask—let alone the temple's patron—meant that . . . A few priests knew much about Thotharn and had always told him not to dabble in such affairs.

"Won't we be noticed in this crowd, freelady?"

"Probably. My stepmother will scold me . . . again, my father will shrug, and no one will think of anything else. Pretend to be enjoying yourself."

That was easy. They looked into the merchants' stalls, then strolled about. A beast-master wearing a scalloped leather cape and hood strolled by. Vassilika cried out in wonder at his troupe of trained marpolets, each with its soft-furred crest dyed a different color, each juggling three gilded balls in its dark-fingered paw-hands. "Come see us tonight!" the man urged. "We're teaming with actors to play *Rustam's Ride*."

I wish we could, Andriu thought. I wish . . . this were real, that I could take Vassilika to the play, buy her a fairing, then walk her home. . . .

They passed the dealers in fine carpets. Vassilika raised an eyebrow. "I don't suppose . . ."

"That I could manifest a flying carpet? I wish I might. But lady, I'm not strong enough to create a carpet that could carry us both."

The carpetseller, rising to greet them, heard them speaking of magic, and his smile of welcome faded. Merchants who enhanced their wares magically lost them and were outlawed.

"Let's leave," Vassilika whispered.

Andriu turned so quickly that he bumped into a pilgrim wearing a red hood and a redder nose, the result of devotion to the winesellers, if not the priests. The man burped in surprise, and Andriu sped him on his way with a shove. He coughed in alarm.

"Down here!" Andriu cried. Here, nearer the temple, it was darker. The smells of water and night air won out over the smells of food, wine, and too many people. And there were shadows in which they could hide. Andriu was almost certain he had glimpsed the scribe.

"Do you want to tell me?" he asked Vassilika. "I can't help you unless I know what's happened. And I want to help."

Vassilika started to laugh, then bit her hand to stop herself. She began to breathe deeply to steady herself.

"No one's said that in weeks," she said. "Thank you. I thought I could wait out the fair until Xuthen went back to being merely one lord among many and this business about the old temple laws faded away. But I can't." Her courage broke along with her voice. Andriu took her by the shoulders and shook her. Nothing in the ballads had prepared him for women who threw up or shook with horror. For goddesses, yes. For frightened, pregnant women, no. He had missed out, he thought.

"When did Lord Xuthen become such a firebrand?" he asked.

"I won't act like that again. Forgive me," Vassilika said. "Lord Xuthen? If you were born here, you know he was always scholarly, rather a recluse. The wrong sort of study has proved his misfortune . . . and mine. As you heard, my stepmother prefers old says. She claims a lady needs no more of reading than to settle her household's accounts. But I—Father knew I was bored and hired me tutors. I can read not just the

270

tongues of Ithkar and Rhos, but also write and speak trade talk, and even a little of the temple dialects.'' That was cause for pride, Andriu thought. ''There was some talk of my joining the classes there. But my stepmother sulked so long . . . it wasn't worth it. About that time, Thyrth joined our household as my stepmother's tire-woman. She's an easterner and skilled, as many of them are, in the care of garments. And other things besides—like women's magic.''

''Freelady?''

''Oh, yes, we have magics. Little things like throwing pins in a well. Casting shadows into a fountain by the light of the moon . . . tiny spells. Nonetheless, they have to be paid for,'' Vassilika told him. They reached the temple. Its gates were still open for the benefit of pilgrims who wished to see the wreath of offering.

''Let me show you,'' she said. She knelt on the rim of the fountain where they had met and drew a tiny pin from her sleeve. She held it to her face, breathed on it, and dropped it into the water.

With a crystalline chime it sank beneath the ripples. The water trembled again, in a direction counter to the night wind. Then it went utterly calm and figures started to form in it. Andriu bent forward, impressed. He could not visualize that clearly unless he sang.

Vassilika was restless, but Thyrth boasted she had a cure. One of her friends was steward to Lord Xuthen. Could Vassilika but win his liking, he might let her choose books from the lord's library. So into the trap Vassilika walked . . .

*　　*　　*

The water blurred.

"No," she said. "It's too shameful. I'll tell you, instead. Thyrth went with me. There was a mask on the wall of the library. I didn't like the looks of it, but Thyrth told me to look closer; who was I to question a lord's taste? I remember something that . . . there was this smell . . . a demon with his face, Xuthen's face . . . blurring into the mask. Hours later I woke up. The house was empty, so I fled home. Thyrth never returned. Why should she? She'd done what she planned."

"As Xuthen's agent?"

"As Thotharn's."

When had it started? Had a merchant with a grudge against Xuthen brought him his first taste of the proscribed lore of Thotharn? Or had he himself become bored and turned to it of his own will? Xuthen proved the warning of the priests true: those who looked into the mask might find themselves wearing it. And he had dared present the wreath today? No wonder it had not blossomed.

"Thotharn dwells within him now," Vassilika said, looking down at her hands. "And Xuthen is at an age when men look to have heirs. Why should a demon be different?"

How would a demon perceive old age? Xuthen was at his prime, as men reckoned it. But perhaps the river Ith's dampness set his joints to aching, or his teeth shifted. Perhaps his eyes were blurring.

"I tell you, I will not bear such a child, and to be used thus! I thought perhaps, if my uncle rowed upriver for the fair, I could leave with him. Downriver, Thotharn's taint would not touch the child, and I would not be scorned among my mother's people. But he did not come."

"If you want me to speak to the master of the ship I came on—" Andriu caught his breath. He had not coughed for hours, he realized. "I think he's gone, though. But other ships . . ."

"I have no passage money. And my jewels . . . you saw this morning."

"Listen to me—" Andriu spoke quickly. "I'm a dream-singer. I can *sing* you gold enough for passage, lodging . . . and for an exorcism for the babe. He'll need it, I fear."

Using personal magic for gain would get him outlawed . . . again. But he could only be arrested once and had no goods for the courts to confiscate. So it made no difference. Still, he would have liked more time, time to know Vassilika better. There had been times when he might have sung her heaps of grain-bright coins and then entertained her with five ballads. Now his voice was rusty; the coins he would manifest would be tarnished, nicked, and worn as if they had passed through many hands. And he would be lucky if he had strength enough. . . . No, doubt was fatal. He could do this, he had to. A roll of five-goldens should serve.

He saw the trust, the faith in Vassilika's eyes, and began to sing. Coins began to chink out of the night air and into Vassilika's lap. He felt energy flowing out of him.

Vassilika gasped and pointed. In the corner by the gate, a blot of shadow was forming silently into a masklike shape. Beneath it, into the temple precincts he had already profaned, stood Xuthen, several fair-wards with him. Why couldn't they see how evil he was?

Vassilika swept the gold into her surcoat and leapt up.

"As I suspected . . . unlawful use of magic, for a start," said Xuthen. "Well, Sergeant?"

273

"Run!" Vassilika cried. Light-headed from his song, Andriu followed her. For a time, his lungs pleading for breath, he kept pace. He could almost feel his life's blood bubbling up toward his lips.

"Get away!" Andriu staggered away from her down an alley and brought up against a stall with enough force to double him over. At least Vassilika stood a chance of escaping without him. And he might escape notice. Andriu looked up, tears of pain blurring his eyes . . . and saw the mask grinning above a scribe's desk. Of all the luck . . . if it were foul luck and not fouler magic! A sweet smell, too sweet, wafted from that open mouth. . . .

"Ah," Xuthen's voice purred at his shoulder. "A novelty." Cool and slender fingers traced his brow, down his cheek, and raised his chin toward the light carried by one of the lord's servants. Andriu wanted to scream at that touch. Instead he gagged and spat up blood. Still, the sweet scent flowed from the mask's lips. Heat spread from the touch of those well-cared-for, evil fingertips and burnt away his consciousness.

Andriu felt disappointment. Not dead, then? He floated slowly back to his body. Surely it would not be long. He felt the warmth of rich, piled fabrics, down-filled cushions, a room filled with braziers. No prison boasted such comfort. Probably he was in Xuthen's town house.

"My own dream-singer," gloated Xuthen's cultured, hateful voice above Andriu's head.

"You'll get no music from this one, lord!" Another voice . . . the steward?

"Ah, but I can heal him. Will he not be grateful as youth

274

and health return? I shall taste that gratitude. But he will know only a reprieve. His health will fail again, and I shall taste his despair. But who knows? If he sings well, perhaps I will truly heal him."

"He is shamming sleep, master," said the steward. His bony, old man's fingers gripped Andriu's shoulder, twisting into the joint until he cried out. Even above the roaring in his ears came the mad piping of his fever—and Xuthen's laugh.

"Open your eyes, dream-singer."

Andriu saw that he lay on a low couch. Above it was a huge mask of Thotharn wrought in the antique eastern pattern and inlaid with dazzling, threadlike swirls of precious metals. Heavy hangings and deep-piled rugs caught the shadows cast by lamps wrought of pierced copper. Their light danced off the metal inserts in the heavy, carved furniture.

The shadowy lord and the mask that ruled him—they would devour Andriu.

"An interesting idea," mused Xuthen. "Lord Thotharn has had lords, scribes, stewards, serving-women as his servants. But never a dream-singer."

"No!" Assuming Xuthen would let him near knife or poison, Andriu would kill himself. Lying on the narrow couch below that mask, he felt like a sacrifice on its altar.

Why aren't you content? he asked himself. You wanted to do one good thing before you died. You did it. Vassilika is safe. That no longer seemed enough.

Xuthen reached out to touch Andriu's face as if he were a toy. "You must be cleaner—and quite a bit stronger—before you sing." He lifted a tiny hammer and struck a bell that stood upon a nearby table.

Before a servant could come, Andriu heard voices raised in

the entryway of the house. "The lord is busy now, lad. Come tomorrow."

"Lord Xuthen told my master that he should be brought any gems come in by caravan from the east as soon as they were unpacked."

That was no boy's voice. Curse the little fool, why hadn't Vassilika fled? She had gold, and he'd given her time enough to get away. Now she had ruined Andriu's only chance to do something decent before he died. But there was no point in cursing her. They were both damned now. Xuthen would never let them go.

Vassilika, muffled in a drab cape of the sort worn by apprentices, appeared at the door. Before the noble could do more than rub his hands together, she had dropped the package she carried and had taken from beneath her cape a green branch.

"I wanted to buy you time," Andriu couldn't help crying out.

"This branch has been truly blessed," Vassilika told Lord Xuthen. He backed away from it. "Come, Andriu. I couldn't let you buy my self-respect. So I came back. This will hold him . . . long enough. . . ."

Andriu swung his legs from the couch. He felt stronger. Was that Xuthen's doing already—or the branch's? But he dared not think of Xuthen or the mask from which he drew his power, not as long as Vassilika stood trembling with the effort to hold up the branch.

"Would you leave me already?" asked Xuthen, his voice silken. He turned to face the mask and raised his hands to it. Andriu and his rescuer started backing toward the stairs.

"Stay. . . ." cried the mask's brazen tongue and lips.

276

"Stay . . . eee . . . eee. . . ." The mask's voice sounded like the wailing of the lost. Echoes from nowhere trembled and clutched about them. As Andriu faltered, one hand going to his chest, Xuthen's steward sneaked up behind Vassilika and struck her down with a heavy metal statuette. She crumpled on the dark stairs, and Andriu's strength evaporated.

"Stayyy. . . ." the mask cried again. Its breath, sweet yet corrupt, drifted toward him from the shining lips and turned him giddy. It brushed his nostrils and his will was no longer his own, he was staggering back up the stairs, half fighting, half consenting, he was reeling into the library where Xuthen awaited him smiling.

"Sit down," he ordered. Andriu sat. He wanted to scream, to grab Xuthen and shake him till his neck snapped, to tear down that mask from the wall and drive his foot into its grinning mouth. If Thotharn drank pain, let the demon start with that!

"I have had enough violence for tonight," Xuthen decided. He tapped his bell lightly, and a servant appeared. He wore gray livery which bore what Andriu recognized with loathing as a stylized version of the mask emblazoned over his heart. The true horror of such a device, Andriu thought, half in a daze, was that unless you knew precisely what you were looking for, you wouldn't understand what you saw.

"My master wishes?" asked the servant.

"There has been an intruder. A woman. Summon the Watch."

The day after, Andriu stood in the court before the temple. A platform had been built there. Today he wore gray, the

277

livery of Lord Xuthen. At least he had been spared having to wear the sign of the mask.

He had wanted to stand as far away as possible from that platform, with its shameful post for securing prisoners, but Xuthen's steward forced him closer. Vassilika, he thought, would forgive him for witnessing her punishment. That hurt him. She would endure what she had to. But tonight—most likely tonight would see her floating facedown in the river. And Xuthen/Thotharn could still claim the child. . . .

"Watch," hissed the steward. Xuthen had given Andriu to him to be schooled as one might school a wild beast. But the steward had no need of whip or chain. Andriu could smell the breath of the mask. His knees grew weak, his chest began to ache, and the high whine of fever started up in his ears. His health was a gift that could be withdrawn.

Stubbornly Andriu jerked up his chin. He wanted his memories of Vassilika untainted by today's shame.

"I told you to watch," the steward repeated. Andriu choked. He was going to have to cough, to breathe in the mask's breath. . . . He watched, hating himself.

Father Demetrios and Lord Xuthen walked toward the platform. "For the last time"—the priest's voice was urgent but, being a dream-singer's voice, carried to the farthest reaches of the square—"in the name of the Comforter herself, let me implore you—"

"I stand for the old law of your own temple!"

"Temple law this may be," retorted the old dream-singer. "But it is not justice and will have its price."

The sergeant of fair-wards brought Vassilika out onto the platform. She wore only a shift. When he took her by the arm to guide her to the post and its dangling manacles, she met his eyes, and his fell. She shook her heavy braids down over her shoulders to give herself some covering when they ripped her shift from her shoulders. Then she placed her hands within the metal rings before she was compelled to. When the sergeant offered her a strip of leather to bite on, she turned her head away.

The crowd sighed in horror. Andriu saw Vassilika's kinswomen sobbing. The man beside them twisted his hand on his knifeless belt.

Andriu winced as he heard the sharp rip of Vassilika's shift tearing. He couldn't just stand here, could he? Not when he had nothing not even his soul—left to lose. What if he stepped forward and declared himself the father of her child? . . . He would be arrested . . . and he would get free of Xuthen, perhaps long enough to die clean. As if sensing his intent, the steward reached over to silence him with a hand on his shoulder. Again Andriu smelled the breath of Thotharn and his head spun. He was reeling, staggering over the smooth flags of the square, away from the steward, he had opened his mouth to protest . . .

As Vassilika caught sight of him, a tear slid down her cheek. Ever so slightly she shook her head at him: This is pointless, she was telling him.

But it wasn't. For fifteen years he had sung, had nursed his disillusionment and bitterness. Then he had met her. And she had manifested (without dream-songs) what he had long forotten—the core of him, that still believed in innocence and justice.

He opened his mouth to shout but found himself singing instead.

At first his voice quivered. Then he collected and stitched

together the rags of the fine voice he had once had and made his dream-song. He sang of Vassilika's manacles turning to bracelets. Suddenly her wrists were laden with gold.

He never knew for certain what scraps of poetry he lifted from the old ballads to wrap about Vassilika as he longed to set his cloak over her bared shoulders. But as he sang, for the first time during that long, shameful morning, Vassilika blushed. She raised her hands to cover her full breasts, and the gold from the transformed chains rang on her wrists. There was strength and shelter in those arms, Andriu thought. But it was not fitting for Vassilika to stand revealed before the crowd. He recalled words from one of the oldest of the priestly hymns. "Strength and dignity are her clothing," he sang. Father Demetrios held out an arm to restrain Xuthen. His eyes were very bright with recognition, and with joy. Andriu wondered why he ever thought he needed to hide from him—or that he could. It was all so much simpler now.

The people in the court looked at Vassilika not because they wanted to see her humbled, but because she glowed like a festival gown with the radiance with which Andriu's song had invested her. That was but her outer shell. Could he show them the Vassilika he knew? He had to.

As he continued to sing, he became aware of that other life within her, part Vassilika and part something utterly alien and hostile to her. It was the demon seed she had been tricked into bearing. It could not be tolerated. Yet the child was also half hers, might have her spirit, her generosity . . . He could not extinguish its potential. Andriu's voice soared effortlessly into the difficult high notes. Even as he marveled at its range and power, he knew that it flooded into that growing life and shaped it anew. It was as much his now as hers, even though they had never lain together in love. He could claim it now and not be lying.

Xuthen snarled and stripped off his cloak. He wrapped its heavy folds about his hand and grasped the iron intended to brand Vassilika in disgrace. When he drew it from the brazier, its tip flowered, red and baneful.

Andriu tried to leap forward and got to the steps of the platform. Then he felt the chill breath of the mask stealing over him, draining the strength from his voice. His power to sing life into manifestation was fading with his own life . . . too soon.

Vassilika's hands came up to her mouth and she began to sing. It seemed as if her cupped hands caught her voice, caressed it, and cast it forth, stronger for their touch.

She was not a dream-singer. Rich and pleasant her voice might be, but it was simply that of a woman who might be expected to sing over her weaving or to please friends. Andriu thought he could have listened to it forever. It made him think of harvests, of woven baskets heaped high with fruits, wines ruddy and gold, fires that welcomed travelers at sunset, when the air turned frosty and there was a hint of smoke in it, and the flashes of green and copper at the horizon subsided.

It strengthened him. He staggered onto the platform and opened his mouth again. Just let him claim the child as his and this ordeal would be over. Then there would be an investigation, and they would have Xuthen . . . wouldn't they? His eyes met Vassilika's, hope and questions in them.

She tossed her braids back from her shoulders and stepped forward, her flesh shimmering. When Andriu's knees gave out, she eased him down and knelt beside him. Cradling his face with its cracked, bloody lips against her breasts, she touched her mouth to his forehead briefly and went on with her song. Her voice took on an added luster.

It was not dream-singing, but something equally as powerful. It lifted him, bathed and healed him, then moved out beyond him to embrace everything in the temple. "Blossom," it commanded. "Flourish, grow for me!"

Awe on his face, Father Demetrios hastened to the doors of the temple and went within. Andriu heard him cry out in wonder, then run deeper toward the sanctuary itself. Then the old priest stepped out into the light. Clasped in his arms was the wreath of Xuthen's blasphemous presentation to the Comforter. As the old priest moved, the green stalks quivered. The golden heads of grain drooped with their own weight and shifted as the breeze from the water touched them. Sun shone off the dew glistening upon them. Vassilika held out her arms to receive the wreath from the dream-singer as lovingly as if it were her own child. I helped, Andriu thought in wonder. I really did. My faith helped change this.

Xuthen screamed. "Will no one punish this shameless bitch?"

The iron he clutched in his hand had burned through his cloak and charred flesh so that his entire arm began to smoke. But the demon in him transferred the agony away from his consciousness to whatever might be left of Xuthen-the-man and lunged at Vassilika. As the iron touched her shoulder, Andriu heard her flesh sizzle.

Then Vassilika laughed. Where the iron had touched flesh, the only mark made was a stalk of grain which faded, even as a blush fades.

"Red hot!" screamed Xuthen. "Witch!"

"That's a lie!" Andriu shouted, just as Vassilika's father leapt onto the platform.

"False charges," cried the man. "I call challenge on you, my lord. Sergeant, arrest him!"

Father Demetrios came forward with the guards. His first words ignored Xuthen and went straight for Andriu's heart. "My son! I wept when you ran away, and I tried to find you. Now . . ." He looked as if he might weep again. "Where had you disappeared to? It doesn't matter, now. Thank the Three you are home again."

Andriu kissed the priest's hand. He had a sudden, incongruous picture of Vassilika wearing a black robe and an air of enforced sanctity, or of himself attempting once more to school his fondness for rude ballads into the teaching of choirboys. Vassilika, he knew, had no talent for contemplation; her gifts were all for life. He hadn't been much of a contemplative, either. When that failed, he had run wild. He would try living instead of rebelling now.

But there were matters to tend now, and Vassilika seemed to have them in hand. She stepped forward and handed Andriu the wreath. Holding the stalk of grain that she had drawn from it, she advanced upon Xuthen and brushed it across his face. He screamed as if it had seared him . . . and it had. Andriu had no other words for it. Xuthen was withering from that touch, shriveling in upon himself until his body crumbled into ash. A guard went to the fountain, drew water in his helmet, and washed the place where the demon enfleshed had fallen.

"Are you ready to come home, daughter?" asked Vassilika's father.

Andriu swept his arm and cloak over her shoulders. She

grinned at him in a deplorably unladylike fashion, and that grin answered all his questions. She would be going home at least long enough to collect her clothing. It occurred to Andriu that she must also have a dowry; the thought dazed him. And then they would both go to the temple, at least long enough for Father Demetrios to wed them before the transformed wreath.

And then what?

Andriu sighed in pure contentment. He had his health back, he had been forgiven, welcomed by Father Demetrios, and he had Vassilika. Despite a life filled with songs and with dreaming, he had never dreamt of a Vassilika. And to think he had returned to Ithkar expecting to die and wanting only to do it in his birthplace! What a ballad this would make! He could sing it up and down the Ith. . . . Oh, but would Vassilika want to sing it with him? A bard's life wasn't for everyone.

She smiled at him, and he remembered how she had complained of boredom. She would love traveling, and she would never be bored again. He'd see to that! And he . . . he'd never be lonely. There would never be enough he could do for her because she had taken away his loneliness.

He couldn't have sung himself a better future!

Andriu smiled and kissed his bride-to-be.

THE PRINCE OUT OF THE PAST

Nancy Springer

Kam Horseleech awoke with a start, not knowing for a moment where he was. That always happened to him at Ithkar Fair, starry sky overhead instead of the familiar thatch, no warm form of wife. Usually the drunken cries of ill-assorted fairgoers served to alert him, but there was no noise, it must have been that most hushed time of night a few hours before dawn. What had roused him?

Still groggy, he sat up and glanced around. Moonbeams, shadow and soft light, tents and wagons. Smells and sounds— quiet stirrings of all sorts of animals, someone's nag stamping, lop-eared rabbits rustling in their cage and a cheetah in one farther away—nothing untoward. Kam yawned, his mind moving hazily. Sleep after a trying day, that nomad's mare foaling breech and the cut on that supercilious noble's prize ambler, the man peering over his shoulder as he worked. No matter. Go back to sleep.

Yet he had felt a summons, firm as the grip of a hand on his upper arm. But no one stood near.

Well, it would do no harm just to have a look about. . . .

Kam got up, stumbling slightly over his own sizable feet. Automatically he ran a hand over his shock of hair and through his rough beard, picking out bits of straw. A big hand, not at all clever by the looks of it, but good with horses. . . . He stumped off at random, trying to be wary. It went against his nature to be suspicious, but this was the most disreputable sector of the fair, as he had been warned many times by both friends and experience. All those who stank, whether animal or human, were pushed outward from the sweet-smelling temple center of the fair to lodge here at the fringes. So if he did not want to be knocked on the head by bravos or to step on a snake-charmer, he had to be careful. What lay in shadow of tents and trees . . . and that moon-glade, now, just ahead. It would not do to step out in it without having a bit of a look around. . . .

He stepped out in it nevertheless, for he was one who liked the light, and a most unaccountable feeling took hold of him.

Now what was that grip, gentle, invisible hands of— moonlight?—on his bony wrists, tugging at him, on his shoulders that were round and stooped from toil, guiding him? Not even crying out—but with bushy eyebrows arched high in astonishment—Kam found himself threading his way quite surely through a haphazard maze of sleeping bodies, past the offal of distant food booths to a region that smelled strongly of manure—

Until he came to a stop, and all the stench and squalor

around him seemed distant and unreal, for he saw only those who stood in the moonlight before him.

Being what he was, he noticed the horse first. It stood very still, white flanks mottled gray by leaf-shadow in moonlight, shimmering, almost spiritous, but so big, a destrier without peer, massive neck highly arched and the small ears almost hidden in mane, noble nostrils, dark eyes, ripple of muscles in great shoulder—and standing with one hand resting lightly on the great shining curve of barrel, the master—

Kam turned his eyes slightly to see who it was who owned such a steed. Another mincing noble, he judged it would be. But no—this man looked to be neither perfumed noble nor worldly priest nor commoner nor nomad nor soldier nor merchant nor any other sort of man that Kam could put a name to, nor even one of those nameless overseas barbarians. He was—what was he, in the moonlight? He met Kam's stare quite equably.

"Goodman horseleech," he said, "thank you for coming."

Young, he was very young, and handsome—and yet the curls of his fair young head shone pure white. And something in his voice was not young at all—there were ages of quiet in that level voice. A glint of sheen about him—crown, or helm, or sparkle of armband, or brooch at the cloaked shoulder? Kam was never to remember clearly, for he was caught in a trance of strangeness and shifting moonlight. And that face dimly lit and the eyes deep pools of shadow—he was perhaps not of unusual height, perhaps of a height with Kam if Kam had straightened fully, but he seemed tall, even when he bent to run his hand down his horse's sleek side.

"It is the hock, here," he said.

Kam noted the swelling, moved closer numbly to explore

287

it with large, deft, and gentle fingers, noting in the same trancelike fashion that the steed bore not a thread of harness. "Spavin," Kam said, his voice coming out curiously rusty.

"I know. That last battle, too much, the terrible weight—he had been lame for a long time, and has worn the hoof all uneven with it. What can you do for him, goodman Kam?"

He hated to answer truly. He swallowed first. "Very little," he said finally. "If I could have treated it sooner, just after it happened—"

"I know. I lay abed, a spear-tip buried in my thigh, and by the time I— Well . . ." The stranger paused, glancing, if Kam could judge, obliquely upward, toward where the moon hovered, gathering thoughts. "The talk of Ithkar Fair is that you are the best healer of horses south of the mountains," he went on at last. "Surely there is something you can do."

There were remedies. Kam had tried them at various times, reluctantly. "Some men burn the spavin with white-hot iron to draw the devil out," he said, his voice as quiet and even as that of the one he faced. "Others pierce it with tapestry needles or slender knives."

"And you say?"

Kam tried not to scowl. "I say let ill enough alone. Pain and disfigurement—"

"And small enough result. Yes." The stranger turned slightly, his hand still on the great steed's back. "Have you no magic, goodman Kam?"

A chill that was not the night breeze touched Kam—fear, but not of the stranger. It was the well-inbred fear of one well mannered who has always obeyed the law. "You know the priests guard magic quite jealously," he said too hastily, too anxious to tell the other that which should not need saying.

288

"Magic is forbidden in Ithkar except when judged harmless or a minor part of a man's stock in trade."

"Well, then say that I forced you to do my will." There was not the slightest hint of threat in the youth's voice—only eagerness. "With this," he added, and from a scabbard under his cloak he drew forth a long, slender sword that shone like new silver in the moonlight.

A sword!

Kam gaped, knowing now quite certainly what he had managed not to know before: that this man, this horse, were not of earthly sort. The fair-wards let no weapons into Ithkar Fair, whether lance or dirk, whether on noble, cleric, or commoner. None. Years had taught him that the rule was as dependable as the sunrise. And here stood one with a shining sword in hand—he could not, then, be one who had entered this place by any earthly gate.

"Who are you?" Kam whispered.

The other seemed suddenly abashed and sheathed his sword. "Does it matter?" he asked.

"To be sure, it does!" Kam exclaimed, though he could not have told why. "Who—*what* are you?"

"The prince out of the past."

Names of dead heroes, champions of the Three Lordly Ones in the noble times long past, filled Kam's mind in disorder, like half-remembered music. "Who—which one?"

"All."

Kam stared, beyond his depth, uncertain whether to kneel, pledge fealty, kiss the moonlike glint of a ring. But he was a plain man, he could do none of those things. Only one thing could he do for this prince, and silently he turned to the horse to attempt it.

"Even the spirits are drawn to Ithkar Fair," the champion said, all in a soft rush, as if he had at last found someone he could talk to. "This fair draws all to it, best and worst. . . . We walked here side by side all the long way, the steed and I. He is limping worse than ever now. I wish I could have carried him, for he carried me many a sore time."

Kam had placed one hand on the horse's flank and the other on the hot and tender hock, and he stood puzzled and distraught. "Lord," he said, "I cannot feel him."

The youth smiled quizzically. "He's solid enough."

"Yes, but I mean—I cannot feel his being, his . . ." Kam did not know the word for "essence," but he knew horses, their shying, their slobber, their passions—for grass and home and each other, their oblique thoughts, their fears—his body bore the half-circle moonlike marks of their hooves. And he knew that what stood so tamely under his hand was not horse as he understood it.

"What is he?" Kam asked.

"All." Now it was the prince who fumbled with words. "The . . . greatness, the majesty of . . . all such horses, as I am . . . of men."

Kam closed his eyes, tried to remember the tales he had heard as a boy, tales of a golden time of high court and high courage, long ago when the Three ruled. . . . None of them came clear, but a sort of vision drifted to mind of the steed that bore the champion joyously across the countryside, that lent its weight to the blow of his lance, that took him curvetting out of the hands of the enemy—under his touch the great kingly destrier stirred, lifted his lovely head, and softly whinnied.

"Yes!" It was the prince, an excited whisper.

Kam placed both hands on the hock, embracing the injured part with their warmth, and let the magic come. "Lordly Ones," he whispered, "Lordly Ones on your seven pillars of cloud white as pearl, white as moonlight, white as white gold, help me. . . ."

It shot through him with javelin force. He heard and felt that the charger reared up with a great neigh, and he felt the prince catch him as he fell backward, strong arms and warm, but he could see nothing, and in a moment he knew nothing more.

He awoke some hours later to bright sunlight and the unwelcome sight of a fair-ward standing over him, scowling under the shadow of his brass helmet.

"Up, horseleech, and come with me," the fair-ward ordered.

Kam did not get up. He felt far too weak. Instead, he looked around him. He lay on a pile of straw in an unfamiliar place—where were his blankets? A half-grown urchin stood nearby, and a nice-looking shaggy gray pony with thick mane on a well-arched neck. Dapple gray—or was the gray mostly dirt?

"Caught red-handed," the fair-ward grumbled, prodding him with his bronze-shod quarterstaff.

Kam struggled to a sitting position. "What is the charge?" he asked.

"Magic! When I came by here yesterday that pony was spavined so bad ye could see it with no eyes. Today it's sound. Get up."

The news rather than the order brought Kam scrambling to his feet. The urchin faced him at the pony's side, unsmiling. A curly-headed, freckle-faced lad, his hair sun-bleached nearly as white as tow, he stood no higher than Kam's chest. But

291

his eyes, startlingly dark, looked merry and wise and very old. Struck in his belt he wore a long stick.

"Come along," the fair-ward said, and Kam went without a word.

The priest who heard the case was young, golden-robed, newly shaven of head, and newly cynical since having become privy to the inner workings of the temple. He regarded Kam impatiently.

"Have you any defense?"

Penalties for the use of magic were severe. Kam could be declared outlaw, lose his home and possessions and his rights as a freeman. Most practitioners resolved this matter with a simple bribe, for the priests were mercenary. Kam had no bribe and no defense except the truth.

"The champion . . ." No, it would not be truth to say that the prince had made him do it. The healing had been Kam's gift of the heart. "The Lordly Ones empowered me to help the horse."

"Pony," the fair-ward corrected.

The priest sighed hugely. Ai, the credulousness of these peasants! Would they never learn anything other than their literal-minded, superstitious beliefs? Still, the man was evidently not a shyster or a sneaking wizard. Even the fair-ward admitted that Kam had a reputation for honesty.

"If I let off everyone who spoke of the Three," the priest said rather sharply, "the fair would be topheavy with trickery, shoddy wares sold under a veil of glamour."

Kam glanced up from where he had been studying his large toes. "Well, if it is trickery to heal a suffering beast," he said just as sharply, "then I stand guilty."

"There is a need for codification of these matters of

healing," the priest grumbled, more to himself than to Kam. The problem was irksome, and he had not had his morning pastry. He decided to delay judgment.

"We'll see if you have anything more to say after a night down below," he told Kam, and waved a slender hand in dismissal.

"Down below" turned out to be a cell with chains and shackles and nothing to eat. Kam sat there disconsolately through the day and into the night. But when moonlight began to make its way through the single high window, Kam felt misery leave him, to be replaced by a quite unreasonable hope. He watched as, the moon traveling toward its setting, pale shafts of light inched nearer and nearer to him. At last, just as he had known they must, they touched the shackles on his wrists—

And the chains fell apart with a faint silvery clink, and invisible hands helped Kam to his feet. Utterly astonished in spite of his hope—for it is one thing to expect the impossible, and another thing to see it happen—Kam let himself be led through a moonstruck and unlocked door and a maze of temple catacombs to a seldom used entry that opened dustily before him. Moonlight fell on cobbles outside, and the prince out of the past and the steed of all steeds awaited him as before.

"Why do you not ride?" Kam asked anxiously. "Is the horse not well?"

"Well and whole. You ride. You must be weak. Have they beaten you?"

"No." Kam was touched but not surprised by the concern in the champion's voice. "Thank you, my lord, but I need not ride. I can't, anyway. I—I have never sat a horse."

"Never, and you all your life a horseleech?" The marvel of that smile in the moonlight. "Well, I am blithe indeed that you are not outlawed or hurt. Let us walk together, if you will not ride."

They set off companionably toward the outer sector of the fair enclave, where drunkards brawled and peacocks shrieked and jugglers and horses were lodged, horses for sale, trained performing horses, pack horses and saddle horses, Kam's love and livelihood. As they walked the most wondrous horse he had ever seen walked freely beside him, its hooves chiming against the cobbles, with not a trace of a limp.

But the prince limped. Of course, the wound in the thigh. "Are there no leeches for you at Ithkar Fair?" Kam asked.

"Not such a healer as you, goodman." The prince smiled again. "Never mind. The steed will carry me."

He made ready to ride when they reached Kam's small campsite. He needed the height of a wagon-bed to help him vault to the horse's back. Before he climbed up, Kam took courage to ask him something ignoble.

"Lord—will there be a fair-ward awaiting me with the dawn?"

The prince genuinely laughed, a ringing, lovely sound. "Nay, I think not," he declared when he was done. "The priest has had a difficult night, and some of his notions have been shaken. He is not a bad sort, you know, really."

"Or he would not have given me a second thought."

"Yes. I think you will find he will be glad enough to let you be."

Once again it was the quietest hour of night. The moon was nearly down. The youth sprang to his steed.

"Farewell, goodman Kam," he said, and with a touch he

started to turn the marvelous mount away. Then he turned back and stretched out a silver-ringed hand. "I have no payment to offer you, and I have not even told you—many thanks."

Those eyes, deep pools of shadow . . . Half in fear and half in longing, Kam ardently wished that he could see those eyes more clearly.

"You have made me rich," he replied. "My lord . . ."

"What is it?"

"Who—what lad are you by day? In the light of the sun?"

"Helpless yet, but all hope, unwounded. The prince that will be."

"Ah." It was a sigh of fulfillment. "Call on me, champion," Kam said.

"I will. Kam . . . farewell."

They touched hands, and then he was gone, the sound of his charger's hooves ringing away rapidly in the night. He would make good speed before sunrise.

When even the sound had left him, Kam turned and looked skyward. At the horizon the jewel of white fire that was the moon dipped and sank. Kam felt oddly alone, he who always came alone to Ithkar Fair.

"Prince that will be," he murmured. "And may that day come soon."

COLD SPELL

Elisabeth Waters

"I strongly suggest, young woman, that you consider my proposition carefully. My friendship with your late father will not protect you from my wrath if you do not cooperate." Garak glared angrily at Eirthe, and she glared right back at him. After a moment he abandoned his attempt to stare her down, as she had known he would, and left, swirling his black wizard's cape around him as he stalked off through the fair.

She sighed as she turned back to the tapers she was dipping. Her father had taught her well when it came to candlemaking, but he hadn't thought to teach her how to handle Garak. He and Garak had been drinking companions during the fair in previous years, but Garak had always treated Eirthe as part of the furnishings of the candlemaker's booth. Now, however, her father was dead, and Eirthe was

297

the candlemaker. And she didn't think that she'd care to take Garak, with the hasty temper and pride that covered his incompetence as a wizard, as a drinking companion . . . or any other kind of companion, either. Frowning, she jerked the candles out of the caldron, splashing hot wax into the fire below. The fire responded with a surprisingly loud hiss.

"I'm sorry, Alnath," Eirthe hastily apologized as a patch of red-gold flame moved to another part of the fire and regarded her with unblinking eyes.

"You should be," the salamander replied. "Even overlooking the fact that you're splashing wax on me. You're going to ruin those tapers. You know that they have to be dipped smoothly and evenly."

"I certainly should know; Father told me often enough. I wish he were here to cope with Garak."

"Why? What's that blustering fool up to now?" Alnath separated herself from the fire and came to rest on the back of Eirthe's left wrist. Since this was her habitual perch when she condescended to leave her home in the fire, Eirthe had long since become accustomed to the heat on her skin and no longer found it particularly painful. Her hands were always a mess from hot wax and heavy caldrons anyway. She reached out a callused finger and scratched Alnath gently behind the ear.

"He wants me to make some people candles for him."

"Why not? After all, you are the best candlemaker in the fair. Probably even better than your father was—your candles are more alive."

"True," Eirthe said grimly, "and that's exactly why Garak wants them—in the likenesses of the richest merchants in the fair. If I put enough life into them in the making, even he will be able to bind them to the people they resemble.''

"You mean using the law of similarity? I suppose he could. He does have some magical ability, though not much. But what would he gain by it?"

"Remember the old goldsmith who died last year, near the end of the fair? I know father made a candle of him, but it disappeared. Three nights later the goldsmith burned to death in his bed, and it is said that the blankets weren't even charred. And after that, Garak had quite a bit of money for a mendicant wizard. I think he's running a protection racket.''

"What are you going to do about it? Denounce him to the fair-court?"

"Using what for proof? That was nearly a year ago, and the people who actually knew anything aren't going to want to remember. But I'm not going to make candles for him, no matter what he offers me. I don't need more wealth than I have—especially if it makes me a target for every greedy man around. I'd go mad in luxury with nothing useful to do. I can only wear one dress at a time, sleep in one wagon, and eat and drink as much as will fit in my stomach. And I like making candles. Garak is badly mistaken if he thinks he can turn my head with promises of great riches.''

"Unfortunately, he's likely to try to harm you if you don't do what he wants.''

"Oh, he was making dire, if unspecified, threats when he left. But we both know that his magic isn't up to much. He'll be furious with me, but he'll probably bluster it out and go away, just like he did today.''

"He'll be back.''

"So will the Three Lordly Ones.'' Eirthe chuckled.

"Seriously, he'll come back tomorrow, I'll tell him I won't do it, he'll mouth gibberish at me and make dire predictions about all the terrible things that will befall me, and then he'll stalk off, the very picture of a mortally offended wizard, and life will go on.''

"You're probably right." Alnath shrugged herself off Eirthe's wrist and back into the fire. "If you want to finish that batch of tapers today, you'd better get back to work."

Garak showed up again the next day around midafternoon, all dressed up to intimidate. With his black robe covering his paunch and the hood pulled forward to shadow his face, he actually did look rather imposing. But there are certain difficulties inherent in an attempt to intimidate the daughter of one's drinking companion: it is necessary for her to forget all the times she has seen you slouched on a bench leaning against the side of the wagon, with wine dribbling down your beard and staining your robe. Eirthe was not obliging enough to forget that, and that was the vision which superimposed itself over Garak's shrouded form. Great wizard indeed, she thought.

"Well, young woman?" Garak intoned. "Have you come to your senses?"

"I have never been out of them," Eirthe replied calmly, "and no, I will not make candles for you. Go and play your games by yourself; I'm not interested." She hung the tapers she was holding on the rack and reached for the next batch, confident that Garak would bluster and then leave if she simply ignored him. With that firmly in mind, she concentrated on her work, not noticing what happened next.

Garak drew himself up to his full height, which was about

the same as Eirthe's, and began to chant in some unknown language while waving his hands about in what were presumably magical gestures. Eirthe continued to dip tapers with a steady rhythm, but several passersby stopped to stare.

Suddenly she heard a warning hiss from the fire, where Alnath watched. Sneaking a glance out of the corner of her eye at Garak, she saw him shiver, as if a wind passed through him from head to feet. *What's wrong?* she thought at Alnath.

Alnath's reply formed in her head. *He's invoking Thotharn— and the god is answering.* Alnath sounded uneasy, and Eirthe, remembering the stories she had heard of this alien god, did not feel able to offer any reassurance.

But why should the god answer him? Eirthe protested. *He's not a priest.*

Maybe he's a tool. But Thotharn is definitely with him. Alnath paused, listening. *He's putting a cold curse on you, saying that your candles will never burn, your fire will go out—* The fire went out, and Alnath's scream split Eirthe's head apart as she blacked out.

Her head hurt dreadfully, and she was lying on the ground. Eirthe cautiously opened her eyes. Garak was gone, but so was Alnath, and her fire was still out. She dragged herself painfully to her feet and fetched the tinderbox from the wagon, but her attempts to rekindle the fire were unsuccessful; she couldn't get so much as a spark from the flints. The wax in the caldron was still liquid, so she hastily poured it into a storage crock. There was no point in adding to her misery the task of having to chip out an entire caldron full of hardened wax.

She looked at the surrounding booths, wondering what the neighboring craftsmen had made of the incident. From the determined way in which they all carried on their normal business while being careful not to look in her direction, she gathered that they had all decided it was safer to ignore the whole mess. Well, she couldn't blame them for that. She wished she could do the same.

She picked up the tapers she had been working on, which were near enough done to use anyway, and retreated to the privacy of her wagon to take stock. Garak had said that her fire would go out and her candles would not burn. Her fire was out all right, but she wasn't going to take his word for anything. But her efforts to light the tapers she held were unsuccessful, and when she tried to light one of the molded images of the Three Lordly Ones she had made several days earlier, it wouldn't light, either.

"That's wonderful," she muttered. "Just what I don't need, a retroactive curse."

There was nothing she could do about the candles at the moment; she had enough money, so she didn't need to worry about starving for a while, and her headache was wearing off. That left her free to worry about Alnath. She remembered hearing her scream just before she fainted, but she didn't feel that Alnath was dead. She might be hurt, though, and in any case Eirthe was not about to abandon a creature that had been her best friend since early childhood. She would have to find her.

"So how do I find a salamander? Start with fire; who uses fire?" Eirthe picked up her cloak and went out into the darkening twilight, trying not to think about all the fires that would be lit as the sun set.

*   *   *

Several hours later, well past suppertime, Eirthe purchased a meat pie from one of the food stalls and collapsed dejectedly on a nearby bench to eat it. It wasn't exactly that she felt hungry, but she was cold and very, very tired, and she hoped that hot food might make her feel a little better. All she wanted to do was crawl back to her wagon, crawl into her bunk, and sleep for the rest of her life. Her head was hurting again after hours of wandering around calling Alnath, and there was still no sign of her. She wasn't within range of the goldsmith, the silversmith, the armorers, the alchemists, or the herbalists, she wasn't near the potter's kiln, and she was nowhere in the vicinity of the bakers, cooks, and pastry chefs. Who else used fire?

Eirthe took another bite of her pie and forced herself to chew and swallow it. Idly, with no real hope of receiving an answer, she broadcast another call to Alnath. To her astonishment, she caught an answering flicker, accompanied by a picture of Alnath flaming in a large glass sphere. Eirthe hastily shoved the remaining portion of the meat pie into her mouth and practically swallowed it whole as she went to follow the picture to its source. Alnath felt unhurt, but why was she surrounded by glass instead of being in a fire? Had Garak somehow managed to imprison her?

She hurried away from the food and clothing booths and had almost reached the eastern boundary—her section—when a small ball of flame came flying through the air and settled on her wrist.

"Alnath." Eirthe smiled tremulously and stroked her head. "Are you all right?"

"Yes. I've found a nice place. Warm." Alnath flitted

303

away, and Eirthe followed her to a nearby booth where she settled back into the glass sphere that Eirthe had seen a few minutes before. Now she realized that it was part of the wares of the glassblower's booth, though it was an unusual design for a bowl.

What is that, Alnath? she asked silently.

Alnath shrugged. "Warm." She subsided into the bottom of the strange bowl and flickered contentedly.

"Ah, a fair maiden." A drunken voice issued forth from the shadows cast by Alnath's fire, followed by a young man clutching a wineskin. His brown tunic stretched over a paunch that would have done credit to a priest, and his large chest and callused hands—even worse than Eirthe's—showed the effects of years of glassblowing. All in all, he looked like a short, and not unfriendly, bear. "Have you come to laugh at my misery, too?"

"I have quite enough misery of my own, thank you. I don't need to go looking for any more—even to laugh at." She looked around at his wares, neatly arranged on shelves around them. There were dozens of goblets, all exquisitely shaped, a good variety of animal figures, and the odd bowl in which Alnath was resting. "Why are you miserable? Your work is beautiful." She ran a finger over the smooth glass of Alnath's bowl. "Not so much as an air bubble in it."

"It's absolutely perfect," the glassblower agreed. "My finest work to date. And—until that accursed Garak passed by this evening—it was destined as a gift from the high priestess to her sister. It was to be a home for her ornamental fish—and now look at it!" He gestured dramatically with the hand holding the wineskin, then took another healthy gulp of wine.

304

"Garak certainly seems to have been busy today," Eirthe remarked bitterly. "What did he do to you?"

The glassblower froze, wineskin just touching his mouth, and looked at her over it. "He do something to you, too?"

Eirthe nodded, fighting a sudden desire to burst into tears. She blinked rapidly and felt the wineskin thrust into her grasp as surprisingly gentle hands guided her to a bench.

"Here, sit down. Have some wine, you look like you need it."

Eirthe took a large mouthful of wine and choked it down, feeling it warm her. The second mouthful felt even better. "Thank you, sir."

The man laughed. "No need to be so formal. I'm Cadmon, glassblower."

"Eirthe, candlemaker." She passed the wineskin back to him, and he took another swig and passed it back.

"So. Eirthe, what makes you wander about alone after dark?" Cadmon leaned back, obviously ready to listen to a long story.

"I was looking for my salamander," Eirthe began, indicating Alnath, who was still curled up in the bowl. Cadmon sat up abruptly.

"Is that a salamander?" he asked in amazement.

"Of course," Eirthe replied, puzzled. "What did you think it was?"

"I thought it was just part of the curse." She looked questioningly at him, and he continued to explain. "You see, Garak doesn't like me, and hasn't for a long time. I don't show sufficient respect for his robe—decrepit piece of fabric that it is." Eirthe giggled and he grinned at her. "And I certainly wasn't about to give away my beautiful goblets for

305

what he wanted to pay for them. Besides, he wouldn't appreciate them. No soul.

"Anyway, he came by late this afternoon, in a truly foul mood, and demanded the fishbowl to use in his scrying. Now I rather doubt that he could scry with the whole ocean to work with, but I was polite. I didn't tell him that. I quietly explained that the bowl was a special commission for the high priestess. I expected him to drop the matter right there, but he got really funny. He said that she, and all the priesthood, were children playing with toys they didn't understand, but that he understood true power and soon they would all serve him.

"I must have smiled or something, because he got mad and started cursing me. He said that anything put into my vessels would burn and be instantly consumed. And then he stalked off—and it was true! Look." He picked up a goblet and poured a small amount of wine into it. The wine flamed briefly and the goblet was empty. "I can't even make mulled wine! I—the finest glassmaker south of the steppes—reduced to drinking from a common wineskin." He suited the action to the words. "It's disgusting." He lowered the skin and looked owlishly at Eirthe. "And what did he do to you?"

Eirthe sighed and slumped back against the wall, trying to think of where to begin. "Well, he and my father were friends of a sort, and my father used to make candles for him."

"Oh, you're Bearn the candlemaker's daughter? What happened to him?"

"He died last winter," she replied quietly, and Cadmon made sympathetic noises. "Anyway," she continued, "I came back by myself this year. I worked the last ten fairs with my father, and I'm a good candlemaker, possibly even a bit better than he was. But Garak showed up, and for some reason—only the Three know why—he seems to expect me to be friendly to him and do whatever he wants!''

"Really?" Cadmon looked appraisingly at her. "You're pretty enough, but I wouldn't have figured you for his type.''

Eirthe looked blankly at him for a few seconds before she realized what he meant. "No, not that kind of friendly. He was talking about a sort of partnership—you know, 'do as I say and you'll be rich.' He wants me to make wax figures for him.''

Cadmon drew in a sharp breath. "So he's trying that again!''

"It would seem so, but he's doing it without me. I told him to go play his stupid games someplace else.''

"In those words? How brave of you.''

"Or maybe stupid." Eirthe shrugged. "I really didn't think there was much he could do about it, but somehow he managed to cast a cold spell on me. My fire won't light and my candles won't burn, and I don't know how I'm going to make a living.''

Cadmon patted her hand awkwardly and started to pass her the wineskin. "Oops, it's empty. Let's go get some more; I'm not drunk enough yet. Are you?''

"I don't think so. What does drunk enough feel like?''

"You don't feel anything. Come on." He started toward the wineseller's, and Eirthe picked up Alnath, bowl and all, and followed. After the trouble she'd gone to to find her, she wasn't going to let her out of her sight.

* * *

307

They got two more skins of wine and then decided to go by Eirthe's stall to get some goblets that wouldn't incinerate the stuff. But as Eirthe stepped past the spot were Garak had stood that afternoon, Alnath screamed and her fire nearly went out. Eirthe, with the inside of her skull still ringing, hastily stepped back, and the salamander quieted and burned brightly again. "Don't try to take me in there again!" she scolded.

"I wouldn't dream of it," Eirthe assured her fervently, setting the bowl carefully on the ground and rubbing her aching head.

Cadmon stepped carefully beyond the point and then back. "It really is cold there. Let's go back to my place." He grinned sardonically at her reaction. "Don't worry. Your virtue is perfectly safe. I'm too drunk to do anything and I intend to be a good deal drunker before I go to bed. And if you try to sleep here, you will literally be an ice maiden by morning."

"I'm afraid you're right." Eirthe sighed. "Wait a minute while I get the goblets." She went into her wagon, shivering under her heavy cloak, and hastily filled a sack with some clothes, her hairbrush, and other assorted miscellany, and added the goblets. A couple of her candles were swept in with the other junk, but she didn't stop to worry about them. They certainly weren't a fire hazard! She hurried out to join Cadmon and Alnath in the comparative warmth of the cold night.

She woke in the morning feeling surprisingly good for someone who'd had the type of night before she had. And most important, she was warm, largely because Cadmon was curled up snoring beside her. She slid out of the bed, being careful not to wake him, and went from the wagon into the stall. The leather hides that protected it at night were tied down, but it was far from dark inside. Alnath, still flaming away in the bowl, greeted her with the suggestion that she rebraid her hair and do something about her clothes. "You look as though you had slept in them," she added.

"I did," Eirthe told her calmly. "It was warm." She retrieved her bag from the bench where she had dropped it the previous night and began to root about in it for her hairbrush and clean shift. She shoved the candles on a shelf above Cadmon's display table so she could reach the bottom of the bag, which, of course, was where her shift was. The steady snores coming from the wagon made it seem unlikely that Cadmon would appear in the next few minutes, so she hastily began to change into clean clothes. As she pulled the voluminous shift over her head, she vaguely noticed that the light seemed brighter. Surely the sun wasn't rising that fast? She bent to pick up her skirt and froze in astonishment.

Right next to her face sat one of Cadmon's exquisite wine goblets, and inside it, burning slowly and brightly, was one of her molded candles. Eirthe sat slowly on the bench, skirt forgotten in her hand, and stared at it, sure that it was the most beautiful sight she had ever seen. She didn't hear the snores stop briefly, then turn to groans, as Cadmon dragged his aching body out of bed and into the stall.

He dropped on the bench beside her, trying to shield his eyes from all sources of light, and inquired in a pained whisper if any wine was left.

"Cadmon, look!" Eirthe pointed to the candle.

Cadmon took an unwary look, then winced and covered

his eyes again. "Eirthe, that's cruelty to hungover glassblowers! Blow that thing out."

Alnath made the hissing sound that was her form of laughter. "Try some more wine, Cadmon. There's a bit left in the skin by your left foot."

"Thank you, whatever you are." Cadmon grabbed the wineskin. A couple of quick swigs restored him enough to enable him to notice the world around him. "I didn't know you could talk," he told Alnath, then added to Eirthe, "Are you getting dressed, or do you plan to stay like that all day?"

Eirthe, engrossed by the candle, hardly heard him. "It won't blow out."

"Nonsense. Candles always blow out—usually at the worst possible moment." Cadmon went to hang over it from the other side of the table. "Let me try." He blew directly at the flame, but it only burned brighter—a result, Eirthe thought, of the alcohol content of his breath. He frowned at it. "That's odd." He picked up the goblet and shook it. The candle flew out, and Eirthe, grabbing for it before it could set the stall on fire, found when she caught it that it was not only out, but cold to the touch.

"How strange," she muttered. She picked up another wineglass and carefully dropped the candle in it. It lit, all by itself, as the wick passed the rim of the glass. She upended the goblet, and the candle dropped, cool and unlit, into her waiting hand.

"Cadmon," she said excitedly to the man standing open-mouthed before her, "do you realize what we've got? We've got a lamp that can't be blown out but won't set things on fire if it's knocked over. I bet we could sell lots of these."

Cadmon's face lit up as he looked at his stock. "You're

right. Your candles won't burn, but anything put in my glass burns instantly—so the curses cancel each other out and your candles burn slowly in my glasses. I'll design glassware that will set off your candles, and you can make candles to fit in my glassware—it'll be a great partnership! Deal?''

Eirthe nodded. "Deal. Let's go see what can be salvaged from my place, and then we'll have to go to the fair-court for permission to move my wagon and set up a partnership.''

"We may have a little trouble explaining all this to the court and the fair-wards,'' Cadmon remarked thoughtfully.

Eirthe smiled sweetly. "Not as much trouble as Garak is likely to have when they catch up with him—which will probably be immediately after the court session.''

"You're absolutely right.'' Cadmon looked cheered by the thought. "But there is one thing you should do first.''

"What?'' Eirthe said absently, admiring the effect of the taper she had just fixed in a tall thin glass.

"Put some clothes on.'' He chuckled as she blushed and hastily threw on her skirt.

While she laced her bodice, Cadmon wandered over to study Alnath, who had decided to take up residence in the fishbowl. "Maybe we should make you our trademark.'' He gave a violent sneeze. "Drat! I hope I'm not getting a cold. That's a miserable thing for a glassblower—correction. Lampmaker.'' He smiled at Eirthe as they went out together into the morning sunshine.

BIOGRAPHICAL NOTES

André Norton

1)The name Lin Carter has been associated with the fantasy field for a number of years. Not only has he been responsible for editing collections of little known or near forgotten works of an older day, in the volumes *Dragons, Elves, and Heroes* and *Golden Cities Far,* but he has also written such critical studies as *The Young Magicians.* He has created a hero of his own, Thonger of Lemuria, and has collaborated with Sprague de Camp on Conan tales. It is fitting that this master of fantasy be represented at Ithkar Fair; who has a better right to attend?

2) Winner of two Hugo novel awards, the Balrog, and other honors, C. J. Cherryh has the firm foundation of a classical education, something few Americans can claim in this day and age. From her home in Edmond, Oklahoma, streams a steady flow of tales, both fantasy and straight science fiction.

313

In her own words she "tries out things"—like fencing, horsemanship, and firearms. She is well acquainted with wildlife from lizards to hawks, with more conventional fur and feathers in between. From the first appearance of *Gates of Ivrel* in 1976, her stories have added luster to the whole field.

3) From schoolteaching to writing is a path several writers have followed. However, Jo Clayton has in addition had the experience of belonging to a homesteading family of the West. Who, then, is better fitted to record the adventures of a farmer's daughter at Ithkar Fair and produce so realistic an account of matters natural and magical?

4) Some writers seem able to evoke other times and places with such a sure touch as makes one ready to believe in time travel and personal exploration of the past. Morgan Llywelyn, of mixed Irish and Welsh parentage, may have been city born and bred, but her heritage drew her from those high walls wherein she was a model, a dancer, and followed other modern roles, to become an expert horsewoman and, at length, a writer able to draw different people of different times and cultures with infinite skill. Her primitive fletcher is as alive as the heroine in her recently very well received novel, *The Horse Goddess*.

5) Patricia Mathews started her spell-weaving by writing for fanzines (a method that has been an excellent stepping-stone for many an author). She has been represented by Darkover tales in several anthologies. If her story herein is a bit grim, still, it holds the reader. Her Ithkarian tale carries a germ of what she hopes in the future to make into a novel—and it is as polished as any piece of her jeweler heroine's labors.

6) Out of the wide plains of Texas to misty forelands of her own devising, Ardath Mayhar makes a remarkable transition. Her words sing, which is not remarkable in an author who was first a poet. She is able to recreate skillfully other writers' dreams, also, as in her justly acclaimed addition to H. Beam Piper's legends of the Fuzzies—*Golden Dream*. Then there are the worlds of her own in which one can lose oneself from the first sentence onward—*Soul Singer of Tyros, How the Gods Wove in Kyrannon*, and all the rest. Now she shows how, in Ithkar, one may point a needle and bring evil to justice.

7) Since it fell to my lot to write these "minute biographies," I find it difficult to write this one. I was won to fantasy in childhood by a cherished love of the Oz stories, and I have never looked back. Animals mean a great deal to me—thus my fairgoer is an animal trainer. Ithkar itself was born of an idea conceived in the reading of books about the great medieval fairs—an idea I have cherished for a number of years. I am pleased and proud that it has inspired such fertile response from others.

8) Judith Sampson's creative bent showed early. In spite of physical handicaps she proved there were no bonds on her imagination. In turn, she credits many of her plots to fantasy role playing. Her fiction mixes fantasy and science fiction, weaving new patterns from old threads. But with it all she has a light touch. Who would want to miss that night at Qazia's fairside tavern when that forceful landlady confronts the ferret-fetch?

9) Dr. Roger C. Schlobin approached Ithkar by a scholar's road. A professor of English, he is also the author of a number of noted analytical studies on the subject of fantasy—

its use in both literature and art—as well as book reviewer for *Fantasy Newsletter*. A frequent speaker at conferences and on campuses, his grasp of his subject is well known. "For Lovers Only" is his first venture into fiction and we are honored to welcome him to Ithkar.

10) J. W. Schutz began his writing career in Africa while living in a tin-roofed shack on the borders of the Sahara. At the time he was acting ambassador to the Republic of Niger. He has lived through the hazards of modern diplomatic life, such as anti-American riots and the like, helped fight a fire aboard a ship, and once stole a railroad train for the embassy in Berlin. He says it has been a lively life, but it has not kept him from writing—nor from having a maker of dolls appear at Ithkar.

11) Susan M. Shwartz, having earned a Ph.D. in medieval studies from Harvard, now reviewing and contributing to a number of fantasy anthologies and editing one of her own, is also information coordinator at a Manhattan investment firm. Her interest in the bard as a source of literary lore shows clearly in "Homecoming."

12) Again a mixture of Welsh and Irish blood has brought the field an outstanding writer in Nancy Springer. No one who has read her novels—*The Silver Sun, The White Hart, The Sable Moon,* and others, which create the history of her beautiful, if sadly haunted, imaginative world—can gainsay that she is firmly a mistress of the fantasy genre. Her adventure of the undemanding horseleech brings an autumnal glow to Ithkar's chronicle.

13) A genuine note of humor in fantasy is one of the hardest to obtain, as any writer will declare. But in "Cold Spell" Elisabeth Waters inserts into the Ithkar pattern one of the

neatest turnabout bits of magic to be read in many a year. She has been writing for five years and lives in California with a well-known author, two teenagers, and two cats. Perhaps something in this mixed background has tightened her hold on the power and led her to such careful bespelling.

FRED SABERHAGEN